RAVEN BROUGHT THE LIGHT

KRISTIN GLEESON

OTHER WORKS BY KRISTIN GLEESON
In Praise of the Bees
CELTIC KNOT SERIES
Selkie Dreams
Along the Far Shores
Raven Brought the Light
A Treasure Beyond Worth (novella)
RENAISSANCE SOJOURNER SERIES
A Trick of Fate (novella)
The Imp of Eye
The Sea of Travail
HIGHLAND BALLAD SERIES
The Hostage of Glenorchy
The Mists of Glen Strae
The Braes of Huntly
Highland Lioness
NON FICTION
Anahareo, A Wilderness Spirit
LISTEN TO THE MUSIC CONNECTED TO THE BOOKS
Go to www.kristingleeson.com/music
Receive a FREE novellette prequel, *A Treasure Beyond Worth,* and
Along the Far Shores
When you sign up for my mailing list: www.kristingleeson.com

To R.Young, a great teller of tales

CHAPTER ONE
PRESENT DAY CHINA

I t was his height that first caught Bríd's eye.

He rose from his seat, scanned the emerging crowd and banged his head on the soffit above. Dr John Sheldon, the too-tall Alaskan Indian. Here, in this small Ürümchi airport, poised as it was on the edge of China, he was still too tall. But for all his height, the dusty western clothes and shaggy hair, he could still be taken for Chinese.

Bríd was surprised at his shaggy hair. It gave him a certain wild look. When she last saw him his hair was bristle length, a feature that only emphasized the severity of his expression and darkness of his eyes. The severity was still present and that, combined with something she couldn't quite name, still had the ability to touch a nerve deep inside her. A nerve she thought deadened by the past months. Could she do this? What choice had she, really?

Just as Bríd was about to move forward, she saw a stocky Chinese man approach Dr Sheldon, and coming closer, she could hear the man's inquiry, but understood nothing of its content. Her sometime professor stiffened and frowned. 'I'm not Chinese,' he said.

Bríd bit her lip and pulled back slightly. She didn't want him to know she had seen the encounter, something she knew would not count in her favor. It was important she get off on the right foot with Dr Sheldon. Her PhD career depended on a good report from this dig. She steeled herself, moved forward and offered her hand.

'Hello, Dr Sheldon. I'm Bríd Ní Laoghaire. I'm Paul's replacement.'

John Sheldon looked at her with a puzzled frown. 'Bridget?'

Bríd reached up to tug a long braid and met only short curls. Another reminder of who she was. Or wasn't. Should she go back to Bridget? She couldn't put back the hair she'd cut. Last year, returning to the Irish form of her name seemed the right thing to do. Now, with her hair freshly shorn, she wasn't so sure. 'Bríd Ní Laoghaire is the Irish form,' she told him. She pronounced 'Bríd' slowly and carefully, emphasizing the 'eee' sound of the 'i'.

John Sheldon looked her up and down and shook his head.

'Oh. But it's you all the same.' He leaned over picked up her bags and started off for the door, making his way through the milling people.

At a loss, Bríd followed him. He had that ability to confuse her when she'd taken his class a few years before. It was a class she'd taken reluctantly, to fill a requirement. She'd heard much about John Sheldon, the tall, stern Alaskan Indian. Mysterious and deep, her friends had told her, a statement that only made her laugh. She'd no interest in any "noble savage" act and sat in his first class full of misgivings as John Sheldon issued the course instructions with a stiff formality and minimal words. Bored, she twiddled her braid and consulted the calendar on her phone, counting off the days she would have to spend in his class as she waited for the "noble savage" act to begin.

Then, just as she wrote the number twelve on the pad in

front of her in flourishing circular motions, he'd begun a tale. His resonant voice penetrated her count and she lifted her head and focused. John Sheldon transformed while his voice enveloped her and his dark eyes mesmerized hers. His hands and arms shaped the story, while his voice painted the words of his tale. She entered the tale, became part of it and never wanted it to finish.

But it was outside his tales, when he talked and lectured to the class about the theories and histories, that he confused her most. Her own love of the story, the myth and its underlying meaning, had escaped into her enthusiastic response to his tale. But he'd met her enthusiasm with suspicion and something just short of distaste. So she had curbed her tongue and with it, her enthusiasm for him and his gift to see inside the soul of the tale. Until, just every so often, she would catch a look, directed, she thought, at her, which unsettled her so, she could only blush to the roots of her very red hair.

Bríd stared at him now as they approached the battered SUV parked just outside the airport. In the raking light of the blistering mid-day sun his face looked drawn and tired. Beyond that she had no sense of his thoughts. As before, he was an enigma.

Once on the road, she settled back into the seat and gazed out the window. She soon realized speaking was out of the question. It wasn't Dr Sheldon's taciturn company, but the engine noise and the jolts from the rugged landscape. Besides, she felt tired after the endless journey.

Outside, the vast dusty landscape seemed to match her mood. They were just north of the Täklimakan desert where a few millennia of climate changes had dried up its river beds, depleted its vegetation, and redefined its inhabitants. Until recently, the ancient silk route that had threaded its way from the Mediterranean to China was the only thing that had broken the isolation of its tribal communities.

It was the stark isolation that struck Bríd now. The harsh, bleaching light seemed to lay bare every contour of the rocky terrain, apart from the distorted haze of distant mountains. Such a landscape frightened her at the same time it held a deep rooted attraction that reflected her own emotional state. Desiccated. She looked down at her right wrist and traced the circles of the recent tattoo and felt soothed.

Dr. Sheldon glanced over at her and instinctively she pulled her sleeve over the tattoo and looked away, but not before she saw the glint in his eye. Was he judging her?

'You've had time to read the background material?' he asked, his voice neutral.

She nodded and tried to calm the anxiety that arose in her. She'd read the material many times in the last few days, panicked at this last-minute chance to salvage something of her career prospects. She'd been so grateful she hadn't given herself time to consider that she might not be able to meet Dr Sheldon's high expectations. But now, the enormity of her decision awakened the huge doubts she had managed to suppress during her hasty departure from Ireland. What kind of daftness made her think that as a third-year doctoral student researching ancient Irish migration patterns she could work on dig in China with a professor obsessed with old Tlingit myths?

Bríd gave Dr Sheldon what she hoped was a confident smile. 'I'm as well briefed as I can be without actually having been to the site. Is everything here going okay? Well apart from me, that is.' She felt herself redden as she tried to explain. 'Having to fill in for Paul, I mean. I know you valued Paul's abilities and that he would be difficult to replace, but I'll do my best.' Difficult to replace was the best she could manage in lieu of saying she was sorry she wasn't Navajo like Paul and she was sorry she didn't have Paul's vast array of knowledge of native mythological structure.

'I hear you sing?' Dr Sheldon said.

Startled by his question, she cast him another glance. There was a slight curve to one side of his mouth. Did she detect a smirk? 'Yes. Well, I did,' she answered. 'But not the kind of thing you might be thinking of.' What use was singing on a dig anyway?

'I hear you sing well, that you've won awards.'

'They would be Irish awards. For Irish singing.' Where was this going? As usual he had managed to put her off balance.

'Well, Paul can't sing worth a damn.' A smile spread across his face, a rarity that transformed his whole demeanor and defused any indignation she might have felt.

It was later, after a few more mundane conversations, that Bríd could bring herself to ask him any more questions about the work ahead.

'The campsite is all set up and a small group of locals have done some of the preliminary digging,' Dr Sheldon replied when she asked about it. 'There are few enough of the rest of the staff, but with all the complications from the Chinese government, it's just as well.'

'What sort of problems?' Though if all the stories she had heard were true, she would be surprised if there weren't problems. But still, she felt a flutter of anxiety. 'Is it anything you can't overcome?'

'No. Well, I hope not. We do have two Chinese apparatchiks observing us officially, to ensure we comply with their guidelines. Their real purpose is ensure that anything we discover is dealt with in an appropriate manner.' Dr Sheldon raised an eyebrow that left Bríd in no doubt that "an appropriate manner" would not necessarily mean furthering the cause of knowledge.

'It's because the area is very politically sensitive. There's been unrest and resistance to Chinese rule and this site, in an area close to the Silk Road, anything we unearth would be of interest to the Chinese. They have a very strong view about their unique place in history.'

Bríd searched her patchy knowledge of Chinese history. 'They want to maintain the belief that their culture and inventions developed independently of the western world?'

Dr Sheldon nodded. 'Something like that. I suppose it gives them their strong sense of cohesion in a vast country. But an outlook like that does get in the way of research. Thankfully, they don't have too much of a problem with my interest in locating the origins of a group of ancient people who left the area and went to Alaska.'

Bríd laughed. 'An early Chinese export. I would think they would be pleased with that view.'

'Well, to a degree. The period I'm talking about is before the time of the Chinese we think of today.'

Bríd groaned inwardly. Already she'd waved her ignorance at him like a big red rag.

'Sorry, it was a feeble joke, anyway.'

'Don't worry. You're not alone in that mistake. But we have Dr Chou's expertise to help any kind of problems like that. He joined us a few days ago. We owe a lot to him for getting clearance for the dig, as well as his earlier thoughts about locating possible sites for exploring my theories.'

Dr Sheldon's theories. Jesus tonight. He actually believed that his Alaskan clan's origins were so far west on this continent they were practically on the doorstep of the Kazakhs in Eastern Europe and other newly emerging mounted peoples. If it had been anyone else when she'd first heard his theories, she'd have laughed and told them it was great *craic*. But Sheldon was serious.

Forget the ancient land bridge. Forget the ten, twenty, thirty thousand years of migrations that Native Americans and scholars argued over, John Sheldon believed that his particular clan came late, driven by drought, migrated across the continent, then took to boats and made its way to the Alaskan region. Hilarious. And the only reason she got this place on the dig. Who in their right mind would want to work with such a fool? Besides Paul, of course. Except there was something about him, something underlying that made you want to believe it might be true, just because he wanted it to be true.

'How does Dr Chou view your chances of uncovering some evidence for your theories, Dr Sheldon?'

There was a moment of silence. 'You should call me John, I suppose.' He glanced at her and she felt herself redden. Was that doubt in his voice? She wasn't certain she could call him John, anyway.

'As for Dr Chou, he's fairly hopeful. Some years ago, he found artefacts with possible cultural links and Paul's reading of the mythological and physical landscape, he thinks, is promising.'

He cocked his head slightly at Bríd. 'But that's in the material I sent you.'

'I just wondered if there was anything else he might have said recently, since he arrived.'

John grunted. 'Since his arrival most of our conversation seems to have been directed off into tangents. Usually by his new assistant, some fresh-faced Chinese guy who studied at Berkeley named Jin Wang. But Bob Kirby says he's good, so I guess he's all right.'

Bríd cringed slightly at the mention of Dr Kirby's name. Yes, he was smooth and sophisticated, and at every department or university event his Nordic good looks charmed everyone while John Sheldon hugged the wall and looked strangled in his suit and tie. Despite all that, she'd thought Dr Kirby still looked more like the bottom-pinching, arm stroker she'd heard about and had resolved to keep under his radar, lest she end up under him instead.

BY THE TIME they arrived at the field site, Bríd was exhausted. Conversation had long ceased and all she wanted to do was to crawl into bed. But it was not to be. As soon as she stepped out of the SUV she could see several people approaching. She recognized Dr Kirby's shock of white hair and impeccable tan under his immaculate shorts and shirt. Looking at him, she could see the clear resemblance to his uncle, the world famous archaeologist of the fifties. Behind him was his shadow, Scott Gordon. The others she didn't know.

Dr Kirby draped an arm around her, drawing her closer to the group. 'Ah, Bridget, you've finally arrived. Come and meet some of the group.' He fixed his deep blue eyes on her as she fought the urge to pull away. 'Bríd,' said John quietly from behind. 'Her name is Bríd.'

An annoyed look crossed Dr Kirby's face for a brief moment, only to be replaced by smile of great charm. 'Of course. And you must call me Bob.' He gave a slight nod then gestured to the others grouped around him. Bob Kirby had never matched his uncle's fame, but you wouldn't know it now, the way he behaved like a celebrity everyone wanted to be with.

'Scott Gordon you probably already know. Next to him is Miffy Langdon.'

A shapely blonde woman smiled, but her eyes had narrowed slightly. 'It's Millicent really, but everyone calls me Miffy.' Her voice had a slight edge.

Bríd forced her own smile and greeted Miffy before turning to Scott.

'How are you, Scott?'

She'd expected Scott would be on the dig since he was Bob's assistant. How else would Bob manage if he didn't have Scott's meticulous eye for detail and dogged energy to do his work? And though she'd never met Miffy, she could only assume she was Bob's latest in a long line of protégés. Would Miffy have any field skills at all, or would they lie in other directions? Against Miffy maybe she wouldn't come up too short.

After a few muffled words from a red-faced Scott, Bob stepped aside and allowed Bríd full view of the two men behind him.

'Let me introduce you to our Chinese colleagues, Dr Yiban Chou and his assistant, Dr Jin Wang.'

The two Chinese men acknowledged the introductions with a polite nod. Dr Chou, the shorter of the two, ran a hand nervously through his narrowly cut grey hair, while his younger assistant, Dr Wang, extended a lanky hand.

'Call me Jin,' he said and then laughed. 'You must be very tired. And we just keep you standing.'

His laughter was warm and easy and his eyes met her in a friendly twinkle. Suddenly Bríd was conscious of her unkempt hair and rumpled clothes. She noted his tall, slim frame, the stylish cut of his black hair that a lock of it had defied and fallen into his dark eyes. He was not at all like any Chinese colleague she could imagine.

Behind her John shifted. 'Right. I guess you can meet the others later. In the meantime, Miffy can show you your tent. You're sharing with her.'

Bríd turned back to the SUV to get her gear out of the back, but John beat her to it. He motioned her towards Miffy and she reluctantly made to follow the retreating figure to the row of tents erected to one side of the clearing. On the other side were two small trailers and a larger open tent with a stand and bowls and a gnarled tree that provided some shade from the retreating sun.

As she neared the row of tents, she halted suddenly to avoid colliding with a stocky Chinese man. 'Sorry, sorry,' Bríd said. 'I didn't see you.'

The man stood in front of her, neither particularly tall nor imposing, but his posture, like his eyes, was intractable. 'My apologies, Miss O'Leary. I should have made my presence known sooner. I am Lu, Xiang Lu.' He gave her a brief nod.

'Oh, no bother, Mr Lu.' She made an effort to make the reply calm to conceal how much he startled her. She returned his nod then hurried after Miffy, keenly aware of John close behind her. Why had he said nothing to that man?

As if he heard her thoughts, John came up behind her, just beside the tents, and spoke in a low voice. 'That's one of those government apparatchiks I mentioned.'

Bríd nodded even more unnerved by the man now. Of course he would have been briefed about her arrival. Probably Bob or John had told him. She hoped so.

She entered the tent and John followed behind her to deposit her things. He gave Miffy a brief nod and Bríd a 'see you in the morning,' before leaving in a manner that seemed almost like beating a hasty retreat.

Bríd glanced around the tent. Miffy sat on her cluttered camp bed in a haze of designer perfume. Her shirt buttons strained under the press of her breasts. Around her, clothes poured out of designer suitcases and cosmetics, shoes, towels and other paraphernalia were scattered on every available surface, obscuring any signs of a second camp bed. Bríd felt the urge to follow in John's wake.

'You'll find the camp bed somewhere over there.' She gestured vaguely to the other side and gave Bríd a dark look.

'This tent is much too small for even one person. I don't know how they expect me to share it. I wasn't supposed to.'

'I don't need too much space,' said Bríd.

Bríd tried to hide her annoyance. After all, she had to share this space with Miffy for several weeks. She gritted her teeth and picked up a few towels and shirts and located the metal frame camp bed that was to be hers.

'Blankets?' she asked. John had said it was cold at night and already she could feel the chill descend.

Miffy gave her a petulant look. 'I don't have any to spare. You'll have to ask John. Bob and I both feel the cold, but John, being an Alaskan, well I guess ice runs through his veins.' Miffy laughed.

Bríd gave a feeble smile. She didn't feel like tracking down John again. In the morning she would be more able to deal with this. Now, she just wanted to crawl in bed and sleep.

Miffy frowned at her and sighed dramatically. She grabbed a small blanket from her bed and handed it to Bríd. 'Oh, here. I suppose we won't miss it just this one night.' She gave a light giggle. 'If Bob and I get cold I'm sure we can come up with a way to keep warm.'

Bríd had no doubt about the truth of her statement as Miffy rose and left the tent for the night.

CHAPTER TWO

'I'll show you the lab and the office later,' John said. 'First, we'll get started on making a grid of the chamber at this end. Then we can tackle the remaining layer covering the chamber. It's some kind of mat, so we need to be careful removing the dirt that's on it.'

Silently, he handed her a few tools and string. She took the equipment and began her work, trying hard to quell her butterflies. John watched her closely as she marked off the grids with his assistance. He corrected one of her grid calculations at one point, but said nothing. When she'd finished, she selected some tools from the box, knelt beside the grave site and began to remove the layers of dirt with a small brush. John looked up from his tablet where he'd been entering the data and went over to squat squat beside her.

'Relax,' he said. 'No need to be so cautious.' He handed her a much larger brush. 'We don't want to be here until Christmas.'

She nodded, conscious of his strong, callused fingers. The place where she had her tattoo tingled, but she put it down to nerves. She'd felt awkward and nervous around him since she arrived. Not that he had been harsh, or unduly critical of her, it was that he'd watched her so closely, scrutinized her every action as she worked.

She scanned the grave. It was about ten meters or so square. A little ways off, the local workers had piled the half-meter of earth that had covered it originally. The area around it was flat and nondescript, no outstanding natural markers of stone, or anything else that would indicate it was significant. But it was significant, something in her told her it was. It had nothing to do with Dr Chou's careful gathering of indicators and local information, or John's tireless pursuit of any tiny lead. No, there was something here in the air she felt only Gran would understand.

She looked at the other staff working, to see if she could detect in them any suggestion that they felt it too. In one corner Scott squatted with a tape measure and a tablet, deep in discussion with Dr Chou and some local workers, a camera hanging from his shoulder. He was animated and excited, yes, but it was nothing more than that. The others were in the lab trailer, she guessed. She stole a glance at John. He was explaining the use of the different brushes. She could sense nothing else there, either. She sighed. Nerves, just plain nerves.

She set down to work and tried to focus working with the correct brush while John worked beside her in silence. Slowly, the two brushed away the layers of earth covering the large grave chamber. She could feel the sun beating through the canvas hat that covered her head, raising prickles of heat on her hair and dripping sweat from her brow. The bandana around her throat she'd dampened earlier had long since dried and her tongue was thick against her teeth. She looked up and saw that Scott and the others were heading off to the mess tent.

John stood up. 'We'll take a break now.'

He removed his bush hat and wiped his brow, moving to the side the long tongue of black hair that lay plastered there. 'I'll show you the office.' Without further word, he made his way over to one of the trailers. She rose and hurried after him.

Bríd greeted the coolness inside the office with a shiver. Outside she could hear the generator's loud hum. An area air conditioner stood to one side of the desk at the far end of the room. At the desk Jin sat working on a laptop. He stood when John and Bríd entered.

John frowned. 'Is there any problem?'

'No, no,' said Jin. 'Not at all. I was just checking on some data.' He looked at Bríd. 'How are you finding it, Bríd? The heat is a killer, isn't it? Especially after coming from Ireland.'

'Have you been to Ireland?' Bríd asked.

'No, I went to Stanford University, but later I lived in San Francisco and Seattle, and they aren't all that different, I think. I hope you don't start wishing you had never left the lush lands of your home.'

'Ah, no. It'll be grand. I'm sure I'll get used to it.'

John handed her a bottle of water. 'Make sure you drink plenty of fluids when you're here.'

Though his tone was neutral, she thought she could detect an edge to it. She felt her anxiety rise again, conscious of John's tension.

John looked over at Jin. 'Is there any data I can help you with? Something that you need to clarify?'

'No, it's okay. I got what I needed.'

Jin shut the laptop and moved over to the door. 'I'll see you later at the mess tent, Bríd.' He opened the door and left.

John walked over to the laptop, opened it up and scanned the files. After a few moments he looked up at her and frowned.

'Is anything wrong?' she asked.

'What?' He looked puzzled for a moment. 'No. Nothing's wrong. We don't have the internet here and we can only use satellite phones, so we have to go to Ürümchi periodically, to send off our reports. So I like to be sure the files on here remain uncorrupted in any way.'

It was later, after he had showed her the computer files recording the dig, the various reference resources and the few hardcopy texts at the other end of the trailer, that John no longer seemed distracted. She knew this only because, once again, she felt his intensive scrutiny, even as she left the trailer and went to wash up. She sluiced her hands and face and she could feel him watching her. As her awareness increased, so did her uncertainty over her feelings about the watchfulness.

All her disturbing thoughts vanished when she arrived at the crowded space of the mess tent. It was noisy in a friendly way and Bríd felt herself ease after a moment. She happily navigated the three folding tables and four benches carrying her plate of bread, some cheese and some fruit and bottle of water from the food table. She was surprised to see Jin slide over and gesture to her to come and sit beside him, opposite Bob and Miffy.

Jin looked at her sparse plate as she took the place indicated. 'I hope you aren't too put off by the basic menu here. We all pitch in and do our turns at the food. The schedule is in the office.'

'Oh, I'm sure it'll be fine. I'm just not that hungry now,' said Bríd.

Bob turned from his conversation with Miffy and looked over at her. 'Ah, but you must keep up your strength. We don't want you to lose any of those perfect curves.'

Bríd shifted under Bob's sweeping gaze, conscious of Miffy's tense posture beside him.

'It wouldn't hurt her to lose a few pounds,' Miffy said plaintively. She played with the bits of bread on her plate. 'Though with this stale bit of brick that is supposed to pass for bread, it should be easy for you.'

'It's the air,' said Scott from the other table. 'If you could remember to wrap up the bread and then put it in the cooler, it wouldn't be so stale.'

'My expertise is not in food management, Scott. Just because I'm a woman, you can't expect me to do these domestic things.'

'It's hard on all of us to be expected to share kitchen duties,' said Bob. 'Have a little patience, Scott.' Miffy gave Bob a bright smile.

'All I was saying, that with a little care... ' Scott's voice trailed off.

John entered the tent and glanced around the tables. He patted Scott on the back and took a seat between him and Dr Chou, opposite Mr Lu and Mr Chang.

Bríd stared at her plate and wondered at Scott's forbearance. She thanked the gods again that Miffy spent her nights in Bob's tent. What did John make of the two of them, though? Surely, he could hear them in the tent he shared with Scott next door. She stole a glance, but he was engaged in quiet conversation with Dr Chou and she couldn't read his expression.

'I hope you don't mind doing your turn at the food, but if you like, I can switch with you and you can do my turn at the dish washing instead,' said Jin in a low voice. He gave her a warm smile and she relaxed.

'No, no. I don't mind cooking. Really. I always used to help my gran in the kitchen,' said Bríd. She reddened at what she knew was a bold faced lie, but she didn't want him to think she was anything like Miffy.

'That would be in Ireland, I suppose,' Jin said. 'How is it an Irish girl ended up at the University of Pennsylvania?'

Though she was used to this question by now, it still touched a nerve that she tried to suppress. 'My mother moved to Philadelphia when I was fifteen and I went with her. But I went back to Ireland in the summers, to be with Gran.' She had missed Ireland so much in those in-between months. Summer was what she had lived for.

'And your father? Is he still in Ireland?'

His tone was sympathetic so she allowed herself only a moment's anger at her father and made herself answer. 'I don't know where my father is. He left home when I was young. He's a musician.'

'A musician. How interesting,' said Jin. 'And would you have any interest in music?'

Bríd smiled, and answered without thinking. 'Yes, yes I do. Music is a great part of my life.' Then the memories flooded in and she frowned. 'Well it was.'

'Was? It's not anymore?'

'No,' Bríd answered with quiet force. 'No. That's part of my past. Now I have to think of my studies and move forward with that.' That answer, however incomplete, was the best she could manage, even for someone as sympathetic as Jin.

LATER, as Bríd relaxed under the shade of the gnarled tree waiting for dinner, Jin came over and sat beside her.

'Your hair is as flame-colored as those mountains over there,' he said and then grinned. 'And I bet your skin would match them, too, given half a chance in this sun.'

She laughed. It felt strange to do it, it had been so long, but it felt good.

'You should laugh more,' said Jin. He gave her a long look. 'It makes your eyes lighter in color.'

Bríd laughed again. 'You'll have me red in skin now without any sun, if you keep saying things like that.'

'Not at all,' said Jin. 'I'm sure you've had your share of compliments.'

'Not the way they tripped off your tongue just now. Where did you learn English—it's so good.'

'I've spent a lot of time in the States. First at college, and then working for a few companies and then giving lectures and appearing on panels.'

She was impressed. 'Were you working with Dr Kirby then?'

'No, no. I only just met Dr Kirby and Dr Sheldon.'

'Oh, are you a colleague of Dr Chou's?'

'I knew Dr Chou. But I am a scientist. A geneticist by training.'

'A geneticist? And you're here?'

'There are all types of expertise that are required at field sites. My expertise has been used many times now.'

'Of course. Sorry,' said Bríd. 'You see, except for a few days on an Irish dig, this is my first real field experience. Hopefully, it won't be my last.'

'Don't worry. I'm sure your knowledge of the whole project exceeds mine,' said Jin. As if to prove the point, he began to quiz her about the work and her knowledge of John's theories. She answered his questions readily enough, surprised at her own level of expertise. She shared her knowledge with a growing confidence, and in the end she found she was grateful to him. It was only when he asked about her opinion of Bob and John that she grew more guarded.

'As I understand, Bob has many connections worldwide. That makes him quite an asset when trying to raise money and support for any kind of archaeological enterprise. I'm sure John is appreciative of his abilities.'

'But John's theories. What do you think of them?'

Bríd looked down at her hands, searching for the right

words. 'He has a deep belief in them, I think. And his determination to prove them is very strong.'

'But what do *you* think?'

'I hope that the dig will give him the answers he needs,' Bríd said finally. She wondered if it would give her any answers. If she could find a sense of peace, she would be happy with that.

THAT NIGHT, as she sat on her cot alone in the tent, the thought of Jin raised a smile. He was so easy to be with. He didn't assess her all the time, like she felt John did. And he was certainly easier company than Miffy and Bob. Miffy filled the space of their tent with more than just her belongings and heavy perfume.

Bríd began to remove her gear from her backpack and placed them in the little crate at the foot of her camp bed. As she pulled out her pair of jeans, something fell to the ground with a ringing clatter. It was her tin whistle. Now what would that be doing in her backpack? She stared at the whistle. She would never have brought it. Not ever. That was over. Finished. She picked up the whistle and stuffed it back in the backpack, and as she did so her hand came across something hard between two shirts. Carefully, she pulled it out. It was a handsomely carved wooden box, small enough to hold in the palm of her hand. Her grandmother's treasured possession. No. It couldn't be. Tears filled her eyes. Hastily she stuffed the box back into the backpack and shoved it as far down to the bottom as she possibly could.

CHAPTER THREE

Bríd heard the raised voices as she approached the small trailer that functioned as the office. She paused, not knowing whether to knock or to go away.

'That is my final word, Dr Sheldon,' said a voice she recognized as Xiang Lu's.

'I don't think it's reasonable to halt work at such a critical stage,' said John, his anger barely suppressed. 'We really don't know what's inside the chamber, so how can you be sure we need permission to enter it?'

'I am sorry our procedures seem arbitrary, but I assure you, they are not.'

'Well, until I see something written, I won't halt the work mid-stream,' said John. 'I have no option but to proceed as scheduled.'

'That is not a wise choice,' said Mr Lu. The tone was unmistakably menacing. 'I count on you to think it over carefully. Good day to you, Dr Sheldon.'

Bríd ducked to the side of the trailer just as Mr Lu came striding down the few steps and across to his tent. What was going on? Would the dig be canceled? How would John handle that, and moreover what would she do? She'd only been here a few days and already she found much that caught her imagination. Besides, the thought of returning to her mother's house in Philadelphia was more than she could bear. And Ireland was out of the question, even though her research, her things—including her harp—were still there. The research could be sent. And though her heart wailed at the thought of losing her harp, she knew she couldn't go back, not now, maybe not ever.

It would be best, for now, to go on as though nothing was changed. But she would leave the reference sources for later. She changed direction and made her way towards the wash stand over by the kitchen. When she was finished, she pulled a comb from her pocket. In some ways she was glad she no longer had the thick, long braid that used to hang to her waist. Here it would only get in the way and make her feel even hotter than she was.

Bríd went over to the familiar spot on the rock to relax under the gnarled tree, taking advantage of its precious bit of shade until the meal was ready. Maybe Jin would join her and she could pass the time with him. Her turn at kitchen duty didn't come for a few days yet and she was in no rush for it. Despite all of Gran's coaching and coaxing, her bread was hard as a rock and her brack tasted more like the metal charms they contained. It was music that had brought her alive.

She studied her fingers. The blunt nails so good for the harp, whistle and fiddle were now dry and cracked from the arid environment. She flexed them slowly, easing out some of the stiffness. Would they be so agile now if she played? What if she had lost that nimbleness that carried her across the strings and air holes? Suddenly, she needed to know if it was still there. That flying. Was she able for it? Would she try to play the whistle Nellie had slipped into her backpack when she'd hurriedly gathered her things together to flee the house, flee Ireland? Who else but Nellie, Gran's longtime friend, would have been so bold to pack the two items bound to upset her most? But now it seemed more of a challenge than anything distressful. What harm would it do if she played—it wasn't really playing, there was no audience to see her fail.

Before she could change her mind, Bríd went to her tent and retrieved the whistle. She settled on the rock again and put the whistle to her lips. With only a moment's pause, she launched into the first bit of music that came to her head, tentatively picking out the notes at first, careful of the tune, careful of its pitch. It was only a ditty one, a bitteen tune she'd learned for her first *fleadh ceol* when she was six. But it settled in her heart, swelled it too full and then pushed itself into her throat, cutting off her breath. She stopped.

'Go on.'

Bríd whirled around and saw John standing near her. She swallowed her tears and narrowed her eyes in suspicion. 'Ah, no. I don't think I can play more. It's been too long.' She would not give him the satisfaction of watching her fail.

'Keep going with that same tune you were playing before.'

Bríd gave him a doubtful look. His tone seemed sincere, but she wasn't sure. 'No, no. It was far from good, even though it was a simple tune.'

'What might seem simple at first can be riddled with subtle complexities. So often we're confused into thinking the ornate is the better, the preferred way.'

Bríd sifted his words through her mind, working hard to discern just exactly what he meant by them. Then she smiled, a hesitant affair quickly ended. 'Yes,' she said quietly. 'You can do so much with a simple tune. It can allow you room for growth, to go forward, expand upon it, decorate it and then bring it back to its original beauty.'

'Exactly,' said John. 'But maybe you need to try with the

simple and see where it goes.'

She looked at him carefully, wondering again at his words, her whistle still poised in her hands. With an intake of breath, she tentatively brought the whistle up to her lips again and began anew. This time the tune came out strong and lively, as it was meant to be played. This time she felt only the tune, its simple melody catching hold of her, whizzing through her mind as she played a little with its possibilities, things she never would have dared at the *fleadh ceol*. The judges would have frowned her off the stage.

Bríd finished the tune. '*Sin é,*' she said. She'd done it. She'd played something. Bríd looked up at John and felt a wave of gratitude.

'Was that the name of the tune, *sin é*?' asked John.

Bríd laughed. It came out rough and raw and it surprised her. 'No, that wasn't the name. That was Irish for "that's it," meaning it's finished, done.' She didn't mention the other meaning she had given it. 'The tune is *The Kesh*. It's a standard tune played often at *fleadh ceols*.'

'*Fleadh ceols?*'

'Ah, sorry now. They're music competitions for all different instruments and ages held regionally and then nationally to promote Irish music.'

John looked thoughtful. 'Really? That's amazing. And you've competed in them?'

'Mmm.' She'd lived and breathed them until she was twelve. 'Camping in soggy fields with soggy tents, praying the harp would hold its tuning and the fiddle wouldn't break a string. It's a wonder we all didn't get pneumonia. Though one year Ciarán got such a bad cold I'd thought his dripping nose would clog his flute.' She stopped short before that thought, her mind closed down, and the liveliness that had seized her a moment before died.

John stood patiently before her, waiting for her to continue, his own face alive with interest. She looked down at her feet and willed away the tears.

'I find it impressive that you Irish are so dedicated to preserving your culture. I knew there were Irish pubs and societies in Philadelphia and that music was a big part of it, but I wasn't aware that there was such a structured, embedded approach in place. I only wish the Tlingits could boast of such an extensive program to keep the culture alive.'

'I'd say there are a few more Irish out there than Tlingits,' Bríd said with a wan smile.

'True. But that doesn't mean to say their efforts shouldn't be praised.' He gave her a studied look. 'Would you play another tune?'

Bríd looked down at the whistle, gauging herself. With a determined grip, she pulled the whistle to her mouth and dashed out the beginning of a short set of hornpipes. The bouncy tune took hold of her in a few seconds, lifting her up and setting her on course for its follow up. John's foot began to tap and she let that push her on, keeping the drive, the rhythm and the joy of it that ran down her fingers and into her bones. Yeeees. She finished on a flourish.

'You have good breath control,' said John.

She looked up at him, puzzled. 'You play?'

He hesitated a moment before answering. 'Well, I play flute. Not all that well.'

She wiped the fipple quickly and offered the whistle to him. 'Have a go.'

John looked down at the offered whistle then over at her, a dark, assessing expression filling his face. After a few moments it cleared and he took the whistle.

'It's in the key of D,' Bríd said.

John nodded and put the whistle to his mouth. After a few

runs up and down he settled into a slow tune with a haunting melody that ran eerily through her. It was simple, it didn't have a huge range, put it was persistent, it got under your skin and drew you inside, into that part of you that was not connected to this world, but the next. When he finished Bríd found she was disappointed. Disappointed because she wanted him to continue, to keep her in that other world a world that was not *Gort na Carrig*, was not Philadelphia.

'*Go halainn,*' she whispered. 'That was beautiful. What was it?'

'It's something I learned from my uncle.'

It was the first time she had ever heard him mention anything about his personal life. 'Your uncle?' she asked tentatively. 'Was that in Alaska?' How stupid of her, of course it was in Alaska. But for some reason she wanted to know more about him and she didn't know how to ask him, what to ask him.

'Yes, my uncle in Alaska.'

'He plays the flute, too?'

'Yes, a bit. He was trying to get me to see the world differently.'

She nodded as if it was clear to her. He had quizzed her carefully about her own home despite the pain it raised, yet there was something that prevented her from pressing him too much about his own background.

She caught sight of Lu making his way over to the mess tent and remembered the argument earlier. Well, she certainly wasn't going to ask John about the status of the dig now. He would know that she'd overheard something and she was certain he'd wish she hadn't. He had no need to worry, she would keep his secret, if not for his sake, but for her own. She would rather not discuss the meaning of the conversation with anyone else, even Jin, because she'd long ago learned in any academic department it was best to remain as much as possible outside of all the various petty rivalries that run rampant in academia and wrecked many a career. But though she might not want to admit it to herself, she found she did want to protect John from any needless questioning or doubts from the others.

In the kitchen tent, Bríd found most of the team members already seated around the table, busily eating a simple meal Scott had prepared. Bríd could tell it was Scott by the carefully sliced carrots and precisely squared potatoes in the stew. She filled her plate and then chose an empty spot next to Jin. In the past few days she had found Jin selecting the seat next to her at meals, so she decided to return the compliment this time. His shirtsleeves, carefully rolled back, revealed strong, sinewy arms. He greeted her warmly.

She glanced over at Bob, who still looked fresh and unruffled after a day's work. He was smiling as Miffy talked about her house in the Hamptons. John, who'd followed her in, took a seat next to Bob, his own crumpled shirt and dirt-stained shorts looking only slightly neater than the bandanna tied carelessly around his head. He bent his head to Bob and spoke in low tones, obviously updating him about the discussion with Lu.

Bob turned his full attention to John. 'I don't understand. I thought we'd cleared all the hurdles before we got here. In fact I'm sure of it. What reason did he give?'

'Something to the effect that this now promises to be a culturally significant discovery and requires special permission to proceed,' said John, his voice low.

Bob glanced over at Chang, seated at the other end of the next table, beside a local Chinese worker and his eyes narrowed slightly. Where was Lu, anyway? She'd seen him earlier heading to the tent. Bob rose and made his way over to squeeze next to

Chang's wide frame. He spoke in Chinese, his voice low and firm.

'Did I hear you right?' Scott asked John. He was seated next to Miffy, opposite Bríd. 'We have to wait to go into the chamber until we get further clearance?' John nodded and Scott sighed. 'Isn't there anything we can do? Any evidence we can provide to support the need to go ahead as planned?' Scott carefully listed some examples he thought might work. 'How about some of the cultural or linguistic connections to this region?' he finally added.

Bob looked up from his discussion with Chang. 'What a good idea. John, why don't you give Mr Chang some insight into the extensive work you put into selecting this site. Tell one of the clan tales that show some of your ideas.'

'Yes, John,' said Jin. 'Please do. I would be very interested to hear the clan tales Bob speaks of.'

Bríd caught her breath and looked at John. Whatever would he make of such a request? He was very particular about when and where he told his tales, a quirkiness she knew was somehow connected to his cultural background.

John frowned at Bob, then looked downwards, as if he was drawing from something inward. After an unreadable glance at Bríd he rose. 'I'll tell you the Tlingit creation tale. It speaks of Raven bringing light to the world when he released the sun, moon and stars from the cedar wood box.'

John's voice dropped into a rhythmic cadence, each word measured and rich in timbre. Its resonance found its way inside their bodies, slowed their breathing, and eased them into the tale. It wrapped around them like a light cloak and pulled them away on the Raven's wings...

Raven, revered by all Tlingit for his gifts to The People, was born of the sister of the Creator Nascakiyiel, who lived at the head of the River Nass. When Raven traveled around the world he saw it was dark for all The People. Eventually, he heard that Nascakiyiel had the sun, moon and stars locked in a cedar wood box. So Raven turned himself into a hemlock needle and floated in the River Nass where Nascakiyiel's daughter drew water. The daughter drank from the river, swallowed the needle and became pregnant. She gave birth to her son, Raven, who was the light and heart of his Grandfather, Nascakiyiel. As he grew, Raven became more precious to Nascakiyiel until there was no wish he could refuse Raven. One day, spying the cedar wood box against the wooden wall, Raven asked his grandfather if he could play with it. After refusing three times, Nascakiyiel finally gave him the box and Raven opened it up and released the sun, moon and stars into the air and up the smoke hole. Raven transformed himself to his original form and flew off after the newly freed sun, moon and stars. The light from these wonders spread out along the land, stronger and stronger. The People became afraid, so they scattered to every corner of the earth....

By the time John had ended the tale, a hushed silence hung in the air. For a moment it seemed to Bríd that no one dared breathe. Then Jin shifted slightly and Scott began to clap, inspiring the others to follow suit, except Bob. Bríd refrained too, since she knew that John would find it inappropriate, an accolade that shouldn't follow something that neared the ritualistic. They'd never clapped in class, not from any instruction from him, but an almost instinctive understanding that they shouldn't.

'Everyone knows that tale,' said Bob, annoyance clear in his voice. 'That's a general Tlingit tale, not one of your clan's. Tell one of those.'

John gave him a dark look that lasted only a moment. 'I think that tale is enough.' He nodded to the others and strode out. Bríd followed him with her eyes, wishing she could go after him and ask him more, but she knew she didn't have the courage.

CHAPTER FOUR

Bríd walked over to the trailer to try once again to check those texts she'd wanted to earlier. She also wanted to see if she could find some of the Tlingit mythic tales, specifically the ones from his clan that he wouldn't tell earlier. She'd heard him tell the raven tale before, but she'd forgotten what beauty he brought to it. Well, she hadn't forgotten, really, but hearing him tell it again, she knew it was a power that had to be felt to understand. It couldn't be described, nor could it translate to paper, which is all she'd been reviewing the past few weeks.

She sighed. Though she'd understood his reaction after he'd told the tale, she couldn't help but wish he'd be more like Jin. Jin was open, charming and easy. He always had an encouraging word for her. She knew John had spoken under duress and felt very personally about his clan tales, but she wasn't sure about the reason he left so quickly. He was such a closed, suspicious person who kept people at a distance. She sometimes found it hard to believe that he'd been engaged and later jilted when he was still a PhD student. His hair had been waist-length then, and he had all but dressed in buckskins. Or at least that's what they'd said.

It was hard to imagine John with his hair waist-length and traditional jewelry adorning his neck and wrists; a young John, full of enthusiasm and love, until now. Now she felt she'd seen some glimpses of that person, and with his shaggy, longer hair softening his face, he did seem younger and occasionally more approachable. It was not an emerging 'noble savage' that she saw, but an undercurrent of vulnerability and sensitivity that made her want to know his thoughts and ideas, and, if she were to be honest, his feelings.

Bríd looked up at the sky, taking in the huge dusting of stars that shone overhead and told a myriad of tales of their own. Orion, Arcturus the Bear, the Seven Sisters. So many tales and so many stars filling the heavens and in some place and time shaping people's understanding. She thought of the tales that shaped her own perceptions. The tales that made her who she was. These tales she herself had told, after hearing them dozens of times from Gran or her friends. Tales of war, jealousy, wisdom, sorrow and humor, all giving her a sense of who she was and where she came from. Some of these tales she had sung as a *sean nós* song or a ballad that told of a history, a way of life not forgotten. It was through her love of these stories, songs and ballads that she understood John's connection with his own tales.

Lost in her reverie, Bríd stepped inside the trailer and flipped on the overhead switch. She made her way over to the temporary shelves at the back, to the various texts and files that hadn't been scanned for the computer. Tools and other paraphernalia cluttered the floor and she picked her way through.

'Is there something I can help you with?'

Bríd whirled around to see John sitting behind the desk at the other end.

"Sorry, I didn't mean to startle you,' he said. 'I just wanted some space to think and didn't bother turning on the light when I came in.' He gestured to the small window. 'The stars are so bright.'

Bríd stared at him for a minute, trying to collect her thoughts and still her pounding heart. 'I-I can go, if you like. I only wanted to check some texts.'

'What texts?'

'Well,' she floundered, 'the texts on the tales, mythic tales. Like the one you told tonight.'

John smiled slightly, his eyes full of humor. 'Ah. You'll find the main tales there. But the ones specific to *my* beliefs'—he emphasized the word my—'now those won't be in the journals or texts. They're from my clan. I didn't publish them. Not yet. Not until I have proof.'

'Are they written down anywhere else? May I read them?' How else was she supposed to get a full understanding of the connections? Ah, for the love of God, but he was difficult.

John gave her a long, intense look then gestured to the chair opposite him. 'Sit.'

Bríd did as she was told, feeling the cold metal of the chair on the back of her legs. Across from her John's eyes began to cloud slightly, taking on a distant look.

'Among my people, my clan, there's a particular tale, a tale of our beginnings, before we came to Alaska.' He took a deep breath, closed his eyes briefly and then began.

When the Sun came, bright, red and strong, The People lived together as one, but many. The light amazed them with its brilliance, its fire, a flame color that matched the mountains of their home. But the Sun grew big and powerful, feeding as it did on the fields, the animals and then the People. Some of the People died, the animals left and there was little to eat. Then the beautiful and bright Sun of suns was gone. Nothing was left. The People decided it was time to leave, time to find a new sun. So they journeyed towards the East, the place of New Beginnings. After much travelling, they came to the edge of the land. Halted in their journey, The People wondered if this was the place to stop. Then the huge trees surrounding them sang a song. A song of Floating on Water. With great thanks they crafted the trees into seafaring canoes and took to the water. Eventually, they came to a great floating white mountain, a glacier. They knew this was the special place for The People because it was clear Creator had put the obstacle there so no one else could enter. But how were they to enter? Then the glacier sang a song to them. It was a song of going underneath. Trusting the song, The People sent three women through in a small canoe—three widows. The women returned and said there was beauty beyond. Slowly, The People went underneath, and eventually came out on the other side. To the Place of Beauty. The Place of The People. And there they stayed....'

John's voice trailed off and around them was silence. It was a silence filled with images, emotions, intangible yet overwhelming.

Bríd blinked. 'Yes,' she said. 'Yes, I can see.' She looked down at her hands.

'Why did you agree to join this dig?'

Bríd looked up, startled by his question. 'I—well.' She couldn't possibly tell him it was the only dig with an available place left because it was so last-minute. All the unspoken parts of the question—her different field of interest, her year away from Penn last year—hung in the air. She took a deep breath, reached for the empty air at her neck. No braid. 'I'm interested in mythic origin tales,' she finished lamely. She fingered her wrist, tracing the circles.

He gave her a skeptical look. 'You were in my class, granted. Your paper was good. But your dissertation subject is far removed from Native Alaskan, or even Native American mythic tales.'

'Ireland has mythic tales,' Bríd said sharply. She took a breath, calmed the defensive pose she took so readily since leaving Ireland. She attempted a light tone. 'Ah *begorrah*, we even have our own tales about our beginnings, so we do.' Her accent was thick and strong, filled with all the stage "Oirish" she could muster. 'Ah now, kind sor. Sure, but you've heard of our own Cuchulain, the mighty hero, or the fight of the Fir Bolg and the Fomorians? Or the taking of Ireland by our very own Milesians?' She gave dramatic sigh. 'Our own heroes are clear in Amairgen's poem.'

'I'm sorry,' said John. 'You're right. And you have your own language, as well.'

Her moorings gone, Bríd looked up and saw the puzzlement on his face. But he said nothing else. Desperate to be alone, to gather up those moments of feeling whole again, she made to leave.

'Sorry, I guess I'm more tired than I thought. I'll say goodnight.'

'Don't go yet,' he said.

She looked at him, tried to penetrate the neutral expression that masked his face. After a moment she detected a small glint there. The question was out of her mouth before she could stop it.

'What do you hope to find in the chamber?'

He raised his brows. Silence fell between them and Bríd dropped her eyes.

'A relation,' he said. His voice was quiet.

'A relation?' She was puzzled. Did he mean a relationship to his theories?

He shrugged. 'We have a geneticist.'

She opened her mouth to speak but nothing came out. He wanted to find a link to his stories by using his own DNA and

matching it against what they found. She hardly knew what to
say to that. 'I see,' was the best she could attempt.

INSIDE HER TENT she was relieved to find Miffy's cot empty. She
could only hope that this would be one of Miffy's amorous
nights and she could be alone with her thoughts. She sat on her
cot and traced again the design on her wrist and waited for the
calm to descend. She thought back to her recitation, the feeling
she'd had as she spoke the words. It had never happened to her
before, that filling up, that 'becoming part of the meaning.'
Never in that way. The closest she could match it was how she
felt when she got carried away with the music. When the notes
shaped her, fit her into their jiggetty jig or their bending sorrow.
She'd never questioned that, it just was. Since she was little.
Since she picked up the whistle at God knows what age.

But now this with the words. Right there in front of John.
After his way of challenging her, getting under her skin. And
then to come out and say that he hoped to match DNA with the
remains they were about to unearth. Ah janey, what could she
say to that. She remembered Jin's question about what she made
of John's theories. Would she say anything different after
hearing this? The thought of Jin made her smile. He always
knew how to bring out the best in people, make them feel they
were capable. Unlike John.

She caught sight of the whistle lying on top of the crate and
leaned over to pick it up. She fingered the holes absently and
assumed the familiar positions. After a moment or two, she
brought the fipple to her mouth and quietly played a little tune.
She smiled. There. That wasn't so bad. She played an air, a long
piece that had been one of her favorites, while she focused carefully on the items around her. There, in her backpack, just
poking out from her jeans, was the wooden box. And though the

tears formed in her eyes, Bríd put down the whistle and picked up the box.

Swirling designs were carved across the top and on the side of the box. She remembered it well. Gran had it on her table upstairs, next to her hairbrushes. As a child Bríd used to trace the designs with her finger, until her mother or someone would catch her and shoo her out of the room. She seemed to remember Gran showing her something about it once, when she could barely walk. It opened. Yes, that was it. Bríd held the box in both hands and tried to open it. Nothing. It wouldn't budge. She turned the box on its side and held it to the little camp lamp by her bed. Was there a seam? With some effort she tried to find it with her thumbnail, but failed. She sighed. She would just have to try in the daylight.

With thoughts of sleep filling her head, Bríd grabbed her toilet bag and headed to the wash stand, glancing over to the trailer. Beyond it, just at the edge of the small patch of scrubland, she could see two figures. One had its back to her, but she could make out the stocky figure of the other in the bright starlight. Who was Lu talking to and why were they talking so far from the campsite?

CHAPTER FIVE
CHINA C.1500 BCE

Tlachtga glanced back from her horse and watched the cart rattle along across the clumps of grassy little hillocks and hard packed earth under a too bright sun. From his perch on the cart, Mog Roith squinted against the glare, pulling on the reins to bring the cart to a halt. The horse stomped a little, as if to express agreement with the decision to stop. Mog climbed down carefully and stood beside the cart, while his fosterling and nephew, Buan, stretched, then jumped down to join him. The landscape spread around them—a vast expanse, broken only occasionally by clumps of low gnarled trees and brushy shrubs. A range of mountains the color of flame straddled the distant horizon.

Tlachgta smiled wryly, turned her horse and ambled back to them. The two men stood side by side, one white head, one golden, each with a hand raised to shield their eyes against the glare, scanning the horizon.

'Is all well, Father?' she asked. She dismounted with fluid grace, her hair blazing in the sun, her bright plaid tunic a flash of color against the duller brown of her trousers and boots. She patted Medb and murmured calming words to the panting horse.

'Yes, my daughter, I just thought to pause a moment to check on the harness, it seems to have come loose on one side.' Reaching over to the Segda's bit, he gave Tlachtga a reassuring smile. His blind eye was clouded, but his good eye twinkled.

Tlachtga's laughter answered his look. 'That is poor play, Father, to put your need to ease your backside on Buan's harnessing abilities,' she said. 'It will not be long. I see up ahead a long cluster of trees, where there is surely some water. That should be a good place to make a camp. We will be there well before nightfall.'

'All right my daughter, you have found me out.' Mog bent and stretched his legs. 'Just give me a short space to recover the feeling in my lower half and create a more harmonious feeling towards *Greine*.'

Tlachtga smiled, knowing that Mog would never feel ungrateful to *Greine*, the sun god with whom he had a special sacred connection. His many years as a powerful *Drui* vision poet had not dimmed his sense of humor, though. Once again, she touched the disc around her neck and thanked *Brija* for blessing her with such a father. He had been good to her. Especially after her mother died in childbirth during Tlachtga's third summer. Mog had raised her, guided her in the *Drui* way as he had been, but he had let her find her own sacred connection. The whole tribe recognized Mog's power and wisdom, and many of its members had called upon Mog to advise and direct their decisions.

It was *Greine* who had called them here now. One of his visions had shown him he must journey forth for many seasons, gathering knowledge from the furthest reaches of the great lands. Tlachtga never doubted her father's power or wisdom, but she couldn't suppress a private thought that his interpretation suited his desire for knowledge all too well.

IT WAS three summers since they'd left. Three summers since she'd left Fintan and made the promise to marry him when she returned. Her doubts about the journey had not quietened in that time and she hoped and prayed every day that Mog would turn back. She looked around her at the parched land and her doubts deepened.

Mog climbed back on the cart and Buan behind him. Tlachtga cantered on ahead, her long braid bouncing against her back, taking care to Medb's pregnant girth. Up ahead she saw a grove of trees, tucked in the small gorge by mountains colored a brilliant red that matched her hair. There, that's where they should make their rest. She was certain this was the place the Sai had described to them. The grove of trees should be beside a long stream. She drew closer and could see the grass underneath the trees was green and fertile with little flowers scattered among them, bringing welcome color. She glanced to the small, grassy plain nearby. That must be the place they planted their summer crops. It didn't look much, but perhaps they supplemented their needs with game and a little fish, though even so it was hardly a place of abundance.

TLACHTGA STARED at the bundles still piled in the cart and sighed. Behind her, Buan and her father sorted the poles, skins, felt and lacings needed to make their dwelling. Experience, accidents and friendly advice from others had taught the group efficient and effective shelter construction for the various places and seasons of their past travels. She turned to watch Mog and Buan erect the center pole and then surrounding support poles.

Once the felts were in place, they tied up the flaps to take advantage of the growing cool breeze of evening.

The dwelling erected, Tlachtga turned back to the cart and finished unloading. She carefully carried the pack that contained her father's sacred objects: the eagle headdress, the bull hide, the leather bag filled with power objects and his wheel.

Despite all his medicine and power, it was all she could do to save him in their first year traveling when he fell on a jagged rock and injured his eye. For almost the span of one moon Tlachtga had tended Mog, pouring infusions and tinctures down his throat, until she had been forced to make the dangerous walk to turn his soul from death. It had worked, and eventually he had recovered, but she felt protective of him, still.

Her own sacred bundle was not so large and she lifted it out easily, along with their metal pot, clay bowls and sack of conscientiously accumulated medicines and herbs. Finally she gently lifted out her most precious bundle of all, the harp her father had obtained from a trader two summers before. It was wrapped in a skin bag that she kept well oiled, to protect it against the weather extremes they encountered. Tonight, finally, she would play the harp and perhaps find some peace.

'Ah, Daughter, this meal is indeed medicine for the body this night,' said Mog. The three of them sat companionably around a small fire, small wooden trenchers now empty. 'You have worked wonders with the spare store we have left. These people we heard of will arrive soon and hopefully they will be able to trade to fill our store as well as our minds.'

Tlachtga smiled at her father and thought his years of searching that had brought him here to find one of the wise ones who were called *Sha Man*. These *Sha Mans* could travel to the cosmos. Mog wanted to know more, he wanted to learn this magic, if he could.

Tlachtga reached over for the skin bag that held her harp and withdrew it from its case. She placed it on her lap and plucked a few of the gut strings. Its simple but graceful design drew her hand along the slight curve of the pillar, across the arched neck and down the square box that held the sound. The motion was her prayer before she played. She plucked a few more strings to test the accuracy of their tone. Her father looked over at her in delight.

'A tale this evening, to see us to our sleep?' she asked.

Nods from both Mog and Buan gave her their answers and she plucked again, the bell-like sound intoning a reflective mood. Casting her mind around, Tlachtga decided on an old favorite to offer as thanks for a safe arrival. It was one of the tales of Finn, whose many exploits and deeds taught young and old alike in countless ways. Though they knew the tale well, it was not worn out in the telling, especially when Tlachtga gave it. The harp tinkled its own laughter through the tale, mocking Finn, warning him and enjoying the lesson well taught.

It was the tale of the wise fish. In the tale Finn hears that the wisest creature in the world is a fish that resides in the stream near his home. Determined to have such wisdom, Finn searches for the fish and finally, after much calling and thrashing about the stream's banks (for Finn is afraid of water and getting wet), the fish appears. He tells Finn that certainly, he will let Finn catch him and eat him, on one condition. Since the wisdom resides in the belly, Finn must first tickle the fish's belly in order to awaken it. Finn leans over, stretching further and further to the belly that always seems just out of reach, and he falls in. The fish escapes and Finn is never able to find the fish again.

Buan and Mog's laughter rang through the air, their enjoyment clear and easy in this night of rest. After a short while, each tired, they rose reluctantly to bed down for the night. Tlachtga moved to tend the fire, their hearth. She divided the hot ash into three piles, invoking *Brija* to protect them throughout the night. The ritual complete, she banked the fire for the morning.

THE NEXT DAY, before the sun had made much headway across the sky, Tlachtga was on Medb, her bow and arrow quiver slung across her back, looking for more substantial food to replenish their meager stores. Buan had made the same quest on foot, in another direction, hoping the stream would provide some tasty offerings, too. Mog had remained behind to mend the harness and make other necessary repairs delayed in their long journeying to this area.

Tlachtga followed the stream up into the foothills, scanning the sky for birds in search of their own prey. Even this early, Tlachtga could feel the strength of the sun on her body, penetrating her tunic. The cloth clung damply to her back under her quiver. The stream suddenly looked very appealing and she decided to take advantage of the private moment and bathe in its deeper waters. After cooing a few playful words in Medb's ear, Tlachtga loosed the mare for a drink and some grazing. She felt little need to hobble her now, not because she was heavy with her first foal, but because of the deep bond between them.

With Medb settled, Tlachtga reached for her braid and unraveled the wavy lengths, her fingers taking care with any tangles. Its coppery color glinted in a sun only partially shielded by the few trees and hilly landscape, easing its strength a little. She stripped off her woven trousers and felt-lined leather boots. Untying the braided yarn belt, she removed the plaid knee-length tunic wrap of blended blues and greens that skirted out around her when she rode. Tlachtga had adapted this outfit to her own needs after seeing the Sai and other mounted tribes ride their horses with more ease than her own long shift tunic had allowed. She grinned down at the outfit now at her feet, thinking there had been some real benefits of her travels. Medb was another benefit she could never dream of giving up. Smiling, Tlachtga stepped tentatively into the deep stream. More confident after a few moments, she reveled in its coolness, easing her limbs outwards slowly. On a whim, she plunged underneath the water.

The water flowed over her body, polishing her skin. It reminded her of her initiation in her ninth summer. She'd gone to the sacred pool to offer her own special gift of poetry when she'd slipped and fell in, sinking to the bottom, her long tunic catching on an imbedded root. She flailed her arms wildly, trying to win free, fighting off the panic that threatened to overwhelm her. Then, with no warning, a strong calm radiated through her, starting in her chest and spreading outward. The Lady, *Brija*, appeared in front of her, freeing Tlachtga and whispering the words of a far-off time. Whispering words of a great path, a great destiny. Afterwards she had fashioned a disc piece etched with three spokes that combined her father's sun wheel and her own triple-aspected goddess.

LATER, sitting on the bank, drying in the sun's warmth, she viewed the flame-colored mountains before her, drinking in their beauty, listening for their spirit. This area was nothing like the tree-filled lush places she knew as a child, but she sensed a strong spirit presence. Turning on her stomach, she scanned the stream, looking for a quiet spot where the water's flow was barely perceptible. The water was Tlachtga's easiest link to the spirits and she was unable to let this opportunity pass to see a glimpse of the future.

Though she would never say a word to her father, she could not shift her uneasiness about this place. The animals were nervous and hard to find, the plant life was working too hard to live in this dry soil. She knew it was drought, but for how long? Would they have to bear it along with these people? Perhaps the drought itself would convince her father to go back. She felt she had learned much. Now it was time for her to return home, marry Fintan and begin this path chosen for her.

She would try now and peer in the water, to scry the future for what clues could be had. She chose a suitable spot and reached for her small pouch of sacred herbs, removing the tiniest bit of leaf. It fluttered from her fingers into the water, her eyes following its journey, her lips intoning the invocation. When the fragment touched the water, she shifted her gaze slightly outward, then disengaged it entirely. The image began to form slowly, the colors and shapes defining themselves. It was her face. Not her reflection. Her face, contorted in pain. Just as quickly as she recognized her own image, it was lost in a blur of blood-red water that spread over it.

Yaloa squinted against the bright sun and tried to block out the sounds of bleating goats and sheep that were calling for attention. There was little enough grass to sustain them, he knew, but there was nothing he could change about it at the moment, so it must be put aside. Now, he tried to locate the familiar stream that marked their seasonal resting place. After a few moments, he could make out the small cluster of bedraggled trees in a distinctive triangular shape and knew that it was the place. He sniffed and smiled. Even now, the stream scented the air.

He squinted carefully, again, focusing on the figure he'd just noticed under the tree, but it failed to disappear. He moved closer and could make out a person sitting beside a small dwelling. Nearby was a strange animal and something else. Another dwelling? One of the dogs barked.

'There, up ahead!' cried a voice behind him. His sister, Teslintoo, came up by his side.

'Do you see, Brother?'

He nodded and sighed. He could tell by her tone she wasn't pleased to see that two strangers appeared to be camping at their site. What might intrigue him, his sister would mostly likely view with suspicion. He gestured to Qalaktc, his brother-in-law, and Gutao and a few other men. They moved forward, their knives not far from their reach.

As Yaloa and the small advance group moved closer, he could see that not only was the man extremely tall and his dress strange, but his skin and hair color was even more remarkable. Pale beyond imagination. The old man rose as they neared and Yaloa could see that that one eye was clouded and his hands were held open and empty. The tension eased between his shoulders.

'Greetings to you,' said the old man. He used trader language, a combination of words and gestures. 'I am Mog. I have traveled far with my daughter Tlachtga and my foster son and nephew, Buan. I hope you will not mind sharing your shelter space with us.' The words seemed awkward on the man's his tongue, but his tones were accurate enough. He looked at Yaloa hopefully.

Yaloa stared at him a moment, taking in his words, while his mind sifted through all that was before him. He eyed the animal eating some grass. It was huge. Much bigger than the dogs that usually pulled their bundles strapped to poles. This animal, he realized, could easily carry things on its back as well as pulling huge packs on poles. He eyed the wooden construction beside the animal. It had long poles attached to wooden panels that formed a large rectangular box. All of a sudden, he understood. He viewed the old man with new appreciation and smiled.

'I am the leader,' he said slowly and carefully, lest the man misunderstand his meaning. 'You are welcome to share our shelter. I invite you into my home.' He raised one brow. 'When it is ready.'

Mog returned the smile. 'My daughter and son should be back in a short while,' he answered. 'They went off to try to replenish our stores.' He looked out in the distance beyond the group and the milling herd of animals. 'Ah, there's my daughter, now.'

Yaloa turned and followed Mog's gaze eastward. In the distance Tlachgta's mounted shape, a silhouette in the blazing sun, came towards them at a fast pace. As the shape became more defined, the bright light caught it from overhead and lit up the flame-colored strands that flew out from its center like rays from the sun. For a moment, it was as if a ball of fire had dropped from the sun above and was moving towards them. Yaloa's eyes widened, uncertain what to make of the apparition before him. Around him, Yaloa heard gasps, murmurs and the whoosh of warding hand motions. Should he pray to the spirits of the mountain?

CHAPTER SIX

PRESENT DAY CHINA

The tension and energy in the air was so palpable Bríd could almost taste it. They were all gathered around the rim of the excavated hole. It was a chamber, really, and the layers of soil, branches and woven grass mats that covered it were now carefully removed. It was time to discover its contents.

Scott hovered over Bob as he adjusted his harness straps, pressing last-minute clarifications and questions on him about video camera angles. Jin stood poised at the rim with his own digital camera in hand, staring silently into the hole while Dr Chou fidgeted nervously with his tablet. Bríd could feel John's tension as she quietly fastened the harness on him, adjusting the straps and clips. Behind him, Miffy sorted crates, bags and other packing materials in readiness for whatever lay below.

Lu and Chang stood off to one side, frowning visibly, Chang's corpulent figure already sweating profusely under the glaring sun. Chang had informed them in no uncertain terms that they were acting against his instructions and he'd gone ahead and phoned the authorities to report. John had brushed aside his words with a curt wave of the hand. He was too close to his moment of truth to stop now.

After a brief, grim glance at Bríd, John gave the nod and Scott, Bob and Jin lowered John carefully inside. Bob followed closely behind, with John to guide and support from below. Bríd peered over the side. When they had both settled on the chamber floor, they switched on their headlamps illuminating the brick and timber that comprised its walls.

Their lamps moved to the center of the chamber. Bob let out a low whistle. Timeless and silent in its well-preserved state on a wooden bed was a blond Caucasian mummy.

Miffy gasped. 'Oh my God. That's amazing.'

Bob grinned up at her. 'This is the big one.'

John remained silent as Bob held up the camera and started filming.

Bríd sat outside for a moment's rest before dinner, playing idly with the carved wooden box. She'd brought it along to distract her, to focus on something while her mind unwound. Though she was exhausted after a hard day's work, she was excited, too. She wanted to clear her head before she thought any more about the day's events that crowded in nearly to the point of overwhelming her.

She stared at the box, ran her thumb nail around the seam absentmindedly. It was no good. She couldn't get the events to leave her thoughts. John's stoic attitude as he meticulously followed all the archaelogical protocols, taking notes, making sketches while Bob filmed away, making noises of delight and enthusiasm, nearly brought her to tears. Amid all the excitement and chattering that would easily play havoc with John's carefully planned strategies, John was still able to give an occasional smile and keep everyone on track while she and the others removed the mummy and the items buried with it. The others seemed oblivious to John's muted behavior, too lost in sharing their wild views and opinions. Everyone except Jin. She remembered now that Jin had been quiet, too.

It was difficult not to be excited and speculate on the mummy's origins. The quality of the preservation was so near perfect, it was hard to believe it was probably 3000 to 3500 years old. At least that's what Bob had estimated. He was so visibly elated, he could hardly contain himself. Chou had been more circumspect. The government wouldn't be pleased at another example of early racial diversity within China's borders.

From the turn of twentieth century to the 1920s, a few explorers had dared to trek the formidable Täklimakan Desert, searching for links to the silk trade route and the Buddhist faith and had unearthed human remains and artefacts that suggested an early Caucasian presence. At that time, though, limited technology meant it was impossible to date them accurately. The explorers' records had surfaced again after a few Chinese colleagues like Chou began unearthing artefacts and remains in this region. But the expanding desert, Chinese politics and funding problems had slowed the research to a crawl.

But who was the mummy? Where did it come from? It was the artefacts and the clothes that excited Bríd the most. But she needed a closer look before she would voice any of her theories. Theories that left a tense knot in her stomach. Was she really up to such a discovery? Was she crazy? She'd made so many bad choices recently, who was to say that she was right this time?

'Can I help you with that?'

Startled, Bríd nearly dropped the box. She looked up with a weak smile and acknowledged Jin's offer with a nod. 'I'm not sure you can. I think I remember that it opens, but I might be wrong. You see, it was my grandmother's. Well, my great-grandmother's, really, and it's only now that it's come to be mine.'

Jin smiled at her and held out his hand. She gave him the box and he studied it. 'I thought as much. It's a Chinese puzzle box. No amount of prying or pulling will open it, but it does open. You just have to know where to press.' He turned it over and around in his hands, pushing gently at different spots. Suddenly, it sprang open. He offered the box back to her and grinned. 'See?'

Inside was a wad of black cloth. 'My God. Who'd have thought it? You're amazing.' She took the box, turning it around in wonder. How on Earth had her great-grandmother come upon such a thing?

'The box looks quite old,' said Jin. 'And of fair quality, too.' He pointed to the carvings and the mechanism, explaining briefly how it worked.

The wad of cloth inside shifted and fell onto the ground while he talked. As Bríd leaned down to pick it up, a metal object fell out, clattering on a small stone. She picked up the object. It appeared to be a medallion, silver in color with some markings she could barely make out. Near the edge was a small hole where a chain or ribbon might have passed through. A necklace? She turned the medallion over. This side was worn to a smooth patina that glinted in the late sun.

'How unusual,' said Jin. 'May I see?'

Bríd held it out to him, her mind racing. Where had that come from? She had no memories of ever seeing that around Gran's neck. She tried to think. Had Gran shown it to her? Had she ever mentioned it? She shook her head in an effort to recall.

'A very interesting piece. It certainly has a quaint air about it. Did your great grandmother collect antique jewelery?'

Bríd laughed at the thought. 'I don't know. But I would say not. Nor my grandmother. There really was no money for that kind of thing. They were farmers. My grandfather felt that if it didn't work or produce something, then what was the use of it anyway?'

Jin studied the medallion, slowly turning it over. 'An understandable sentiment in a hardworking rural environment. But still, lamentable if we were all to take that view. It would be a shame to have a world devoid of beauty because it didn't fill a function, other than gratifying the eyes.' He wrapped the medallion back in the cloth, placed it in the box and handed the box to her.

'I will say my grandfather did appreciate music, and a fine story. So he wasn't a complete philistine.'

'I would have been surprised to hear otherwise, considering your talent.'

Bríd felt her color rise. 'Ah, no. I suppose you've heard me play the whistle out here a few times. But, I'm no good at all, really.'

'You shouldn't be so humble. You play well. As does John.'

'You heard John play?'

'Yes. Only the once. It was a very different piece to your own.'

'I know. It was one he had from his uncle.'

'Yes of course. That would explain it. It had a certain "tribal" feel about it.'

Bríd stiffened almost imperceptibly. Was there something ever so slightly condescending about that statement, or was she misreading it? 'Well, now,' she found herself saying. 'You could call my tunes tribal, too. If you wanted to.'

Jin smiled, but the smile didn't reach his eyes. 'You're right of course. And I'm sure John would agree, too.' He paused. 'Though I would hazard that John has other things to worry about at present. It must be very difficult for him to deal with the disappointment of today's discovery, after all his work.'

Bríd looked at him curiously. Just what did he think about it, himself? 'I'm sure John will set aside his disappointment and approach this in a professional and scholarly manner. The artefacts and mummy are just full of challenges and will provoke a huge amount of interest across the world. That will bring him a lot of respect and recognition, which would surely make up for the disappointment.'

Jin looked thoughtful for a moment, then touched her shoulder. 'I'm certain you're right, Bríd. And you will be able to help and support this, too. I hope I can be a part of it, just as you are. There is so much unanswered as yet.' He continued in that vein, his excitement gathering, listing some of the possibilities. 'Do you think I could help you with the inventory, tomorrow?' he added.

Bríd squeezed his arm, her own enthusiasm rekindled with his words. 'It is something you want to be a part of, isn't it? I don't know what John and Bob will want to do, but I can mention it to them, if you prefer. I'm sure Dr Chou would put in a good word for you, too.'

Jin's expression was neutral. 'I think Dr Chou would defer to whatever Bob and John might say. So I would be grateful for anything you might tell them on my behalf.'

Bríd ran her fingers along the wooden box in her hand. 'I will, of course.'

It was only later, back in her tent, that she removed the medallion from its box, after some tries, pressing along the sides. On impulse, she took a cord from her backpack, threaded it through the hole and tied the cord around her neck. She was surprised at how good it felt, as though in some way her grandmother was with her now. Her breath caught in her throat. Yes, she could think about her now without the stabbing, choking sensation. Perhaps her grandmother, in whatever realm she might be now, had forgiven her.

'What's that?'

Bríd looked up startled. Miffy stood with her hands on her hips, her eyes narrowed.

'Did you take that from the dig? Are you stupid or something? You know that's not allowed. And putting it around your neck like you're some kind of ancient goddess, or something, is worse. Take it off now before you get anymore of your body oils on it.'

Bríd reddened. 'It's not from the dig. It's mine.'

Miffy gave her a skeptical look. 'Jewelery on a dig? Really. What do you take me for? Besides, you haven't worn it before, why now?'

'It is mine. I-I just didn't realize it until now. I mean I had the box in my backpack and....' She pursed her lips. 'It's none of your business. Just take it from me, it's nothing to do with the dig. You can ask Jin if you don't believe me.'

'Jin?'

'Yes.' Bríd felt herself redden again and cursed her fair skin.

'You and he having a thing?'

'What? No. He's nice and all, but I wouldn't....' She was going to say that she wouldn't have a relationship with anyone on a dig because it wouldn't be professional, but that wouldn't have gone down well and she wanted Miffy to drop the subject.

Miffy sat down on her own cot heavily.

'Aren't you going to Bob's tonight?'

'We don't have to be in each other's pockets, you know,' she said hotly. 'Sometimes it's better to have a little time to myself. It keeps things fresh.'

Bríd nodded weakly and kept her thoughts to herself. It was obvious Miffy had just quoted words that Bob had recently spoken to her. Trouble in paradise? She allowed herself a smile as she knelt down to put the box in her backpack, away from Miffy's prying eyes. The necklace swung out and hit her in the mouth.

· · ·

THE NIGHT HAD SETTLED IN, an inky blackness, devoid of moon and stars. Bríd scanned the sky, looking for some traces of light as she gathered her thoughts and, she admitted, her courage, as she made her way to the office to talk to John.

She had seen John go toward the trailer earlier, while Bob held her captive at dinner, monopolizing her company and the conversation. John had skipped dinner, as had Jin, Chang, and Lu. That left Dr Chou, Scott and of course Miffy. Today Bob had chosen to sit next to Bríd instead and talk to her animatedly about the dig. He was ecstatic about the discovery and convinced it would attract unimagined publicity. Miffy meanwhile, sat in sullen silence on his other side. Bob had then invited Bríd to go with him to check on the artefacts and mummy in the lab trailer before they turned in, but she'd politely declined and he took Miffy instead.

Though she badly wanted to see the artefacts once more, she decided to risk John's company and look at the digital images and video clips rather than endure Bob's unwanted attentions. John certainly seemed the safer bet.

But now, as she hesitated outside the trailer, she tried to reassure herself that John would welcome her desire to study the images. Would he be equally welcoming of her thoughts? But after all, wasn't his own theory just as farfetched? She took a deep breath, opened the door, then entered.

John sat at the desk studying the laptop surrounded by notebooks, sketches and a tablet. He looked up when she entered, the effects of fatigue etched on his face.

'Sorry to disturb you, but would you mind if I looked at the images along with you? There was so much going on today, I was hoping I could study them in more detail, now.'

John nodded with a resigned air, his eyes narrowing. He

gestured towards the folding chairs at other end of the trailer. 'Pull up a seat.'

The words were neutral, nearly devoid of emotion. She released her breath carefully, set up a chair beside John and sat down. The tan on his muscular legs seemed dark against the pale skin of her legs. His legs and shorts were still dusty from the day's excavation. It seemed in addition to skipping a meal he'd had no time to spare for a wash, either. His arm brushed hers as he reached across for the tablet. The warmth of his body, still hot from the day's exertions, enfolded her, dispelling any remaining chill she'd felt in the cool night air. She bit her lip and looked at the tablet in an effort to distract herself.

An image of the mummy filled the screen. It was lying as they first found him, on the bed of a cart with a wheel on either side of him. He was dressed in a tunic of blue-green wool plaid weave held closed with a red and blue yarn tie. Under the tunic he wore mud-brown woven wool trousers that were tucked inside felt-lined leather boots. There was also a kind of hide draped around his shoulders and strapped to his head was a wooden head piece finely carved into the shape of an eagle. A person of prominence, thought Bríd. Possibly a leader of ritual. At his feet were pots and bowls filled with various items and food remains.

Bríd studied the image intently, making mental notes of all the astonishing details. John silently typed away beside her on the laptop. It was a lot to take in. The tunic alone took her breath away. Woven wool plaid? Woven plaid cloth in this area, of such antiquity, was remarkable from what she could remember from her own research. And plaid! Her fingers itched to touch it. But it was the placement of the mummy that really caught her attention. It was lying on the cart bed, between the wheels. She wished her professors were here, for her own expertise was limited. Should she say anything?

John leaned over and enlarged the image to focus on the boots. They were nicely tanned and stitched.

'There's a lot of care and skill gone into those boots,' said John.

'There certainly is.' She was at a loss. She was acutely aware of his presence next to her. Could she make him listen, give her time to make him understand? How should she begin? What should she say first?

John shifted the screen's focus to take in the trousers' careful weave and the tunic's vibrant colors.

Bríd searched her mind for opening words. 'The level of preservation is remarkable,' she managed to say.

'It's the arid environment. It inhibits the growth of bacteria and other elements that hasten the breakdown of materials.' John continued to explain the details of the climate preservation advantages while Bríd gathered herself to make the plunge. After a little more explanation, John stopped abruptly and gave her a puzzled look. 'Sorry, I've bored you,' he said. He paused then nodded to the screen. 'Well, what do you think so far?'

He shifted position, his knee bumping hers and Bríd found herself blushing as a rush of heat surged through her body. He seemed so remote again. Distant. How could she put her own ideas to him? Especially after the disappointment he must be feeling. Was there anything she could say to him that would help? She found herself hoping that it might be possible.

'It's the last thing I expected to find,' she said. She continued to look at the screen. 'And in such a well preserved condition. Not just the mummy, but the items and the clothes found with it.' She licked her lips, urging herself forward. 'The clothes are especially surprising.'

'I know,' said John. He turned to study her, his own eyes unfathomable. 'Woven wool plaid. That suggests so many things.'

Bríd looked at him carefully. Did he know what she was thinking? 'Wool plaid, this far east? This ancient? Surely that's remarkable and would draw significant interest from other scholars. And give you enormous credit,' she added quietly.

John nodded, still studying her face, his own still unreadable. 'I've no doubt it would, as would many other aspects, such as the layout. The cart, wheels—what do you make of that?'

She looked back at the screen, fidgeting nervously for a moment under this gaze. 'Well.' She drew her breath and began again. 'Well it does seem to have some similarities to the Celtic burials at places like Hallstatt and other parts of Europe. But this is so much earlier.' She sneaked a glance at him.

He nodded slowly. 'Yes, I thought it might,' he said. 'I know little about it. He gave a wan smile. 'Maybe there was a reason for you to come on this dig after all.' He rested his hand on her arm briefly. She looked down at the worn skin and chipped nails that showed how passionate he was about his work. It was a passion that, at that moment, she thought she might possibly come to share.

Bríd made an effort to concentrate. She wanted to tell him her ideas, especially since he already seemed to have accepted the possibility she was about to explain. But John had turned back to the screen and moved the tablet's focus up to the head, where the carved eagle headpiece was fixed.

'But this is what interests me at the moment. The headpiece. There's something about it. A connection. I feel it.' He stared at it for a moment and then sighed and shook his head. 'I don't know. But it is remarkable workmanship. I'm not sure of the wood, but I suppose that doesn't matter.'

Bríd stared at the face on the screen, her aching sympathy for John vanishing as suddenly the face took on life. In her mind's eye she could see the face, now a part of the whole man as he stood by the fully assembled cart, ready for use. His tunic flapped in a passing breeze and he began to lift bundles out from the cart's bed. When he turned again she could see his face clearly, one eye blind, the other a bright twinkling blue and his hair a golden blaze in the sun. She blinked again and the image was gone, replaced by an overwhelming faintness. Darkness rose up and threatened to close in on her.

'Bríd! Bríd!' John's arm was around her, shaking her gently.

She blinked again, then looked up at his face hovering over her, his eyes full of concern. She attempted to sit straight, though she was reluctant to release herself from his embrace. 'I'm fine.' Her voice was shaky, denying her words. She took a deep breath. 'I'm fine.' She forced strength into her voice. 'Really.' She shook her head. 'Sorry about that,' she said. 'I don't know what came over me.'

She stared at the screen in front of her, the head still a mummy, any life long gone. John rubbed her arm gently.

She bit her lip and looked at him. 'I saw him,' she whispered. 'Just for a moment. One eye was blind, but the other was a deep blue.'

John frowned, puzzled by her words. 'Who?'

'The mummy. Only he was a man. With bright golden hair, standing by the cart.'

'Where? Where did you see him?'

'Here, just now. Well not here, but I saw an image of him in my mind. He was unloading the cart.'

'An image?'

'Yes. No. I don't know. It was a brief flash, a clip.' Bríd tugged at a curl at her neck, trying to make sense of what she'd seen.

'A vision?'

'What. No—oo.' She gave him an incredulous look. 'It's nothing. Maybe too much heat.' Bríd's voice trailed off helplessly.

'What exactly did you see?'

She sat up straight in an effort to recall it all. She began slowly forming the words carefully, missing no detail. John listened intently. When she finished, he nodded thoughtfully and remained silent for a few minutes.

'I'm not sure what this is, or what caused it,' he said finally, then shrugged. 'I think you've made a strong connection here. Maybe you should assist Bob tomorrow as he works on the mummy. He suggested it earlier today and I said I'd think about it.'

A mixture of emotions surged through Bríd. Though she loathed the thought of being under Bob's eye too much, she dearly wanted to examine the mummy. Would Miffy be there? Then she remembered. 'Could Jin work with us, too? He's very interested in what we've discovered and has asked especially if he could be highly involved with the examination and inventory work.'

John's eyes clouded. 'I'm not sure. It might be better that Jin works with us tomorrow. Chou and I are compiling some preliminary reports for our funders.'

'Oh, right. Of course.' Bríd could sense his withdrawal and wondered at it. Was it Jin, or something she said? She cast around for a topic that would be more neutral. She began explaining burial patterns that she knew, caught up in a babble of words to block out the tumult of emotions inside. 'Are there any similar patterns in your own culture?' she asked finally. Perhaps there he might find some connection he was hoping for. There were a few tiny, niggling differences.

'Tlingit burial patterns?' John's face tightened and she felt his body stiffen against her. 'Exhuming corpses isn't exactly approved in my culture. Though cremation is the general custom, there were exceptions with shamans. They were interred in elaborate burial huts constructed on remote summits or an island's edge. People gave them a wide berth. They also avoided sites where people had died tragically, in order to prevent any encounter with the Kooshdaka, the Land Otter people who tried to claim the souls of the living. Those were the old Tlingit customs.'

These comments, hinting at a personal reference, a personal conflict, surprised Bríd. She carefully tried for more, unable to resist the urge to explore his world. 'What happened during the cremation?' she asked.

John's face eased a little. 'The family cremated the body during a memorial potlatch held to ensure there was a proper transition to the afterlife. During the potlatch they recited the accomplishments and life of the deceased. They would aso recite the clan's genealogy and history recitation. The history was integral to the clan's sense of community, and it guided future actions.' John paused then added, 'My great-uncle is our clan's history keeper.'

His explanation fascinated her despite his stiff delivery. The last bit of information about his uncle set her mind in a different direction. 'You talked in the past tense. Doesn't anyone still believe or practice these rituals? What about your great-uncle?'

'I can't say for sure what he practices now. I haven't been back in years—we have different views.' He looked over at her, and a brief flash of pain crossed his face. 'Well, I used to think we did. Now, I'm not so sure.'

Bríd walked back to the tent, mulling over the events at the trailer. What had happened to her when she'd come over faint? Was it the heat from the grueling day, her runaway emotions in the face of John's presence? What exactly did she feel about John that he caused such confusion in her? She wasn't certain she was ready to admit the growing pleasure she found in his company, or the pleasure at his touch. She would concede that she found him interesting and she wanted to know more about his family

—his reasons for his estrangement from his uncle, for instance. He'd said little more after his initial response, changing the subject back to tomorrow's schedule. Through his neutral tones and the few words of concern for her wellbeing just as she departed, she'd felt the unspoken ban against any more questions about his family.

When she was in the shadow of her tent and paused to unzip the flap, she caught sight of a figure moving towards the lab trailer. The lights were off and it was clearly shut up after Bob's visit. She couldn't identify him, for it was a man, she could see that much. The man fumbled at the door, obviously having a problem turning the key, then slipped quietly inside. It was late for any serious work, but perhaps they couldn't sleep because of all the excitement today. Bob probably. Suddenly, sleep didn't seem impossible for her, it seemed the only thing.

CHAPTER SEVEN

CHINA C.1500 BCE

Tlachtga made a face at the stew she stirred, its juices bubbling in a friendly rhythm. She hoped the noise indicated a good result. Laughter drifted over to her from the group sitting under the tree where Yaloa and his family sat talking with her father and Buan. They were all gathered to share a meal to mark the passing of one moon since their portentous encounter. Though she felt disinclined to share in the celebration, for some reason she wanted the meal to taste its best this evening.

Tlachtga grinned at the memory of her first meeting with these people. With her hair flying in all directions, traveling at a fast and unfamiliar pace, these people had taken her for some kind of sun spirit. When she realized their mistake, she had momentarily considered using it to obtain the learning her father sought, so they could be on their way. But she knew it couldn't work that way. And more important, she knew her father would never have cooperated with such a pretense, even though Buan might have seen its humor. No, Mog had immediately set the people straight, though he had taken pains to emphasize the wonder of the skills and learning they brought, and their *Drui* priest status among their own tribe.

Right now, Mog was explaining his harness construction and how his design ensured a secure fit. She saw Yaloa followed Mog's trader dialect carefully, so not to mistake the exact meaning. Yaloa's native tongue was much different and more difficult to grasp and so Mog used it only for simple statements at the moment. Tlachtga was a little better, her ear for new language sounds had been sharpened through her practice at the harp.

She had accepted the task to learn the language with eagerness. Not, as Buan teased her, so she could spend time with Yaloa, but so she could increase the speed to complete her father's quest here. Now, she found it difficult to admit even to herself how much she had enjoyed the time with Yaloa. That she found him warm and kind. That his straight black hair and mustache, his tilted eyes and broad, high cheek bones, so different to the features of her own people, were deeply appealing. And that all her fears from the scrying in the stream and her anxieties about her surroundings vanished in his presence.

She tried to reason that all of Yaloa's family were equally well favored and kind. Except for his sister, Teslintoo, who for some reason had taken a violent dislike to Tlachtga. As the sister of the unmarried tribal leader, she held a position of authority. She seemed to wield it with an energy even her husband, Qalaktc, did not dispute. Yaloa was the only exception to her successful control of people's actions. Tlachtga thought privately that the woman was as mean and sour as an old sow anyway, so it mattered little.

Squeals of laughter penetrated her thoughts. She turned and saw Yaloa tickling his nephew, Yakwun, who screamed and giggled with with delight. Teslintoo looked on, a smile softening her face for a moment. Yaloa caught Tlachtga's eye and winked. Unable to resist the good humor, Tlachtga grinned at him and raised her brows. Teslintoo intercepted the exchange and frowned. The frown reversed when she saw a group of young women passing near.

'Cousin!' Teslintoo cried, avoiding addressing the woman by name, as was the custom.

Tlachtga watched a young nubile woman make her way over to Teslintoo, her long black hair swaying with the extra force she gave it when she walked. Tlachtga sighed. It was Kayáani. Every bone in Kayáani's body was arranged to create a sense of imperiousness and entitlement that her expression did little to discount. Tlachtga had noticed that the only kinds of attention Kayáani recognized were subservience and admiration. The only exceptions she allowed came from the two she now greeted with a grand smile.

'Cousin,' said Kayáani, taking Teslintoo's hand. 'You are well?' she asked as custom demanded. With Teslintoo's nod, Kayáani turned to Yaloa, her head tilted for its best effect. 'And you, Cousin, I hope your health is also good?' Kayáani raised her eyes, directing her glance at Tlachtga.

Tlachtga knew that neither culture would excuse her for failing to issue an invitation for Kayáani to join them in the meal. Pursing her lips in resignation, Tlachtga made her way over to Kayáani and said the necessary words. The acceptance was no surprise and Tlachtga moved back over to the pot. Her fingers itched to reach over to her medicine pouch and retrieve the herb that induced vomiting. A few pinches in one bowl were all she'd need. Her evening's pleasure had more or less been spoiled. Kayáani was certain to dominate the conversation, with the help of Teslintoo. She was not fluent in the trader language —she could barely manage a greeting. So for politeness's sake, they would have to speak in these people's language.

It was clear to Tlachtga that Teslintoo wanted Yaloa to take Kayáani for a wife. If anyone listened to Teslintoo, Kayáani was everything a man could want in a helpmate. She wasn't sure that Yaloa did listen to her, although he gave Teslintoo polite attention the countless times she pointed out one of Kayáani's wondrous attributes. Kayáani was beautiful, Tlachtga thought dispassionately. She watched Kayáani chattering away to Yaloa. Her high cheekbones set off dark doe eyes rimmed with long lashes. The colorful red and blue threads that weaved through her skirt and tunic top set off her rippling black hair and her even-toned skin. Tlachtga caught sight of the freckles on her own hand as she began to serve the portions and frowned. Distracted, she didn't notice the broth dribbling off the spoon onto her plaid trousers until she felt the heat on her leg. Clumsy oaf, she thought. She was as different to Kayáani as night was to day, so it was best to put away any thoughts of Yaloa. Her first and only thought should be to leave this place quickly.

After the meal finished, Yaloa stood up and excused himself with a plea of various responsibilities. Teslintoo rose, too, and claimed she too should leave to put her son and daughter to bed. After ordering Gutao to check on the sheep, she asked Yaloa to walk Kayáani to her family's dwelling before he tended his tasks.

Tlachtga and Buan began clearing up as soon as the group departed. As he helped her with the big pot, she heard him muttering a little. He looked over her and chuckled, 'That one could use a special kind of horse bit and harness,' he said. 'She is still young enough that she might eventually be of use if she was given the proper handling.'

Tlachtga dug him in the ribs and laughed. 'Ah, when Teslintoo listed all her fine points, I did not hear any mention of good teeth. Shall we ask about that next time? I am sure she would display them if requested. Perhaps Yaloa has counted them.'

Buan snorted, pulling his dark bushy mustache. 'Yaloa would be addled to consider Kayáani for anything other than something fine to look at. I think he prefers to look at you, Sister.' He grinned. 'Though with the state of your tunic, I can hardly imagine why.'

Tlachtga looked down at herself and reddened. 'Now, what would I be doing with Yaloa? You know I am promised to Fintan.'

Buan snorted again. 'Childhood utterances. They mean nothing, Tlachtga, and you know it. Besides, Fintan is silly and simpering. He is too soft for you.'

"What do you know, you big mullux?" She laughed and shoved him again. "You could do well to keep your own horse teeth under cover the way you keep grinning at Yaloa's cousin, Qualtsixkli.'

'I only sought to help her feel included,' said Buan. 'Her brother Gutao is too shy himself to draw her forward.'

Tlachtga snorted. 'I think I hear too much protest, there.'

'You can both cease your teasing,' interrupted Mog, coming along side of them. "Tlachtga, I want to speak to you on the matter of horses, not those you think look like them. Yaloa asked that he be shown how to ride a horse. I told him that is for you to do. I am too old and my poor eyesight would eventually hinder the instructions.'

'Oh Father, you are far from old,' she said. 'Your eyesight with the one eye is sharper than any hawk. You even see what others cannot.'

'Ah, that is another kind of sight, as you well know.' Mog replied. 'The matter is decided, though. Tomorrow you shall start teaching Yaloa the way of riding. I told him it was best to begin before the weather is too cold to permit it. He will meet you down by the hillock at the river when the sun clears the trees.'

Tlachtga opened her mouth to protest, but then thought

better of it. She shrugged her shoulders and said, 'I shall take Segda, then. Medb, I think, is too close to her foaling time.'

THE MORNING DAWNED. Tlachtga pulled on her fur-lined leather boots and tucked her trousers into them. There was a distinct chill in the air, so she added an extra tunic beneath the plaid skirted one. The added warmth would be welcome on a chilly day spent teaching riding. She braided her hair in one long plait and pulled on a blue felt hood. Picking up a small leather leading strap, she left the dwelling and made her way to Segda. She noticed her father over by the cart talking with Buan and gave them both a wave. They returned her greeting.

She found Segda standing patiently, his roan-colored coat shining in the morning light. His head turned at her approach and the soft brown eyes looked at her expectantly. She saw he was already saddled and bridled and shouted her thanks towards the men. It had to have been Buan, his affection for her always displayed in actions rather than words. Her uncle had sent him to foster with her father in Buan's seventh summer, and in the time since, she had never any cause to doubt his brotherly affection, though she could do without his brotherly teasing. With a contented sigh she turned back to Segda and rubbed his head, murmuring her hello. His nostrils widened and he snorted lightly. She mounted in one graceful motion and leaned down to whisper a promise to reward him come evening.

A short while later, Tlachtga sat humming at the appointed spot by the river while Segda nuzzled a sparse bit of grass. The bright sun warmed her back, lulling her into a light doze as her thoughts wandered aimlessly. Drowsy and relaxed, Tlachtga didn't hear the footsteps approach her.

'A-ah, the sun goddess in meditation.'

Tlachtga started, then rose hastily and turned to Yaloa, her face reddening. He was clad in a hide tunic and leggings, leather boots, and a vest lined with goat fleece. His thick, dark hair blew lightly across his face under a close fitting cap. Humor filled his dark eyes as one brow lifted in a hesitant question. She felt her pulse quicken slightly and her breath catch in her throat.

'Of course.' Tlachtga said, after her wits returned. "You see I have provided a day of bright sun for us."

'The light and warmth of the sun is always near in your presence,' Yaloa teased.

'Such words will only make me burn brighter and scorch us both.' Tlachtga said, trying to match his light tone.

She reached for Segda's reins, seizing on the practical action to cover her flustered state. 'Let's begin by getting to know Segda.'

She led Segda closer and allowed him to sniff Yaloa, especially at his arm pits where his personal odor was strong. She took Yaloa's hand, placed it gently on the horse's forehead and guided it down in a soft stroking motion. His hand, warm and firm to her touch, possessed a sensitivity and intuition she could instantly feel. She forced herself to focus on the task at hand and told herself that would bode well for learning to ride. Perhaps if she completed the instruction in good time, Yaloa would share the teachings Mog sought. Then they could at last travel home and she could begin her own destined path with Fintan.

YALOA OPENED his leather bag and pulled out some flat bread and hunks of goat cheese. Tearing a bit from the bread, he handed the rest to Tlachtga. She took it gratefully. It had been a good morning's work, but he was tired. The sun was overhead now and he was grateful when she suggested a break by the stream. Tlachtga had told him he was quick to learn, but warned him he would still feel his inexperience from the scream of his muscles in the days to come. He confessed to feeling a little strain in his legs, but he was certain that some rest was all he needed to resume another rigorous session.

Yaloa munched quietly on his piece of bread and hunk of goat cheese while he watched Tlachtga eat, her sleeves falling back along her arm with the motion. Before she could return her hand to her lap, Yaloa encircled her wrist with his hand and turned it towards him. He looked curiously at the design of three interlocking circles tattooed on the inside.

'May I ask you what the markings on your wrist are?' he said.

She withdrew her hand from his grasp, her face reddening. Had he said something wrong? Her answer, when it came, was formal, as was her tone.

'They are the sacred symbols for *Brija*, the goddess spirit who guides my path of healing, music and metalworking. When I pray for her help I hold my arms just so. My palms are open, to show my wrists to the sky.' She held out her arms and hands in supplication. 'Through these marks I receive her spirit energy into my life pulse points. From that entry it courses throughout my body, whispering its wisdom and giving its strength. It is a most powerful experience.' She folded her hands together. 'My father is tattooed in the same manner, except his marks are the sun wheel, to connect to *Greine*, his guiding power and spirit.'

Her eyes widened at the close of her explanation, holding Yaloa captive for just a moment. She was so intriguing, this woman. So unlike anyone he'd ever met.

Yaloa gently took her hands again and turned the palms up for a closer look. He traced the circles slowly with his finger, first on the one wrist, and then the other, in a meditative motion. He looked up into her eyes and said with equal gravity, 'Yes, I can feel even now the strength of this spirit coursing through you. You are very gifted and blessed.' Carefully, he laid her hands in her lap.

Tlachtga blushed again, but she held his gaze. He moved a fraction in her direction, but caught himself. He picked up the leather water bag, removed the stopper and sipped, gathering himself. After a moment he spoke again. 'Tell me, how did you come to be a *Drui,* as you call it? He intoned the unfamiliar word *Drui* strangely.

Tlachtga blinked and looked away. She took a deep breath and returned his gaze.

'Well, as a daughter of a *Drui,* I was well aware of the nature of its practice, especially since my father raised me.' He passed the leather bag to her and she took a sip. 'After my mother's death, I traveled with my father wherever he was needed. His reputation as a man of power and wisdom was widely known and I learned much just being with him. Then, in my ninth summer, I had a powerful vision. *Brija* came to me and told me my path. After that, I spent time with other *Drui* who were guided by *Brija* and they initiated me in her ways. That is, until I began this journey with my father.'

'And where will your journey end?' asked Yaloa.

'Father says, when the wheel ceases to turn,' she said with a smile.

'Now that is a true *Sha Man's* answer,' said Yaloa, returning her smile. 'I hope your time with us does not end soon. There is much I would still learn from you both.'

'Ah, Father still has much he would learn here, too.' She looked down at her wrists where earlier he'd traced those circles. Was she feeling his touch, just as he remembered how her skin felt under his finger?

'Tell me,' she said. 'How did you come to be the tribal leader as well as *Sha Man,* and,' she paused, 'why do you have no wife?'

Yaloa laughed and lifted a brow. 'Such a lot of questions in one breath,' he said. He was silent for a moment, removed his cap and brushed his fingers through his shoulder-length hair and thought about his reply. 'So, you know I am a *Sha Man*, too. The tribe's *Sha Man* before me was my mother's brother. It is a great responsibility, combining the two roles, but it became necessary in our small tribe. Only a few clans remain of what was once a large group, many ages ago. Now, we struggle to maintain our size.

'When I was in my eleventh summer, I had an eagle spirit come to me with a message for my clan and my uncle. The eagle spirit told me I was chosen for a difficult task that ahead that would save my people.' He looked over at her with a grim smile. 'It was not a message I was eager to hear, for my father had been training me to be a headman, so I could succeed him when he was gone. I knew this new role would only add to his worries, and my own training. So, from that point and for many, many seasons after, I divided my time between my uncle and my father. The long training period, in part, answers your last question. I have not had the time to think about marriage with all my responsibilities.' His voice softened and he gazed into the distance. 'And I guess I had not yet found the right woman.'

Segda interrupted their conversation with a nudge and a nicker at Tlachtga's shoulder. She rose quickly and released the hobble rope that confined him and led the horse to the stream for a drink. Yaloa watched her closely, glad for the opportunity to do so unobserved. He admired her strength and capability and the manner in which she never hesitated to voice her opinion in mixed company, even though it wasn't generally the custom for young unmarried women among his people. A healer, a maker of music, and a metal worker, she was truly connected to a powerful spirit.

'Would you like me to continue with teaching, or are you ready to return?' asked Tlachtga. Her manner was brisk and Yalo wondered again if he had offended her in some way.

'Yes, I would like to get as much practice as I can, while I can spare the time and the weather is fair enough.' He'd kept his tone light and searched for something humorous to add as he rose. His muscles responded with a groan, but he forced himself towards Segda's side.

Tlachtga moved over to him, cupping her hands together to support his foot and boost him up over the horse's back. Yaloa placed his left foot in her joined palms and pushed down. He started to swing up, but his muscles stiffened, betraying him and his leg. The leg collapsed under him and he fell back on Tlachtga, both of them tumbling together to the ground. A flood of apologies burst from Yaloa, alarmed that he might have seriously injured Tlachtga under his weight and the force of the fall.

She gasped and choked, but he could see a twinkle in her eyes. 'I am fine,' she giggled. 'I just need you to shift your weight so I can breathe.'

Yaloa rolled immediately onto his side and apologized again. Tlachtga laughed harder. He stared down at her and pictured the scene that had just taken place. He grinned and eventually joined her laughter.

'I do not think I will be coursing across the grasslands on Segda anytime soon,' he said when the laughter had subsided. 'I cannot even get on him when he is still.'

'That is just your muscles. You stretched them in unfamiliar ways and they froze up when we were eating. You will be mounting again with no problem, once your muscles have loosened.'

Yaloa grinned, massaging his thighs. 'By the feel of my legs I would judge that to be sometime next season.'

'Not at all. I will rub a special ointment on them and they will feel fine by tomorrow, I promise,' said Tlachtga. She was still smiling.

'I guess I will take the word of my healer, then,' he said. 'I think perhaps we should take this incident as a sign we should make our way back, though.'

He tried to rise to his feet once more but was unsuccessful. Tlachtga got up and extended her hand to help him. Once up, he declined her offer of a supporting shoulder, feeling the need to maintain some dignity, and started to make his way back to camp with a slow, stiff-legged gait. Tlachtga laughed until his dark look stopped her.

'The walk will help loosen and warm your muscles,' she said, her tone suddenly serious.

Did she think he was angry at her for mocking him? He wasn't in truth. He'd only played at being annoyed. Had he misunderstood again? He gave her a reassuring grin, but their walk back remained silent.

YALOA GROANED under the kneading pressure of Tlachtga's fingers. He lay face down on his pallet in the dwelling he shared with his sister's family, while Tlachtga expertly rubbed his calves and thighs with the ointment she'd retrieved from her medicine store.

He was clad only in his simple knee-length tunic, having shed his other clothes under her instructions. Although the massage and ointment would help his stiffness, Tlachtga knew these tools were painful paths to feeling better. Painful to smell as well, she thought, as the odor wafted up. The odor was a sure antidote to any thoughts of sensuality that might have entered her mind in such a situation. When Tlachtga asked him to turn over, she caught sight of the martyred look on his face and laughed. It was apparent he had no such thoughts either.

'You will thank me for this tomorrow when your legs will move at your command and without much pain,' she told him. She continued to massage the front of his thighs. 'But I must warn you that in a few moments—' Her words were cut short by Yaloa's howl of pain.

'I am on fire!'

'—it will start to burn.' She looked at him quizzically and then started to laugh once more. Yaloa gave her an offended look.

'You find my pain and suffering humorous.'

'You will live, I think.' Tlachtga answered, and tried to look serious. 'Don't worry, it will not last long.'

Tlachtga continued to knead his muscles. She looked into his face. He rolled his eyes backward and moaned in mock-pain. The tent flap opened at that moment and Teslintoo entered. She looked over at the two of them, frowned, and then sniffed.

'Brother,' she said in a sharp voice. She frowned at Tlachtga. 'I need to speak with you. Alone.'

Tlachtga saw her look. Without a word, she packed up her ointment while Yaloa began to explain his need for the massage and treatment. Tlachtga left, Yaloa's words of explanation drifting behind her. She made her way back to her own dwelling, her mind on the recent scene, until footsteps and the sound of her name halted her. She turned to find Teslintoo hurrying towards her. Once abreast of her, Teslintoo's angered face was clear to see.

'You have overstepped yourself here,' said Teslintoo, 'It was not proper for you to be there alone with him. A single woman not of his family should not be alone with any man.'

'I was there not as a woman, but as a healer.' Tlachtga drew herself up to her full height and towered above Teslintoo. 'Do you have reason to fear that either of us would act improperly?'

'I am concerned that no taint be laid upon Yaloa. He is to wed soon. He told me of this hope this morning and that tomorrow he goes to speak to Kayáani's father. You must do nothing to affect that discussion.' Teslintoo made a visible effort to calm herself. 'You are not one of us, so naturally you do not understand our ways. It is important that Yaloa marry well, and marry one who understands how to be a proper wife to one of his importance. There are many responsibilities. I know, for I have long filled them.'

'I don't understand why you feel the need to point this out to me. I am acting as a healer and teacher with Yaloa. He is a man with honor, who receives my teaching and healing as just that.'

Tlachtga gave Teslintoo a short nod. She walked off as calmly as she could manage in the face of the fuming anger. When she neared her own campsite, she marched over to the cart and kicked the wheel. Pain shot up her foot, but somehow that made her feel better. She should be laughing, really. It was funny when she looked at it from a distance. But at this moment, she found distance difficult and little humor present. In her travels with her father, she had encountered some men who mistook her outward energy for interest, or someone who was easy with her affection. She had never encountered this kind of tension with another woman. Her own anger at Teslintoo puzzled her. When she examined it closely she realized her anger focused not on Teslintoo's mistaken assumptions about her interaction with Yaloa, but that Teslintoo judged her unfit to be Yaloa's wife. Was it her ego that was wounded here? Tlachtga was not so certain.

For a short moment, she allowed herself to entertain the idea of being Yaloa's wife, savoring the notion of sharing conversation with him, sharing his space, sharing the seasonal tasks. Her thoughts drifted into wondering about the feel of his skin and the look of his muscled body. Tlachtga clapped her hand over her mouth. What was she thinking? Teslintoo was right on one count—she was not one of them. Yaloa, as leader and a *Sha Man*, clearly needed a woman who was of their tribe and understood the role. She could see the sense in that.

A sigh escaped her unnoticed. Reluctantly, she admitted how much she enjoyed his company. And how much she appreciated Yaloa's understanding and respect for her learning and responsibilities as a *Drui*. It was a respect that contained no discomforting awe. This would not do. She forced her thoughts in another direction. He was going to take Kayáani for a wife, and very soon, by the sound of it. His marriage should not stop them from being good friends, though. That would satisfy her until it came time for her to leave. With leaden steps, she made her way to her own dwelling.

Just as she reached the tent, she heard her someone call her again. She turned to see Yaloa's cousin, Gutao. He walked over to her. 'May I talk with you in private?' he said with great politeness.

His manner and words were tentative. She thought perhaps he might have some private question for her healing skill. She smiled kindly at Gutao and nodded. She indicated her earlier place at the cart for their talk and retraced her steps with Gutao following close behind.

They arrived at the far side, away from view. 'How can I help?' she asked.

Gutao looked down at his feet and shifted uncomfortably. 'Well,' he began, 'it is about Teslintoo.' Tlachtga knit her brow and straightened. She had not expected this.

Gutao cleared his throat. 'I want tell you that she is a good woman.' He paused again and looked up at her. 'She means well. Especially when it comes to Yaloa. She thinks the world of him and has been very protective of him ever since a wild beast attacked her the winter their mother died. Yaloa was only six but he killed it. Teslintoo wanted to make up for the loss of their mother and tried to take her place.' Gutao paused, then added with a wry grin, 'To the extent that she has even picked a wife for him.'

Tlachtga frowned. 'She mentioned that Yaloa has decided to have Kayáani as his wife. That he goes tomorrow to speak to her father.'

Gutao snorted. 'I know nothing of that. I do know that Kayáani is not for him. She is a girl child still and will remain one for many seasons, if not always. He does not have the time to give her the attention and pampering she desires.' He sighed and looked off in the distance. 'She has great beauty, though, and her heart is good behind her manner, which comes from a father who always demanded perfection from her.'

Tlachtga examined Gutao and saw his feelings for Kayáani bared before her. With great empathy, Tlachtga took his hand and gave it a squeeze. 'Thank you for telling me this, but I am not certain how I can help.'

Gutao looked over at her. 'Yaloa and I are close. I know him as a brother. He needs someone of his own kind.' He took a deep breath. 'Like you. You are like him. You are a *Sha Man* and understand those ways. Yaloa has deep responsibilities that sometimes weigh him down like a great boulder on his chest. He needs to be able to share those worries with someone who can understand their weight and meaning.'

By now Tlachtga's face had found all imaginable shades of red. 'I understand how you can feel that,' she said, desperately trying to conceal her flustered state. 'I am very flattered that you consider me a good match for Yaloa. However, it is not something that can be decided by any well-meaning thoughts you give it.'

'I know it is not for me to decide, but I wanted you to understand that there was more involved than Teslintoo led you to believe.' He smiled at her reassuringly, turned and then walked away. Tlachtga stared after him in confusion.

CHAPTER EIGHT

Tlachtga sat by the stream with Segda, waiting at the same spot as the previous day. This time she faced outwards and assessed Yaloa approach with a healer's eye, to keep her morning's resolve to regard him only as patient and pupil. It would be easier that way. She couldn't help but smile at his walk, though. His gait was stiff-legged, much more than yesterday. Catching her smile, Yaloa waved.

'You see that I have lived through the night without the loss of either limb?' he said. 'I thank my healer and praise her skills for that. The goats, sheep and everyone within ten paces of me do not thank you, however. And it was all I could do to maintain my dignity during my conversation this morning with Kayáani's father. He sniffed and sniffed and slowly edged away.'

'Unfortunately the ointment's power and force extends to the assault on the nose,' she said. 'I will have to rub in more ointment again after today's riding. Then it should become easier for your muscles after that. You will also have stretched them out enough that they will be used to it.'

Tlachtga forced herself to smile. She had not failed to note that he had indeed spoken to Kayáani's father. She fought the drooping feeling inside her and went over to Segda to cup her hands in readiness for his mount. This time, Yaloa swung up smoothly on to Segda's back. She gave Yaloa's position careful appraisal, making small corrections to his feet and hands. After her nod of approval, he began to canter in a wide circle around her. Segda was a fine, strong horse, lean-muscled from the long treks and irregular pasturage. Despite the hardships and the periodic wearing pace, he still rode smoothly, gliding through the wind. His fluid grace was evident even now, under Yaloa's tentative horsemanship. He had improved already, though. He handled the reins easier and was finding the pace of Segda's stride.

She watched them continue their gallop. Gradually, the two blended their rhythm, Yaloa's hair flying loose, supporting the illusion of flight. They broke out of their wide circle and rode across the broad expanse of dry, grassy plain, both of them enjoying the stretch, savoring the sense of freedom such a pace gave. It was a feeling she could understand.

When the sun reached its mid-point, the two sat down to eat their meal by the stream as they had the day before. Tlachtga caught sight of a fish swimming in the quiet flow of the current and felt encouraged. Overhead, a few clouds gathered, giving the air a slight chill, but not enough to dampen her spirits and the joy she felt after the morning's work. Behind them, Segda found a patch of grass and began his meal. Tlachtga smiled fondly at the horse and turned to their bag of provisions. She withdrew their meal, handing Yaloa some flatbread first and then laying out the remainder of the meal on the grass between them. Yaloa took the flatbread and grinned over at Tlachtga.

'My limbs seem to work much better now, after this day's riding,' he said. 'I feel more comfortable with Segda, too. Perhaps I shall make a passable horseman.'

'I think you will make a fine horseman,' said Tlachtga. 'Truly.

You have done well on Segda. His spirit and strength make him less easy to handle than Medb. If she wasn't in foal, I would have had you learn with her.' She smiled sincerely. 'You seem to have a natural gift for riding and you are also very determined to learn.'

A short silence passed while Tlachtga considered the question that had been gnawing away at her since her father requested she teach him to ride. She looked at him directly. 'Why is it you want to learn this skill?' she asked. 'You have no horses. Do you plan to acquire some?'

Yaloa gazed out into the distant horizon. 'There are many reasons why I want to learn all about horses and how to ride them,' he answered. 'First and foremost, I am looking towards the future. You can see yourself that the drought is becoming worse in this area. We need to find a new place to graze our animals and raise our crops. We cannot travel far enough on foot. With horses we can find some place better and lead the people to it.'

He glanced at her and returned his gaze to the distant view. 'Eventually, I would like to have many horses... and many carts.' He paused, then added softly, 'I fear that someday we will have to leave this area and follow the paths of our peoples from which we parted so long ago. The horses and carts would be invaluable if we make that journey.' He looked at her, his eyes dark and serious, silently pleading. 'Your arrival was like a gift from the spirits. You brought us hope. And an answer. Yet after such a gift I would still wish that you and your family would assist us in this great task. It is much to request, I know, but I feel I must ask.'

'I see,' said Tlachtga, at a loss for words. She had not imagined his need would be so strong and his plans so ambitious and daring. It would be difficult to implement, involve many seasons of planning. But she couldn't help but admire his desire to try. 'I had not imagined such a grand plan as this,' she told him. 'But I can understand why the horses are so important. I am certain Father would help.'

Tlachtga took up the leather water bag and sipped from it slowly. She had meant it when she told him she was sure Mog would help him. It was the kind of bold initiative he so admired. But it was also important and there was much at stake. He would understand that, and regardless of the knowledge he sought, he would feel the need to assist them in any way he could. She was surprised to realize this knowledge made her glad. She was also surprised that she felt just as committed to help Yaloa save his people as she knew her father would be.

'There is much for you ahead,' she said, rising. 'I will do what I can to aid you.'

Yaloa looked up at her intently. 'You have done much already and I am greatly in your debt. You have listened well to my hopes and given me your considered thoughts back. Thank you.'

He rose to stand beside her, his dark eyes just slightly above hers. Tlachtga felt her face color again. She tugged nervously on her disc and looked away. Distracted by their movement, Segda looked up from his grazing and moved towards them. Tlachtga reached over and stroked his side, glad for something to cover her confusion at Yaloa's words.

'Here, I think it is time for you to learn to mount on your own,' she said. This was an area she knew about. She must focus on his instruction and not the distraction of his request or its implications for her own future.

Later, her ease with Yaloa returned under the demands of the lesson, and Tlachtga chatted mildly with him as they walked back. She teased Yaloa about his first mounting attempts. She laughed and nudged him with her elbow. 'I did not know you favored tumbling as a pastime,' she told him.

'I think each day you seek to lower my dignity further,'

answered Yaloa with mock severity. They continued their walk, ambling along in the lazy tiredness of the day's exertion. As they neared the campsite, Tlachtga caught site of Buan running towards them. He waved his arms vigorously.

'Tlachtga! We need you quickly,' he shouted. 'It is Medb. The foal is coming and she is having trouble.'

Alarmed, Tlachtga quickened her pace and rushed to follow Buan. Yaloa stayed close behind them, leading Segda. The group soon arrived at the camp area and headed towards Mog's dwelling. Yaloa hobbled Segda at a nearby tree and joined the others by the cart where Medb was lying sweating and struggling weakly.

Tlachtga knelt beside her, stroked her forehead and crooned soothing tones. At Tlachtga's direction, Buan fetched her healer's sack, a small pot and a bucket of water. He set these items beside Tlachtga. She reached for the sack, rifled around, and withdrew a smaller bundle wrapped in a thick piece of leather. Carefully, she unfolded it and revealed a clump of dried leaves and stalks. She spread out the pile on the leather cloth, selected a tiny portion, and then ground it between her fingers into her palm. She emptied the contents of her palm into the bucket, intoning the sacred prayer over and over. Placing the bucket before Medb, Tlachtga stroked her once again, coaxing her to drink. Buan and Yaloa stood behind her, watching in fearful silence.

'*Brija*, help her,' she pleaded in her mind. They could ill afford to lose a horse. She could afford the loss to her heart even less.

After a few moments, Medb's shifting and struggling lessened. Tlachtga removed her over tunic and rolled up her sleeves. She dipped her hand into the pot beside her and scooped out a large dollop of fat. With deliberate motion she lathered the fat on her hands and arms, covering them thoroughly. When greasing was complete, she carefully inserted her hand and arm inside the horse's womb and focused all her attention on the shape inside, her brow dripping with the effort. Buan leaned down and wiped his sleeve across it, giving her some momentary relief.

She withdrew her hand, and with firm fingers on the outside of the mare, poked, prodded and massaged. She greased her hand again and inserted it. Carefully she felt around again and cursed as the little limbs slipped out of her reach once more. She looked over at Yaloa and Buan, a helpless expression on her face.

'The foal is turned the wrong way,' she said, glancing up. 'I cannot move it the right way. The legs slip from my grasp.' She looked back down and tried once more, her breath coming in pants and her face flushing fiercely.

'Shall I try?' asked Yaloa. 'Tell me what I should do, and I will try.'

She looked at his hard-muscled frame and his strong, long fingers. Buan's hands were far too beefy. Reluctantly she withdrew her hand and she nodded. Before he knelt down beside Tlachtga, she gave Medb a soothing stroke and told Yaloa to follow suit. A few moments later he rolled up his sleeves in preparation for the task. She explained the problem with simple diagrams in the dirt and gave him the necessary guidance to make his own attempt to correct it. Yaloa followed her example and coated his hand and arm with fat before gingerly inserting his hand. He reached around and frowned as he focused on his task. Tlachtga watched him closely and questioned him about what his hand felt. After some time his face cleared and he broke out in a wide grin.

'Yes, yes. This is it!' he exclaimed. 'I have it firmly in my grip!'

Tlachtga allowed herself a flicker of relief before she briefed him on the next step. There was still much to do. Yaloa listened to her instructions, the foal's legs still held firmly in his grasp. She handed him a rope. Carefully he inserted it and looped it around the foal's front legs and head.

After it was firmly in place, Yaloa guided the foal's movement towards the vaginal opening. He handed a part of the rope length to Tlachtga so they could combine their strength for the final pull. Then, after resting a moment, they pulled the rope firmly while Yaloa continued to guide the foal's exit. The two were sweating hard and panting with the effort. In one sudden movement, the whole front half of the foal shot out onto the grass. A moment later, the rest of the foal escaped the womb, to lie beside its mother in a startled, wet heap.

Tlachtga and Yaloa collapsed backwards from the momentum of their strong effort suddenly released. Captivated, they watched the foal struggle to its feet, its gawky limbs wobbling in their new environment. His coat was shiny with birth fluid, but its roan color already showed the promise of beauty. Huge, dark eyes stared out from long fringes of lash. He was a wonder.

Buan laughed loudly, his relief bursting into a roar in Tlachtga's ears. She watched him pat and stroke Medb, crooning words of praise. She smiled at him, knowing his attachment to Medb was as strong as her own, even if his riding skill was not great. After a few moments Tlachtga asked him to fetch more water. There was still some work to be done. Tlachtga knelt down beside Medb again and kneaded and stroked her underbelly to assist the expulsion of the afterbirth. It didn't take long. She allowed the foal to return to his mother's side. Medb, exhausted and weak, still found the energy to welcome her newborn with a whicker.

Yaloa still knelt beside Tlachtga, his hands covered with fat, blood and other markings of his recent efforts, looking over at the mother and foal. She saw the amazement and joy in his eyes and face. Catching her glance, he turned to her and suddenly gathered her in his arms in a big hug.

'He's beautiful!' Yaloa cried.

She looked at his smiling face. It was so close to hers. His eyes burned brightly and his mouth was stretched wide enough to give him dimples. She felt her own joy respond to his and met his embrace with a strength of her own. After a moment, she pulled away slowly, reluctant to withdraw from the force of this shared happiness and special connection.

Tlachtga sighed and looked into his eyes. Dark and unfathomable, they stared back intently. He touched her face and pulled it closer to his, her mouth beside his mouth. She closed her eyes and allowed his lips to meet her own, to press home its need, to taste the tangy saltiness from their earlier labors. She threaded her arms around his neck, unmindful of her greased hands and bloodied tunic. The odors seemed to feed her desire and need. Yaloa pulled her closer, moving his hand along her back. She never wanted to let him go. Then she remembered. He was promised to someone else. With a soft moan she broke away from him.

'I am sorry,' said Yaloa. 'Was that considered improper among your people? I should speak to your father first, of course. I hope I have not offended you. I-I just did not think.'

'No, no, it is not like that at all.' Tlachtga said. She stared at her feet, fighting her raging emotions. 'I just do not understand. I thought you had spoken to Kayáani's father only this morning.'

'I did,' Yaloa said. 'But I do not see where that has a place here.'

'Perhaps it is your people's ways that I do not understand,' said Tlachtga with a hint of coldness. 'Among my people it is certainly not the custom to kiss a woman shortly after arranging to take another woman as wife.'

'Nor is it the custom among my people,' Yaloa said. 'What

gave you the idea that I have just arranged to take another woman as wife?'

'Teslintoo told me yesterday that you intended to marry, and that today you would be speaking to Kayáani's father,' Tlachtga said.

'Well you have the right words, but the wrong meaning. It is true that I told Teslintoo that I was thinking of taking a wife,' Yaloa answered. 'I wanted her to grow used to the idea. I thought I would give her that time while I explored the hope with the woman who had inspired the hope.' He took her hand in his two and added, 'Kayáani's father has nothing to do with that hope. I spoke to him on Gutao's behalf.'

'You spoke to him on Gutao's behalf?' she repeated dumbly.

'Well, yes. Gutao has long cared for Kayáani and now seemed a good time to bring the matter to a formal arrangement.' Yaloa looked amused now.

'But I thought that you and Kayáani....' Tlachtga let her words trail off and she finally raised her face to look at his.

'Kayáani may have been intrigued by such a possibility,' Yaloa said. 'But it would not have been a good choice for her.' Yaloa still held her hand. 'Do you not know anything of my feelings for you? My reason for learning to ride was not just the noble pursuit of my people's future. I wanted to spend time with you, to learn more about you.' He lowered his glance. 'I even held back sharing some of the learning you asked about in the hopes it would keep you here longer.'

'Truly?' Tlachtga was stunned. She shook her head a little. This was all too much for her to take in so quickly. She was clear on the fact that he had spoken to Kayáani's father on Gutao's behalf. A smile broke out on her face that spread to her eyes. She suddenly felt much lighter. Yaloa caught the look on her face, then leaned down to try the kiss once again. He gathered her in his arms and she met his lips willingly. Once again, she inhaled and tasted the odors of sweat, fat and blood that clung to his body. She found them delicious. She allowed herself to follow the growing desire for this man that she loved. There was no doubt in her mind. All thoughts of Fintan and returning home vanished. This was her home, here with Yaloa. This was her path.

THERE WAS no surprise on Mog's face when Yaloa approached him about marrying Tlachtga. He merely nodded and smiled even before Yaloa mentioned things like bride price or any other gifts.

'That will come in time,' he said, waving away his words. 'But I will give my daughter Medb as a dowry gift. She loves that mare and now the two of you share a bond with her after the birth of her foal.'

Buan came up behind Yaloa, gave a large whoop of joy and clapped him on the back. 'If you want, you can offer me gifts in return for the secret of taming Tlachtga's tongue,' he said.

Yaloa grinned. 'Ah, there is no need my brother, I think I have found my own method for stilling any wayward words.'

Buan roared with laughter and it warmed Yaloa's heart to hear such welcoming banter. He knew it would be much different when it came to his sister.

CHAPTER NINE

Bríd looked around the tent through the haze of sleep. Heat penetrated the tent's flimsy sun shield. She could feel the sweat already starting to form on her body. Was it really that late? Her hand groped for the little clock on the crate at the head of her bed. She groaned when she saw its face. Across from her, Miffy lay in a crumpled form. She'd already been in bed when Bríd returned last night, her back turned towards Bríd as she entered. She'd not responded to any of Bríd's attempts at conversation, but remained stiffly silent. Too tired to put much effort into further words, Bríd undressed and went to bed herself, falling asleep immediately.

The prior day's work had taken its toll on her and, it appeared, Miffy too. They were late. Quickly she got out of her camp bed and began pulling on her clothes, trying to clear her groggy head. She called across to Miffy, then louder as the form didn't stir. Finally there was movement and Miffy's tousled head appeared above her sleeping bag.

'It's late, Miffy. We've overslept at least an hour. Bob and John will be livid.'

Miffy rubbed her eyes and yawned. 'Late?' she asked, her

manner offhand. 'Really?' After another protracted yawn her head fell back on her pillow and she closed her eyes. 'Tell them I'll be there in few minutes.'

Bríd gave her a doubtful look, then pulled on her shoes and departed. She hurried over to the lab trailer, running her fingers briefly through her curls to give them some semblance of order and felt the damp at the back of her neck. She was already feeling overheated and her day hadn't yet begun.

When she entered the lab, she found Bob at work clad in a surgical mask and gloves, camera in hand, the mummified body lying on a metal table before him. She looked around hopefully for Scott. There was no sign of him.

Bob looked up. 'Oh, there you are, Bríd,' he said. 'Just in time. Can you come and give me a hand?'

His tone was pleasantly welcoming. Bríd let out a breath she hadn't realized she was holding. She picked up her own set of gloves and a mask to protect the mummy from the effects of skin oil and breath and, once donned, took a place on the opposite side of the table. Though a specialized air conditioner hummed in the background, it did little to reduce the slight smell of decay that hung in the air.

Bob brushed aside her hasty apology for tardiness and asked her to hold the mummy's torso while he positioned the camera and took the shot. The mummy was turned on its side, away from her, its left shoulder exposed, revealing a tattoo of dark indigo.

'Okay,' Bob said finally. 'Let's put it on its back, now. I want to get a few shots of the wrists.'

Gently, supporting its head and shoulders, Bríd slowly helped the mummy on to its back. She glanced down at the face, checking for any sign of damage, then stared hard. Without the eagle headpiece that adorned it in the images and video clips she viewed yesterday, the face, the hair were so recognizable it took her breath away. He was so like the image she'd seen yesterday, even down to the golden hair falling away from his face. One eye socket showed traces of scarring. That's the blind one, she thought.

It was unnerving, staring down into a face she'd seen only the day before full of life and as real as Bob. Her eyes clouded over, the face disappeared and she could see the man again, moving across this harsh terrain, clad in his tunic and boots. He stopped in front of a woman, she could see the thick long braid along her back. As he raised one hand to pull the woman's head to kiss the top, Bríd noticed the tattoo on the inside of his wrist. It was circular and it filled the area. She followed the hand as it caressed the woman's hair. Hair the color of her own.

Bríd started to shake, the image cleared and the now familiar dizziness took over. Somewhere, in the distance, she heard Bob ask her to lift the right wrist and turn it towards the camera. Bríd attempted to steady herself and comply with his request. She didn't need to look at the wrists. She already knew the image that was tattooed there.

'It looks like some kind of sun design.' Bob said. He put the camera aside and leaned in for closer inspection. 'Just look at it, Bríd, isn't it amazing? So clear. It'll make a terrific shot.' He glanced over at her. 'What do you think—ornamentation or some sacred symbol?'

Bríd stared at him, fighting the dizziness. She looked down at the mummy, confusion and panic growing as her breath shortened and her ears roared. 'Sorry, sorry, Bob. I feel terrible just now.'

Bob looked over at her, then set down the camera and came to her side. He pulled down her mask and cupped her chin. 'You do look a little pale. Maybe it's just the cold air after too much heat. Here, sit down a moment.' After removing his own mask, he guided her to a chair and poured her a glass of water. Bríd sipped the water gratefully, her breathing slowing, the dizziness lifting. She looked up and gave him a thankful smile.

Bob's hand, still resting on her shoulder, slid along to her neck and he began to massage her neck muscles. 'It's blistering outside already, and that, combined with the sudden cold in here probably set your body off balance. But this should help.' Before she could protest, he moved behind and started massaging her with both hands, his fingers kneading lightly along her neck and her shoulders. Bríd felt some of her muscle tension ease. She couldn't deny it felt good.

A finger caught the cord about her neck and he pulled it lightly from under her t-shirt until the medallion revealed itself. 'What's this pretty little thing?' he asked. He bent over close. She could feel his breath on her neck.

'It's a necklace. It belonged to my grandmother.'

'Did it?' His fingers brushed her neck as he moved to turn it over. 'It looks quite old. I wonder how she came by it.'

'I don't know,' said Bríd. Her breath started to quicken as her pulse rate increased.

'Well, it's lovely.' He released the medallion and his fingers started to brush and caress her neck lightly. 'Just like the wearer.' His lips grazed her neck.

The touch, so light, shot through Bríd. In one motion she rose and disengaged herself, knocking over the chair just as the door opened and Miffy walked in, followed closely by Scott. Their chorus of apologies tailed as they took in Bríd's flushed face and the tipped chair.

'Is everything okay?' asked Scott. His face was carefully neutral but there was concern in his voice. Bríd shifted under his gaze, unwilling to meet his eyes.

'Everything's fine. Bríd here just had a little episode of faint-ness.' His voice was casual, giving no indication of any discomfort. 'She's better now, though.' He rested a hand on her shoulder. 'Aren't you, Bríd?'

Miffy eyed her suspiciously as Bríd nodded her head. 'I think I'll go get a cup of water, though. And maybe a little something to eat. I didn't have breakfast.'

'What a good idea,' said Miffy with a slight smirk. 'Though Scott and I were both late, we felt it best that we have some food before we started the long day ahead.'

Scott flushed as Bríd passed him, his own mumbled words of sympathy barely audible as she exited the trailer. Once outside, she leaned gratefully against the side of the trailer and closed her eyes, glad to be safely extricated from the lab.

'Are you okay? You look terrible.'

Bríd looked up and saw John approaching, his face full of concern. Suddenly she found she was glad he found her and she felt a strong desire to go to him, to hear his reassurance, if even for her basic health.

'I don't know,' she said. 'The heat, maybe lack of food, and— and, well other things.'

John looked at the trailer, his eyes narrowing. 'Here, come with me and I'll fix you a drink.'

She nodded slightly, not trusting herself to speak. John guided her to the office, his hand against her back their only contact. As they stepped inside the trailer, Jin looked up from his seat at the desk, a tablet in his hand.

'Jin, would you mind switching with Bríd over at the lab for a little while? She's not a hundred percent at the moment and could do with a break.'

'No, of course not.' Jin looked at her quizzically, then rose and took himself out.

Bríd took his seat and let herself relax against the back while John pulled a bottle of water from above a shelf over the desk and then handed that and a half sandwich wrapped in cling film to her.

'Here, try this. It's not much, but it might do the trick.'

He waited while she drank deeply and took a bite of the sandwich. The cool cleansing liquid sliding down her throat eased some of the confusion and panic that still swirled around inside. She closed her eyes, savoring a quiet, still moment, then sighed.

'Now, tell me, what's really the matter?' John said in a firm, low voice.

Bríd stared down at her hands, now folded in her lap. What should she say? 'I don't know,' she began. 'I overslept and rushed over to the lab. Bob was already there, examining the mummy and taking photos. I started to help him and then, well, something happened.' She hesitated.

'What?' John's voice was sharp.

She looked up. His eyes were dark, nearly unreadable. 'It happened again,' she said whispered.

'What? What did he do?'

'Who?' she asked, momentarily off track. 'It was the mummy. Looking at him. He had the golden hair, the scarred eye. Just like I'd seen yesterday.'

'The mummy?' John looked puzzled for a second and then his face cleared. 'He had the same color hair as the man in your vision yesterday?'

She nodded. 'Then I saw him, in my mind, making his way across the ground, in an area just like this. He walked towards a woman, and kissed her head. As though in blessing, like a father might to a daughter.'

'And after that?'

'That's it. After that, it clouded over and I became dizzy. Like before. Bob sat me down and then started massaging my neck.'

She felt herself flushing as she said the words. John's own face darkened perceptibly. She looked down at her lap.

'Is that all?' He leaned across the desk towards her. She couldn't say any more. Bob was his colleague, someone he respected and admired. Besides, she knew the 'turn the blind eye' rule in the academic boys club. John's look, expectant and concerned, told her she would have to tell him something.

'He admired the medallion around my neck,' she said feebly. Bríd pulled it up from her chest in the hope that might distract John.

He gave her a studied look then focused on the medallion. Carefully he took it from her fingers and examined it closely. 'Bob likes pretty things,' John said, his tone neutral. 'He can be fairly persuasive when he wants to acquire something he's taken a fancy to.' He was very close now, his dark eyes and lashes inches from her mouth. 'Be careful, Bríd.'

Bríd caught her breath and nodded slightly. 'There are no worries there.'

He acknowledged her nod with a brief one of his own and looked down again at the medallion. 'I can see why it caught his attention. It's very unusual. Unique, I'd say.' He handed it back to her and grinned. 'Like the owner.'

The heat in her face rose again at the words so similar to Bob's but this time they filled her with pleasure, surprising herself. Though 'unique' was not exactly the same as 'lovely,' it still seemed a compliment. She stole a glance at him, his face still so close to her own. His eyes flickered and for a second he moved nearer, then moved back against his seat.

'These last set of "images" you just saw. Tell me again, only this time in detail.'

With a sigh, Bríd closed her eyes and recalled every detail of clothing, manner and landscape she could, submitting herself to an occasional interruption when he needed something clarified.

'You say the woman had red hair?'

Bríd nodded. 'Just like my own. Or like mine used to be. Plaited down her back.'

John nodded. 'But you cut it,' he said softly.

'Yes,' she whispered. She held her hands tightly to keep from touching the short curls. The tears welled up and she bowed her head. Now was not the time.

'Thanks,' he said finally.

'Thanks?'

'Thank you for trusting me enough to tell me.'

'Oh, I see.' She didn't see, though. Did he doubt her word? Did he think she was making it up to get his attention? From his tone she wasn't sure what he meant.

'This is something unusual for you. It's never happened before, you said.'

Bríd nodded and he continued. 'I was thinking what could cause this. What brought on these visions, or images. It might be that the intensive work, all the cramming you've done to come up to speed, combined with the grueling heat might have manifested in creating an idea, an image of how the mummy might have been.'

Bríd looked down at her hands. Is that what it was? She wasn't so sure, now. As much as she disliked the idea of "seeing," as Gran would say it, it was exactly what it seemed like. 'I saw the tattoos on him first,' she said quietly. 'Before I saw them on the mummy.'

'Tattoos?'

She bit her lip. She'd had omitted that detail when she'd described everything before, but it just slipped out now.

'The tattoos on the mummy? On his wrists?' A moment later he reached for her left wrist and turned it over. With his forefinger he traced the loops stamped there. The heat of his finger was so strong it nearly burned her. She snatched it away.

'You haven't had this long,' he said.

'No.'

'A whim?' His tone was quiet, persuasive.

She sniffed. 'Not a whim.'

'Grief?'

She looked at him and frowned.

'I heard you lost your grandmother.'

Bríd stiffened. 'How do you know about my grandmother?'

His eyes darkened, withdrew. 'I'd heard. One of the other students mentioned it, I think.'

Bríd looked at him doubtfully. 'I didn't tell any of the other students.'

He shifted in his chair. 'I'm not sure where I heard it.'

'My mother, I suppose. She told the college after it happened.' She felt her voice catch and flattened it. 'Thirty-three days ago. I was in Miltown Malbay when it happened. Performing at a festival, or rather I was supposed to have performed, if not for a certain fucking gobshite.'

He stirred on his chair. 'I know what it's like to lose someone,' John said, his voice barely a whisper. 'My parents died when I was twelve. Without my great uncle's help, I would still be lost today.'

She pursed her lips. 'Yes, but I'm responsible. If I hadn't gone to Milltown Melbay she might still be alive. I should have stayed home.' She turned her head away, not wanting him to see the tears that were starting to spill down her face. She felt a hand on her shoulder, strong and firm.

'Bríd, you don't know that. You couldn't have known what would have happened. Why have you taken on this burden? What happened in Miltown Melbay?'

She took a ragged breath, her lungs constricting with the effort. Burden. That's exactly how she had been feeling, as though the weight of all the guilt and shame she'd experienced in those fateful days was pressing so heavily on her she could hardly breathe at times. When she thought about the Willie Clancy Festival. And Ciarán. The performance they were supposed to give. The big launch of their careers and their lives together. That failed miserably when she ran off the stage in embarrassment and shame when she stumbled too much on the harp.

'Miltown Melbay,' she finally said to John quietly. 'It was the end of so much when it was supposed to be the beginning of everything.'

John remained silent, but she could feel his presence beside her. It was reassuring and she found she wanted to explain to him what she could, to help him understand. She couldn't bear to look at him, though, to watch his reaction to what she was saying.

'It was Ciarán. All this time I thought he'd been waiting for this opportunity to make music together, just the two of us. All the summers we played together, travelling to venues everywhere in his broken down van, sleeping in the back.' She picked the lint on her shirt, delaying the next part, wondering if she would say it. 'I thought he loved me,' she finally whispered. 'I thought he felt as I did and wanted to be with me and play the music. But at the Willie Clancy festival he told me that he was offered the chance to record a CD with two musicians and tour the States and maybe Australia. States. Two years, he said. That was all. Then he told me who one of the musicians was. But I still resisted the truth.' Bríd gave a brittle laugh. 'They don't say love makes fools of us for nothing. Then she appeared backstage just before we went off and gave him a kiss. I knew then. The langer. How long had he been playing music with her, was all I could think as I walked on stage and sat down at the harp.' Bríd turned finally to John, though she still couldn't quite meet his eyes. 'She can't play flute for shit,' she said with a wan smile.

His hand was still on her shoulder. John hadn't moved once while she spoke. He gave her a reassuring squeeze and a small smile. 'If you play the harp like you play the whistle, I'm sure there is no comparison with her. Your skill in music and the kind of person you are only reveals Ciarán's failings, not your own.'

Bríd finally brought her eyes to his. Deep and dark, she could read no pity or judgment. Only a kind of understanding. She nodded, then looked away. She appreciated his words, and though she might find them difficult to accept, she realized now that deep down she had thought it was down to her that their relationship had failed. She had not been there enough, wanted to pursue two paths at once and ultimately sacrificed her relationship with Ciarán for her studies. Was she to blame really? It was difficult to think otherwise. She raised her face again to John and gave him a grateful smile. She realized she did feel a little better.

John gestured to the desk then briskly took his seat again. 'Have something more to eat now, and then maybe you can get back to work.'

Bríd blinked, taken by surprise at the sudden change in tone. Had she misread him? Was he really trying to just soothe her with platitudes so she could get back to work? She frowned. Maybe she had misread the situation. She had to admit the past month was so filled with emotional upheaval she could no longer trust her perceptions. Maybe stress was the cause of the 'images' she'd seen.

By afternoon Bríd felt more like herself. The remainder of the morning had passed in relative quiet as John worked through the notes, site grid and diagrams with her. They joined the others for lunch and she managed that well enough, but she was relieved when he arranged it so that she would work with him in the afternoon. The two had only just resumed their seats at the desk when Lu and Chang entered.

John greeted the pair and Bríd took two folding chairs, opened them and placed them opposite her. She could hear Chang's labored breathing as he sat, his size making hard work of the heat.

After brief, polite remarks, they moved on to the reason for their visit.

'I understand you have the mummy and all the items from the chamber housed in the lab now?' asked Lu. His uniform lay crisp and neat along his frame.

'That's correct,' answered John. He elaborated no further.

'Is it secure?' asked Chang curtly. Sweat marked his shirt as it strained across his corpulent belly and arms.

'It's locked whenever anyone isn't there,' said John, his eyes narrowed.

'Who has keys?' asked Chang.

'Bob, myself. Why all the questions?' He matched Chang's curt tone.

'This is an issue of cultural sensitivity. We need to assure ourselves that every precaution has been taken to limit access to the chamber contents,' said Lu. He pointed to the computer. 'We also need to review all the images you recorded yesterday, now.'

'Now? I can understand you want to maintain security,' said John. His tone was reasonable but his eyes revealed the strain. 'Can you wait to look at the images until tomorrow, when we've completed an initial general inventory?'

'No,' said Chang. 'It must be now.'

With an audible sigh, John turned to the laptop and called up the files. When the first image appeared, he frowned. 'Wait, this isn't right.' He searched the files again. His frown deepened. He picked up the tablet that lay beside the laptop and skimmed through the files it contained. 'I don't understand this. There are some images and clips missing.' He looked over at Bríd. 'No one mentioned anything to you about it, did they?'

'I hope you're not trying to deceive us,' said Chang. 'It won't succeed, I assure you. We'll just confiscate your computer and review them ourselves.'

John snorted impatiently. 'I'm not trying to deceive you. Look.' He pulled up the images still remaining and clicked through them, first on the laptop and then on the tablet. One by one images of the artefacts appeared in various angles and sizes. Video clips ran showing the placement of the artefacts in the chamber, but as soon as they neared the mummy they skipped or stopped abruptly.

Bríd sat in shocked silence and watched John as he narrated the images and clips, filling in the bits he remembered of the missing content. 'I don't think it's the laptop,' he said. 'It must be something else. Maybe someone else.' He looked at Lu and Chang, the question in his eyes.

'This returns us again to the question of security,' said Lu. 'You obviously have been lax here. Who has keys to this trailer?'

'The same two,' said John. 'Just Bob and me.' He looked at the two men. Lu raised an eyebrow. 'It wasn't Bob. Bob wouldn't do it. He wants this to be successful as much as I do.'

'Well there has obviously been some kind of breach,' said Lu. 'Which only reinforces the importance of the instructions we have been given regarding this expedition. You must return the mummy to the chamber immediately and the artefacts sent on to the museum in Ürümchi.'

'Re-inter the mummy? Are you kidding?' John's voice rose.

'I assure you, we intend no humor,' said Chang, his voice like iron.

'No, that's impossible. There's too much at stake here. Too much to learn. We can't abandon that.'

Bríd felt a rush of anger and began to add her own protests. 'This find is very important, Mr Lu. Surely you can see that.'

'I'm not here to argue the importance of anything,' said Lu. 'My orders are to ensure that you return the mummy to the chamber and cover it back up. That's all.' His face closed and his mouth was set.

'Can't you give us more time?' he asked. 'A week. Just so we can create a detailed inventory and documentation of all that we found?'

'Dr Sheldon, given your security problems already, do you think we would really consider extending the time?' asked Chang.

'Two days then,' John said with a pleading tone. 'Surely you would give us two more days.'

Lu narrowed his eyes, then nodded. 'Two days. Then the mummy must be returned to the hole and covered up.'

Chang frowned but said nothing. With a curt nod, Lu rose and made his way to the door. Chang stood slowly, his eyes on John, then without so much as a nod he turned and followed Lu out the door.

'Bastards,' said John when the door closed.

'Is there anything we can do?' asked Bríd. 'Any way we can change their minds?'

'They're bureaucrats, Bríd. They do as they're told.' He picked up a pencil and began to tap it. 'We have two days to find another way, though.' He pounded the desk. 'Damn.'

His frustration was palpable. And Bríd shared it. She began to search wildly for ideas. What could they do? 'Is there anyone we can ask for help?'

John stared across the room deep in thought. Had he heard her? 'Yes,' he said finally. 'That's it. We'll ask Dr Lei, at the museum. He can talk to them and convince the powers that be to change their mind.' He looked at Bríd. 'Brilliant idea. I'll tell

Bob and we'll go in the morning. It's the kind of conversation that I wouldn't trust over a phone, here. And I can take some images and clips with us to plead our case.'

'It's a shame that the images of the mummy *in situ* are gone. Still, you can use some of the images Bob took today on the camera.'

John's face darkened momentarily as he glanced at the computer. 'Yes, well, I backed them up on my flash drive, so that's not a big problem. It's the fact that they were deleted that worries me.' He looked at her. 'But we'll keep the fact about the backup between ourselves.'

Bríd nodded. At least he trusted her. Trusted her enough to invite her with him to the museum and keep the flashdrive secret. She would like to see the museum and if she were honest, spending a few days with a shower and John for company was quite appealing.

Just a short while later, Bríd followed John over to the lab. He'd taken extra care in locking away the laptop and tablet in a drawer and securing the office before making his way over to see Bob. Bríd decided to go along with him, not only to witness his reaction, but to ensure that she would accompany John to the museum.

They found Bob in the lab trailer bent over a table on the far wall, photographing sections of the eagle headpiece. Miffy was assisting him. Dr Chou and Jin were there too, engrossed in measuring and noting each detail of the mummy carefully, while Scott examined an item under the microscope. Only Jin looked up when John and Bríd entered. He smiled at Bríd.

'I just had a visit from Lu and Chang,' said John. All eyes turned to him. 'The news isn't good. It seems the bureaucrats want us to re-inter the mummy right away and send the artefacts to the museum in Ürümchi.'

Bob's face turned a deep crimson. 'What! That's outrageous. They can't expect us to abandon this expedition in the middle of things. Think of all that's at stake.'

'Exactly,' said Dr Chou with a sigh. 'Really it's no more than I expected. It's because of what's at stake. The government just will not allow us to pursue the possibility that we might have been influenced by any Western ideas.'

'But surely they would see that it could have happened the other way,' said Scott. 'That the ancient Chinese might have influenced the West, too.'

'It appears it's not a risk they're willing to take,' said Dr Chou.

'I suppose there's nothing we can do?' asked Jin, his tone concerned.

'Well, I have bought us some time,' said John. 'I managed to persuade them to give us two more days to examine the mummy and the artefacts.'

'Can we take samples and run tests?' asked Scott.

John grinned. 'They didn't say we couldn't.'

'Should we ask permission first?' said Jin. He turned to Dr Chou. 'What do you think? Would it be wise to proceed in something that risky?'

Dr Chou took his time with his answer, all eyes on him. He looked over at Jin, his brow creased in worry. 'I don't know,' he said finally. 'Perhaps asking permission would be best.'

John gave Dr Chou a puzzled look. 'Maybe we'll leave that for now,' he said. 'It could work out in the end, anyway. I thought Bríd and I could go to the museum tomorrow and ask Dr Lei for help. He might be able to persuade them to change their minds. I thought showing them images of the finds would go along way to convincing him to help.'

Throughout this exchange, Bob had remained silent while anger and frustration played across his face. After a moment, his face softened and he looked merely thoughtful. Until John voiced his suggestion. His face lit up and he smiled slowly.

'Yes,' he said. 'A great idea. But I think you should also take Jin and Dr Chou with you. To lend support in your presentation to Dr Lei, and to help you out if you get into any language difficulties.'

John considered his statement, while Bríd held her breath. If truth be told, she would really prefer not to have Dr Chou. He seemed so pessimistic. Ready to cave in. Would he really be any help? Would Jin, for that matter? She was surprised at his tentative reaction over the testing. As much as she liked him, if he wasn't going to be wholeheartedly persuasive in English or Chinese, would it be better without him?

'You might be right,' John said eventually. 'At least it might be handy to have someone along who speaks Chinese.' He turned to Dr Chou and Jin. 'That is if you don't mind coming along.'

The two nodded their consent, but Dr Chou felt compelled to add his own doubts. 'It is, of course, well worth a try. But we should not count on a positive outcome.'

'That being said, we'll give it our best,' said John. 'We'll leave first thing in the morning. I'll get the prints together now, but could I have a word with you first, Bob?'

'Of course,' said Bob. 'We'll go over to the office.' He removed his gloves and followed John out.

CHAPTER TEN

The first light of dawn broke through the horizon, casting pink and golden lights and indigo shadows. John and Bríd quietly loaded their gear into the back of the SUV, the beauty of the dawn instilling a reverent silence.

Bríd touched her chest and felt the medallion that hung underneath her t-shirt. She'd taken to wearing it all the time now—a strong connection to her grandmother, something she now wanted to feel, to remember. To remind her of her gran's love and kindness and how Bríd always had more confidence, more skill and felt prettier in her gran's presence. And somehow, with the medallion around her neck, it was as though her gran was right there whispering in her ear, sharing the beauty of the morning with her.

She'd thrown on her clothes after a restless night that had only turned to sleep just before the alarm went off. She noticed now that John seemed to have fared no better than she had in search of a restful night and hadn't spared much time in dressing. His hair was tousled and his hat just shoved on his head. She couldn't help but smile.

John looked back at her. 'What?'

'Oh, nothing,' she said. 'I just think we'll both really appreciate the benefit of a good shower and a real bed tonight.'

John smiled weakly. 'At least some good will come of this journey.'

Before Bríd could answer, Jin and Dr Chou approached, their own bags in hand. After brief greetings, they finished loading the SUV and were on their way, John driving.

Bríd sat in the back, next to Jin, while Dr Chou sat up front with John. Bríd wasn't inclined to talk this early in the day, so she turned her gaze out the window to study the arid countryside. The few scattered trees and distant mountains were silhouetted against the crimson colors streaking the sky. As she viewed the sparse grass that gathered in stoic clumps against the threat of another day in the baking sun, she wondered about the people who had tried to sustain a living here, all those centuries ago. What had brought the mummy's people to such a region? Would they ever find out? If the government couldn't be persuaded to change its mind Bríd wondered if there would be much to show for all their effort beyond the images and notes they'd taken. Would that be enough to establish such a controversial position? And what would sparsely supported theories do to John and Bob's reputation? Not to mention their ability to acquire more funding for any other expeditions or digs they might select. No, for John's sake, if nothing else, she hoped this trip would secure the permission.

'This scenery must seem quite a contrast to what you're used to in Ireland,' said Jin.

She turned to him, reluctantly pulling herself out of her thoughts. 'Yes, Ireland is probably its complete opposite. There's much rain, so it's very lush—the trees, the grass are a strong and vibrant green. The light, the sky, they're different too.'

'Do you prefer Ireland to Philadelphia?'

Bríd sighed. 'I don't know, really,' she finally answered.

Though she'd experienced so much pain and misery in recent months in Ireland, she still couldn't bring herself to perceive it as anything else but home. Maybe it was her mother's apparently easy adaptation to Philadelphia and acquisition of a new husband who wasn't interested in music of any kind. And her refusal to speak in Irish with her criticism of Bríd's activities at the Irish center. But she'd spent the last three years of her schooling in Philadelphia before she went to Penn on a scholarship and in that time she hadn't been short of friends. She'd just missed her real home—the farm, the land, the community and, of course, her grandmother. And Ciarán. Though that was no longer the case. How she could have been so naïve to think that in the time they were separated he wouldn't find someone else, was anyone's guess. But at least he could have told her. Not lie and make her believe they were still the same together, until her eyes had shown her what her heart had already begun to sense. Now she forced herself think about it, curse herself for the eedjit she was until she realized she could give him the label 'bastard' that he deserved.

'What drew you to anthropology and archaeology?'

Jin's question brought her back to the present and she tried to form a coherent answer. 'I'm not sure. Maybe it's because there's so much history around back home. So many mysteries about the peoples there that came before us, whether it's ancient Irish or other folk. And tying it in to the mythology, just makes it,' she paused, searching for the right word, 'more intriguing, I guess.'

'Yet you chose to come on this dig. Not one in your own country.'

'There were some complications,' she managed to say. She had no desire to give him the full reasons. 'I'm glad I've come, though,' she said in a decisive tone. She realized it was true. She was glad she'd come. It had been the right decision from both the personal and academic end. There was no denying that the discovery had definite connections with her own area of study and she had found that the distance and some of the people here had made the events in the past month easier to bear. She glanced over at Jin, mentally acknowledging his friendship. Then she looked at John, who was studying the endless stretch of road, his conversation with Dr Chou lapsed into silence. It was John who'd been the real surprise to her. He was not at all as she first thought him, back when he was her teacher. Now she felt she could count him as her friend, but was it more than that? What would he count her? She realized she was attracted to him, there was something about him that drew her to him. But it was more than that. She cared about him, cared that he would achieve something from this expedition. Maybe it was also that he was the only one who knew about the things she'd seen of the golden-haired man and the red-haired woman.

She gave an imperceptible shake of her head, deciding to put those thoughts aside and turned to Jin instead, asking him questions about his own home and academic interests. She found his responses interesting but vague and when she pressed him, he side-stepped her with questions of his own, until the SUV pulled over and stopped, bringing the conversation to a halt.

'I think we'll take a break here, stretch our legs and have a bite to eat,' said John.

Bríd was glad for the stop. After some hours of rattling along the road she found her body cried out for some relief. She climbed out of the SUV with the rest and looked around. There was a little valley just below with a small stream scattered with rocks. Stumpy trees that promised some shade lined its banks. Beyond the stream were clumps of shrubs and rock outcroppings that were potential private spots to attend to her bladder.

After depositing her lunch bag on the blanket set up for their picnic, Bríd left the others and went in search of a suitable shrub. She finally located a serviceable spot some ways from the others and large enough to screen her from their view. While she squatted there a fit of the giggles seized her as she thought about the many times she had been in just such a situation at her grandmother's farm growing up when she was in the upper fields or on a walk. It was yet another thing her mother had sniffed about.

Bríd finished quickly, but after she zipped her shorts, she decided to sit a moment and enjoy a little time by herself. Her gaze followed the course of the small stream and she wondered if it had ever been a larger river. The terrain around made it difficult to tell. Would this have been a vital source of water in the mummy's time?

The strong light refracted and split off the water's reflection, creating momentary blind spots in her view, until one such surge of light spread out and become another view entirely. A view that showed the golden-haired man, his red-headed companion and someone else, a man with dark features. They were leading horses across the grassy plain to the stream, a stream that flowed with some strength, rippling along its stony bed. As the group drew closer to her, she could see the golden-haired man and the woman touch each other affectionately. He was clearly older than her, but of the same fair coloring. Their clothes were similar, the weave and pattern of their tunics nearly matching, while their boots were fashioned in an identical style. Somehow Bríd knew they were father and daughter. But that wasn't what unnerved her so. And it wasn't just the hair that blazed in this burning sun, no, it was all of her—the face she could see clearly with the green eyes, the curve of the mouth, the tug of the braid, even her stance—all of it was unsettling. She was so like Bríd.

Their companion came up beside the woman while they watched the horses drink from the stream. He put his fingers through the woman's and, bringing her hand to his mouth, he kissed it. He murmured something low and the woman laughed, her eyes alight with the love the two clearly shared, then he looked over across the stream.

Despite the day's heat Bríd suddenly went cold. She couldn't breathe. Still, he looked across at Bríd, his tilted black eyes, black hair and high cheekbones so clear as they stared right at her. She knew that face, knew those broad shoulders.

'BRÍD.'

Water, cold and refreshing, dribbled across her forehead and against her wrists and neck. Slowly she opened her eyes and made out the dark features of the face that hovered over her. Her breath caught again and she struggled to rise.

'Careful, now. Don't get up too soon. Just take a small drink of this first. Give yourself time to get over the faintness.'

Her sight cleared more and she saw the familiar hat, the shirt, as John held the water bottle to her mouth. She gulped down the fluid gratefully and allowed it to spread through her body, cooling it. She sat up a little more and took the bottle from him.

'Better?' John took a seat beside her.

She nodded. 'Sorry about that. I don't know what came over me.'

'When you didn't return after a few minutes I came looking for you. I found you here, in a dead faint, beside this shrub.' He gave her a studied look. 'Is it the heat?'

'No. I don't know. Maybe,' she said. She looked down at her feet, now planted firmly in the scrubby ground. 'John, it happened again,' she added softly.

'Happened again?'

'I saw him. With the woman. They were leading a pair of

horses to the stream there to drink. They weren't alone. There was another man with them.' She put her hand on John's arm. 'John, the man looked nothing like them. He looked like you.'

John stared back her, his eyes wholly dark, his brow narrowed. He turned to look across at the stream, which trickled along in an unassuming manner. 'We'll talk about this later. For now we should get back to the others before they start hunting us down.'

HOURS LATER, they drove into the city of Ürümchi, Dr Chou driving this time. Carefully he navigated the bicycles, cars and stalls that clogged the busy streets. Steel and concrete buildings rose high into the sky to create a modern skyline. Hotels, restaurants and businesses were everywhere around them.

They checked into the hotel John had booked the day before, a small unpretentious accommodation near the museum. After the basic conditions of the past few weeks, it seemed like luxury to Bríd. She scratched her head and thought gratefully of the shower that was close at hand. Besides the experience of thoroughly clean hair and body, she hoped the shower would clear her mind of the doubts and confusion of the episode by the stream.

They made their way to their rooms and Bríd noted with relief that John's room was next to hers. Even though he spoke no Chinese it gave her more comfort knowing he was there than Jin and Dr Chou, who were located further down the corridor.

Once inside the room, she deposited her bag on the bed, removed her toiletries and immediately began to fulfil the promise to herself. She hardly waited to adjust the shower's temperature before she got in and felt the wonderful cleansing water cover her body and hair.

It was some time before Bríd emerged from the bathroom,

clad only in a thin cotton kimono, her wet hair curling loosely at her neck. She went over to the window, pulled back the curtain and looked out. There wasn't much of a view, just the buildings on the other side and the street below. If she leaned over she could see the museum. John had pointed it out as they entered, as well as the museum parking lot, currently filled with cars for sale and repair owned by a businessman who leased it from the museum. Bríd was appalled when Dr Chou told her until he explained that the sale of the lease had been necessary for the museum to earn income to pay the staff. Bríd had refrained from any further comments, but her hopes over the outcome of tomorrow's meeting at the museum sunk to a new low.

What would John do if they failed? There really wasn't enough time to gather all the information he'd need. And what had happened to the missing images? Had someone erased them accidentally? She couldn't imagine Bob or Scott making a mistake like that. Was it one of the other staff? Miffy, perhaps? Dr Chou? Jin seemed too good with computers to have made that kind of mistake. She hoped the images John saved on the flashdrive were still intact.

There was a soft knock at the door. Bríd went over and opened it and John stood on the threshold, his own hair damp from a shower. Before she could say a word he put a finger to his lips and came inside.

Once the door shut, he spoke. 'You can't be too sure who might be listening in corridors, here.'

Bríd stared at him, speechless. Was it really like that? 'Oh,' she finally managed.

'I know. It sounds a bit cloak and dagger, but with things so sensitive over the dig right now, you don't know what the government might be up to.' He sighed. 'I'd just prefer they knew as little as possible right now.'

John sat in the little armchair at the corner of the room and

Bríd took a seat on the bed opposite him. Behind him, the window cast a light that formed almost a halo around his head, reminding her of the vision that she'd thought he was part of earlier in the day. Vision. Was that what it was? Suddenly she was conscious of her wet hair and the thin kimono that came only to her knees. She pulled it a little closer.

'Are you feeling better now?' asked John.

Bríd nodded. 'The shower made a big difference. My hair doesn't feel it has its own ecosystem.'

John gave a wry grin. 'Life on a site can wear rather thin after a while.' His face became serious. 'I was talking about the experience this afternoon, though.'

'Oh, that.' She bit her lip. She'd tried not to think of it in an effort to delay what she now knew was the truth. 'I actually saw it, John. I didn't make it up.'

'What exactly did you see?'

Bríd took a deep breath and told him, making an effort to remember every detail, every nuance of gesture. 'It wasn't the heat. I'm sure of that now,' she added when she'd finished.

John sat in thoughtful silence, looking beyond her. Finally, he spoke, his voice low. 'You know, if Sam were here, there'd be no question about your experience. He would just accept it.'

'Sam?'

'My great uncle.' He looked at her, his eyes a mixture of sorrow and regret. 'He once told me I relied too much on the visible, the provable. He said I missed the whole point of the clan stories.' John grunted. 'He might have been right.'

'Why do you say that?' asked Bríd.

'I don't know. It was a long time ago, the summer after my first year in college. The first time I'd been away from home for any long period. I came back full of my studies and all the new things I'd experienced, and there was Sam, still living in his cabin, the outhouse behind it, carrying his water in daily and his old wood stove barely throwing out enough heat. I thought, "he doesn't still have to live like this, why does he do it?" I wanted to show him that I could bring him a better life. I thought through academic work and digs I could enable our people to take their place in the world as the ancient and important culture they were.' John sighed. 'I asked him to help me excavate the summer camp near our place. The one his clan went to. He wouldn't. He said he would be happy to tell me the stories about it, but he wouldn't dig up anything. That would only cause trouble.'

John picked up the book of matches on the table and toyed with it. 'I wonder now if he wasn't right.' He stared at the matches a moment, then stuffed them in his pocket, out of sight.

'Right about what?' asked Bríd softly, noting his action with the matches. Did it remind him too much of the Raven tale?

He gave a bitter laugh. 'Right about everything. Right about my perceptions, my determination to prove things. Right about digging up artefacts, people.' The last word was said in barely a whisper.

'Mog,' she said. 'I heard her call him Mog.'

'Mog?'

'Yes. I'm sure of it. Just as I'm sure that what I saw was nothing to do with my imagination. Would I give them names? Would I call them Mog, Tlachtga and Yaloa? And why would I give the other man your appearance?'

'My appearance?'

'Yes. He looked like you. Exactly like you.'

'Like a Tlingit, you mean.'

'No. Like you. And the woman looked like me.' She began to flush as a sudden thought seized her. Would he think she was deliberately creating some kind of manifestation of her subconscious mind? She pushed the thought away and tried to keep a neutral expression as she changed the subject. 'Do you think there might be other chambers? Maybe one or both of the other two are buried near this one.'

John brightened momentarily, but then faded after a few moments. 'I'm not sure we'll get the opportunity to find out,' he said. 'If we can't get them to change their minds about immediately re-interring the mummy and closing down the site. Though it might not be such a bad idea to re-inter him. At least after we've done all the necessary tests and documentation.' His face cleared a little. 'Maybe we could get them to agree based on that approach.'

'It's worth a try,' said Bríd. Besides his voiced doubts about keeping the mummy for study in a museum, Bríd couldn't help but notice John had called the mummy 'he.' His dedication to uncovering the past was still evident, but the struggle with his own choices seemed to be growing. She only hoped that tomorrow would bring the results he really wanted.

'You're right. It can't hurt.' He gave her a thoughtful look. 'You know, if we did find another chamber and it contained a mummy of clear Asian derivation it might change their outlook. The only trouble is, how do we convince them of the possibility?'

'You believe me, then?' She found she was flushing again, acutely aware of her exact words to him.

John gave her a serious look, then leaned over and covered her hand. 'I guess I do.'

Bríd looked down at the fingers now clasped around her palm, their calluses rough and reassuring on her own skin. 'Thank you. That means a lot to me.'

John gently lifted her hand to his lips and kissed the inside, his lips covering the tattooed circles. It took her breath away. He rose, pulled her up off the bed and against him, sliding his hands under her head. She tasted his mouth pressing against hers, full and sensuous in its touch. A soft moan escaped him, then abruptly he pulled away.

'I'm sorry, Bríd,' he said, his voice slightly hoarse. 'I shouldn't have done that.'

'Why? Why are you sorry? I wasn't objecting.'

'It's not right. I'm your teacher, your supervisor. I shouldn't take advantage of you.'

Bríd snorted. 'Bob clearly doesn't have those scruples, why should you?'

'I'm not Bob,' John said curtly. 'It's against university regulations. We could both get into trouble.'

'But I'm not your student, John.'

'I'm still responsible for you on this dig.'

'I understand, I guess,' she said finally. Though she didn't. Not really. Strictly speaking he was right, but how many people actually followed the letter of that regulation? Still, she wouldn't argue with him, she wouldn't open herself up to any more rejection.

'I should let you get dressed. We've only a half hour until we meet Jin and Dr Chou.' John moved to the door. 'I'll check the images again, before we meet. Maybe I'll be able to find something that might convince the others that there are Asian links worth exploring further.'

'You brought all the images with you? Including the ones lost from the laptop?' Bríd fought the tears that gathered at the corner of her eyes. She wouldn't let him see her cry.

John pulled out a small flashdrive from his pocket. 'It's all right here. I can look at it on the tablet I brought. Wish me luck.' He opened the door and left.

The tears spilled over onto her cheeks. She stood there for a long time, her finger tracing the circles on her wrist where only moments before John's lips had been.

CHAPTER ELEVEN
CHINA C. 1500 BCE

With such an occasion as Yaloa and Tlachtga's wedding to celebrate, it was only right that every effort would be made to make it an event to remember, despite the drought. The most brightly colored tunics and decorated headpieces were pulled out and made ready. The women expended every effort to produce platters of well seasoned berries and root plants and slowly roasted game that determined huntsmen had brought back. The delicious aromas brought smiles to faces and lit eyes as they anticipated a thoroughly enjoyable day.

When she was ready, Tlachgta appeared with her hair loose about her in a blaze of red flame against the green and blue of her fine woven plaid tunic that hung full and long over a skirt of saffron-colored wool. A wreath of flowers crowned her head, and on her forehead three circles were painted. She came with her father at her side, his own cheeks showing the sun symbols in paint. He was still a large, well-made man and he wore a saffron-colored tunic over dark trousers. He'd draped a woven plaid of blue and yellow across his shoulders and had fastened it with an intricately wrought brooch.

It took Yaloa's breath away, watching the two of them come to join him. He had done the best he could with his own finery, rarely worn but of ancient origin. The skin was tanned to a soft buff and his symbol was emblazoned on it in black and red needlework of fine dyed sinew. His light colored leather boots showed the same quality of needlework. An eagle feather hung from his head, its leather fastener woven deep into his hair. He took Tlachtga's hand and felt her strength and his own rose to match it. He would not fail her.

Around him, the drums struck up and the singing began, the chanting rhythm creating a protective circle around the group. Herbs scented the air, cleansing all evil from the ceremony. Food was offered, little morsels for each of them to sample. Buan produced two cups of finely wrought silver and filled them with a fermented drink that Yaloa and Tlachtga drank. The gathered crowd roared its approval.

Mog stepped forward and intoned the sacred words from his own people. Yaloa couldn't understand them, but Tlachgta had told him earlier what they meant. And on his cue he repeated them as instructed.

'I am blood of your blood, flesh of your flesh, soul of your soul,' he said.

'I am blood of your blood, flesh of your flesh, soul of your soul,' Tlachtga said.

The meaning of the words echoed in his mind as Mog took his ritual knife and lifted an arm from each of them and expertly cut a slash along their wrists. Carefully, he placed their wrists together and wrapped them in a strip of finely tanned hide and tied it twice. A twice-tied knot. Yaloa and Tlachtga repeated the words of binding they'd spoken before. When it was Tlachtga's turn, Yaloa felt something shift inside him. His breath was gone. A moment later a gap in his middle section opened and swallowed something whole and closed again. He glanced down at his belly and could see nothing different outwardly, but he knew inwardly everything had changed. He turned to Tlachtga and she looked at him, wide-eyed with wonder and he knew. His life was now beginning. A new path, a new person.

THE WIND RUSHED past Tlachtga's face, coloring her cheeks, sending her hair flying out behind her. She laughed, exhilaration and joy filling her with a happiness that expressed itself in a head-long race across the plain on Segda. The joy was coupled with an ill-suppressed desire to show Yaloa she could still make him bite her dust if she wished. He was behind her now, mounted on Medb, closing in fast, though his skills were sorely tested. Reaching the stream, Tlachtga reined in and walked Segda along the water's edge while they both regained their breath. The cool air of the morning still clung to the trees and grass, providing a welcome freshness.

She heard Yaloa come up behind her. She twisted in her saddle and gave him a grin. He swung down in a smooth, swift motion, landed with grace and made his way over to her. His face was alight with humor, his stride confident and purposeful. When he reached her side Tlachgta leaned over and tweaked a lock of his hair.

'The day has not yet come when you can match me on a horse,' she teased.

'Ah, I was being kind to my dearest wife,' he said. 'It is good for her to think she can beat me at one thing.'

Tlachtga laughed at his remark. 'And I will allow you to say that tale for the sake of my beloved husband's pride,' she said. 'There is a penalty, though.' With a swift motion she dismounted and moved towards him. Threading her arms around his neck, she kissed him. Yaloa wrapped her in his arms and she breathed in the now familiar scents of his body. Scents that always reminded her of the joy she'd felt since they were wed over five moons ago.

'I have something of great importance to tell you,' said Tlachtga.

'I thought there might be a reason you saw fit to prove your horse skills,' Yaloa said with a laugh.

She smiled back and pushed against his chest playfully. Then she took up his hand and held it against her stomach. Yaloa looked at her with a question on his face. She nodded at his unspoken words. His face lit with joy and he scooped her up off her feet, swinging her around, shouting his delight. When he finally put her down he gave her a great squeeze. 'When?' he asked.

'About six moons or so. Just before the winter.'

A look of concern flitted across his face. 'We will make certain that there is more than enough food store and that you will be able to rest all winter to nurse the babe,' he said. 'Beloved, that is wonderful news!'

She laughed at him, thinking what little he knew if he thought that resting and having a new babe were complementary existences. She smiled, then withdrew a small bundle she had tucked in her tunic and gave it to Yaloa.

'This is for you,' she said.

Yaloa took the bundle, looking at her quizzically. Carefully he unfolded the cloth and pulled out a knife, fashioned with an ornately carved handle. He let out a cry of wonder.

'It is beautiful,' he said, fingering the blade with his thumb. He tested the weight, shaking his head in wonder.

'It is made especially for you,' she said. 'To cut true, to protect in all that is to come. It is a vision knife, warning you of danger when held in your hand.'

'I will always treasure this,' said Yaloa. He kissed her.

'It must never leave your side,' she said pulling back slightly. 'I would not want my babe to be without a father.'

Yaloa hugged her close, tucking the knife in his belt. 'It will remain here,' he said.

'You have Mog to thank for it, really,' she told him. 'He suggested it.'

'Does he know of the babe?' asked Yaloa.

'No, no one knows but you,' she answered. 'I would like to keep this between us, until I have shared it with my father. I would wish to tell him such wonderful news myself, before anyone else might have a chance to tell him.'

'Of course,' said Yaloa and he leaned over and kissed her head. 'This is surely a good omen that the tribe's fortunes will improve. Everyone will see that.'

She smiled at his enthusiasm, though she wondered about the truth of his words. There were a few who would be less than joyous at her news. It was not Kayáani who would mind, her own marriage to Gutao already bearing fruit, softening her disdainful attitude. It was Teslintoo's poison she feared. She had resisted all of Tlachtga's efforts to befriend her, the distant civility turning into poorly masked dislike instead. Teslintoo's animosity had extended beyond Tlacghta to Buan and Mog, her criticism of that pair just as verbal as the thoughts she expressed about Tlachtga. The main complaints were the cart building and horse training in order to migrate east, a path she felt would lead only to disaster.

Yaloa had tried to reassure Tlachtga that Teslintoo would soon come round. Tlachtga was not so sure. Teslintoo sniffed and turned her head every time Tlachtga passed the nearly completed dwelling that Yaloa, Buan and Mog were constructing for Yaloa and Tlachtga. The dwelling was near to Mog and Buan's so that she could still help out there, yet have some privacy with Yaloa. At the moment, the couple divided their time between Mog's dwelling and Teslintoo's. Though Yaloa's custom demanded he live with his wife's clan, Teslintoo clearly did not believe it should apply to him. Mog had understood and suggested this solution.

As if hearing her thoughts about her father, Yaloa cupped her chin and spoke of him. 'It is time that I take your father on a journey,' he said. She looked at him, slightly alarmed. Behind her, the stream seemed to race along, matching her heartbeat. 'The journey is the *Sha Man's* journey he has awaited so patiently. I must visit the time of not time and ask the Star People for guidance.' Tlachtga's heart slowed and she nodded her understanding. 'Our time here is growing short,' he continued. 'We need to acquire more horses, prepare for a great journey. I need to know where we should travel. The Star People—they can see into the next time—they will tell me.'

'When will you go for the horses?' she asked in a small voice. Her pleasure when he mentioned he would at last share his knowledge of spirit journeying with Mog had disappeared when he'd talked about getting more horses.

He looked into her face, his hand stroking her head. 'We will return safely, before the babe's arrival. I promise you.'

She looked back at him, trying to take comfort in his words.

AFTER HER MIDDAY MEAL, Tlachtga strolled over to her father, her harp under her arm. He was sitting under a tree, taking advantage of the meager shade available against the hot afternoon sun to fashion a new harness for Medb's foal. A slight breeze rustled the leaves of the tree, enticing Tlachtga to join him and share her news with her father and find some peace from her worries.

'Am I to have the joy of your good harp for a while?' asked Mog when he spotted her.

'Oh, so it is my harp that gives you the joy,' teased Tlachtga.

'Perhaps I shall just leave it here with you and be on my way.' She lowered herself on the ground beside him and, crossed her legs and tucked the harp in her lap.

'Now, Daughter, you know the harp is nothing without you,' he said with a grin, resuming his work. Tlachtga watched him as he deftly worked the leather and wooden fastenings while she idly plucked the harp strings.

'How goes it with my married daughter?' he asked her after a while. 'Her radiant face with eyes for only one person tell me things still go well?'

'Things go very well, Father. I know I don't have as much opportunity to speak with you alone as we used to, but I still feel you are my best and closest adviser, as well as my very treasured father.'

Mog reached over and patted her hand. 'Don't even think for a moment that I begrudge the time with your husband, who is now my son,' he assured her. 'You have chosen well and your happiness makes mine complete. Buan and I are both filled with pleasure when we see the two of you together.'

Tlachtga smiled at his words and let their warmth spread over her. 'We just need to find a good woman for Buan.'

Mog snorted. 'I think Buan needs no assistance along that line. He ably demonstrates his many qualities every day before a small group of devoted onlookers.'

'Truly?' asked Tlachtga, laughing at the image. She had no doubt about its truth. Buan was as large and well-built as her father, and good to look upon. He also had the instinct for showing it to best advantage. Underneath all seeming vanity was a good heart, though. A heart that was simple and open. There was nothing subtle about Buan. 'Is he favoring any particular devotee?' she asked, smiling broadly. Tlachtga has her own idea about its identity.

'Well, now, you would have to ask Buan that.' Mog chuckled.

'But I would venture my guess on Qaltsixkli. She's a good woman and he would do well with her.'

Tlachtga nodded, her suspicions confirmed. 'You're right, Father. She would suit Buan.' Tlachtga was at that thought. Qaltsixkli, sister to Gutao and cousin to Yaloa, was gentle and well liked.

Tlachtga sat in silence, considering these events, her fingers resuming their play along the harp strings. Mog took up his own work with the harness again, respecting her need for reflection. Glancing over at him, Tlachtga was caught up again in his craftsmanship, the effortless skill he applied in the stitching and the firm fasteners. She knew Yaloa valued Mog's abilities and sought to have Mog pass them on to members of his tribe. They also tapped Buan's knowledge of cart construction, as well as all of their knowledge of horses. She frowned, the direction of her thoughts taking her back to her worries.

'What is it, Daughter? Your face now shows something less than joy.'

She tried to clear her face and ease the frown that creased her brow and mouth. 'Well I'm sure it will gladden your heart to know that Yaloa intends to show you the great *Sha Man* journey. He must undertake a very important quest and he needs your help.' She paused a moment, taking brief pleasure in Mog's look of interest and delight. 'Yaloa knows the time is fast approaching when the tribe must move on. He hopes to find out the destination of this great move when he takes the *Sha Man* journey.' Tlachtga looked down at her lap, her voice becoming small. 'Then you and he are to go and trade for more horses.'

'Ah,' said Mog, nodding slightly. 'I thought as much. The questions Yaloa has put to me these many suns led me to believe he was considering acquiring more horses.' He leaned over to cup her chin, his eyes full of love and concern. 'Is there more that causes this layer of sadness? Do you fear for our safe return? You should not, Daughter. You know we are experienced enough to be assured a safe journey.'

Tlachtga looked at her father's face, fighting back the tears that suddenly filled her eyes. 'It is not that I fear for your safe return,' she said, her voice trailing off.

'What is it then?' He stroked her hair, his calm touch proving some comfort.

She knit her brow, trying to find the words. A tear started down her cheek. 'Oh, Father, it's just that I wish the journey for horses wouldn't start now.' She put her hand to her stomach. 'I fear it will take too long.'

Mog looked deeply into her eyes, then took her hand. 'Does Yaloa know of the child?'

She was stunned at his perception, her eyes opening wide.

'Yes, I can see he does,' Mog said. He squeezed her fingers. 'You mustn't be afraid, we will be here when the time comes. Besides, you'll have Teslintoo's birthing skills to ensure all goes well.'

Tlachtga's mind sounded an alarm, her whole body tensing as her father deftly located the root of her fears. A ragged sob escaped her. 'That's what feeds my anxiety. Teslintoo hates me so. She would never assist gladly in the birthing. And what if something should go wrong and you or Yaloa aren't here?' Her mind reeled at these thoughts, visions of her mother's last breath crowding in upon her.

'Ss-h-h, child,' said Mog. 'You will be fine. Your babe will be fine. Teslintoo is a good and loving mother. Think on that. Tell her of your news and ask her help on birthing and child rearing. On those grounds she will likely soften towards you.'

With great effort Tlachtga took in his words and tried to find comfort from them. Perhaps he was right. Perhaps with such news Teslintoo would find some kindness in her heart towards Tlachtga. She could only hope so.

· · ·

TLACHTGA THREADED her way through the camp towards Teslin-too's dwelling. Children raced by, intent on their games, their laughter filling the air and taking some of the tension from her. She passed a group of women who sat weaving root baskets, their hands flying as quickly as the words that passed among them. Seeing her, they called out a greeting. Tlachtga gave them a wave and smile. The temptation to stop and chat was strong, but she resisted it, determined to complete her errand. Besides, she was careful how often she joined in with the women, her grasp of their language not firm and also she didn't want to appear that she was thrusting herself upon them.

The women were still fairly shy of her. She was in their eyes, after all, a *Sha Man* in her own right as well as the wife of one and this was new for them. The women in the tribe generally confined themselves to things of the hearth. They prepared and cooked the food, skinned and tanned the hides, weaved cloth, fashioned clothes, created pots and baskets for use in cooking and storage. And they cared for the young children, no small role in a tribe fighting for survival. But while the person's clan affiliation came through the mother, as in Tlachtga's own culture, the women didn't seem to have a formal path to voice opinion in tribal decisions. This was not so for Tlachtga's culture, where they had say in tribal matters. So Tlachtga was taking care to find her own path here that ensured much of the role she was accustomed to would be preserved. She found being Yaloa's wife endowed her with privileges, but few close friends among the women. There seemed to be no dislike though. And their smiles were warm and friendly as she made her way past them. She took comfort in that thought.

Tlachtga spied Teslintoo busily weaving cloth on a hanging frame outside her dwelling. She sat cross-legged before it, on specially fashioned pallet, the sun shining over her shoulder on to the loom. Finely spun colored wools nestled in a basket beside her. She seemed relaxed and content. Coming up beside her, Tlachtga admired the expert skill that Teslintoo used to weave the stunning lightening patterns in the cloth.

'That is a fine cloth you have made,' said Tlachtga. 'Is it a special piece?' She knelt down beside Teslintoo for a closer look.

Teslintoo grunted and kept working, her fingers deftly weaving the shuttle through the warp threads. After a few moments she sat back to view her work.

'It is for my daughter. It will be her naming dress,' she answered. All the children were given birth names so the wayward spirits would be fooled and not call the children back to the star people. They kept the false names until they were old enough to receive their true names, after their fifth summer, when their own spirits were strong and clearly visible.

'It is a wonderful piece,' said Tlachtga carefully in Teslintoo's language. 'Truly worthy of such an important occasion. I am certain she will be proud to wear something so beautiful that demonstrated her mother's love and skill.'

Teslintoo looked over in a puzzled manner. 'These are very honeyed words that praise my skill.'

'I am aware you have many skills and gifts, Teslintoo,' said Tlachtga, trying to remain calm. 'You are a good mother and I admire all your accomplishments. And I know you are especially skilled in the ways of childbirth.' Tlachtga paused and took a deep breath and said in a lower voice, 'It is that skill I would ask you about now.'

Teslintoo looked at her sharply. 'What is your meaning, exactly?' she asked in a tight voice. Tlachtga recoiled slightly at the needle-like tone and hard glance. A moment passed. Steeling herself against the venom, she placed her hand lightly on Teslintoo's arm.

'I would ask your help and advice,' said Tlachtga. 'You have skill and experience where I have none.' Tlachtga paused and forced a smile. 'I am carrying your brother's child.'

Teslintoo turned back to stare at her weaving. Her fingers gripped the shuttle tightly and then thrust it through the loom, the twang of the warp threads protesting her force. A moment passed, the angry noise from the loom filling the silence. Tlachtga removed her hand and placed it in her own lap, saying nothing, trying to will her gladness to Teslintoo. Finally, Teslintoo stilled her fingers. She turned to Tlachtga and stared darkly at her.

'So. You are breeding,' she said in a bitter voice. 'And now you want my help. It seems there are some things that you cannot do. Does my brother know you are so ignorant about something so important to women?'

Tlachtga felt as though she had been slapped. She flushed deeply. She took a breath to make one more effort. 'Teslintoo,' she said. 'I do not seek to hurt you or displace you in any way. I would like for us to be sisters.'

'Replace me! You could not replace me if you tried for a thousand summers,' shouted Teslintoo. 'You know nothing of our ways, as I have told you. My brother is blinded by the needs of his body or he would see this clearly. I have no words for you. You, who will never be my sister!' Teslintoo turned angrily back to her work and resumed her weaving, her motions jerky and awkward.

Too stunned for words or actions, Tlachtga continued to kneel beside her. She gathered her wits and rose, the air spinning slightly around her. Wordlessly, she made her way to the small path behind Teslintoo's dwelling, stumbling slightly on some brush. Tears of frustration and anger burned in her eyes, driving her onward, away from the scene that had just taken place. She wanted to remove herself from such poison. She shuddered at the thought of sharing space with Teslintoo. Perhaps she could stay with her father until the dwelling was complete. This would not be easy and she knew that Yaloa would never understand her reluctance to go near his sister. Tlachtga sighed, her eyes still clouded with tears. A hand touched her arm and she turned to see Gutao beside her.

'Do not mind her,' he said. 'She will get used to your marriage.' Tlachtga gave him a weak smile. 'Be patient, it will happen. I am certain.' Gutao assured her. He laughed a little. 'I seem to be always apologizing to you for Teslintoo's behavior.'

'Do not worry about that,' said Tlachtga. 'And thank you for saying those words. As much as I doubt that she will ever become accustomed to Yaloa and me, I have seemed to have added another difficulty for her to accept. I am going to have a child.'

'That is wonderful, Cousin,' said Gutao. 'You both must be overjoyed.'

'Oh, we are.' Tlachtga started to smile in earnest. 'It will not be for some moons.' She sighed, her brief smile fading. 'Joy is not the emotion Teslintoo felt, though.'

'Wait until the babe is here,' said Gutao. He gave her arm a reassuring squeeze. 'She will soften then, I am sure of it.'

Tlachtga nodded to him. In her heart she was not so certain.

CHAPTER TWELVE

Tlachtga watched Mog trace his finger along the design of the rattle he held in his hand as he sat cross-legged before the fire. Yaloa had given it to him a short while ago. It had been one of Yaloa's ritual rattles, his eagle spirit helper painted on the gourd's rounded face. It was a spirit Yaloa felt they both shared when he first saw the carved head piece of Mog's regalia. Mog wore the head piece now, the dark contours of the carving accentuated in the flickering firelight, giving the eagle the appearance of imminent flight. An appropriate image, for in moments it would begin. Yaloa and Mog would fly to the cosmos, journey to the No Time and see the Star People.

Mog tugged on the bull's hide cape that was draped across his bare shoulders. Tlachtga knew he was probably anxious to begin, but he understood that all must be in place, everything must be properly prepared. Yaloa sat calmly beside him, his hair hanging loose against a bare chest, his own rattle lying in his lap. She was glad to see he had the knife she'd given him tucked at his waist. Yaloa smiled at her reassuringly. She sat opposite the two of them, holding a drum and stick like the tribal elders who sat behind her. When all was ready she would lead them in the trance beat. Tlachtga wouldn't be making the journey with Yaloa and Mog this time, because of the babe. Yaloa had told her he felt it would be safer. She would be the trance keeper, the one who kept watch during the journey, ready to call the travelers back at any sign of terrible danger or distress.

The elders behind her would help her keep the beat with their own drumming. They were the designated men, trained for ritual occasions and participation in tribal decisions. Women, with the exception of healers, were not involved in these mysteries and so they weren't even present, except for Teslintoo, who was seated at the back. Teslintoo, as the healer and attendant at births, was the only woman until Tlachtga had arrived to attend an event like this.

Yaloa nodded to Tlachtga that he was ready to begin. He reached for the cup of herbal spirit brew, the first thing other than water to touch his lips since the evening before. He drank from the cup, then passed it over to Mog, and placed the tiny twig he held in his fingers under his tongue. Mog did the same. After a few moments Yaloa picked up his rattle and nodded to Tlachtga. It was his signal. She raised her hand and began to beat the drum, setting the pace for the other drummers behind her. She continued beating the steady rhythm, matching Yaloa's and Mog's shake of the rattles. The two men closed their eyes. The journey had begun.

Tlachtga watched them carefully, her hand striking constant beats with the stick, its sound penetrating her own mind. She fought the desire to succumb to her own trance, knowing they needed her to keep vigil. The drumming went on and Tlachtga lost track of the time, her eyes fixed on the two figures outlined in the fire's flame.

Suddenly, she saw Yaloa's rattle still. His face, his whole body was motionless. All the muscles, held taught and firm a moment before, slackened. Tlachtga maintained her beating, her mind crying out in alarm. She knew something must be terribly wrong. Should she call Yaloa back? He had instructed her clearly that on no account should she interfere unless both he and Mog should fall lifeless to the ground. She looked at Mog. He continued to shake the rattle, matching her beat.

Tlachtga held her breath. Should she journey herself, search for Yaloa?

YALOA STOOD beside Mog beside the bank of a dark river, the landscape bare around them. Before Yaloa could speak, a log drifted towards them and without exchanging a word, the two seized the log and mounted it, their feet dangling in the water. Leaning forward, they used their hands to paddle across to the other side.

'How deep do you think this river is?' asked Mog.

'You mustn't concern yourself with the river. That is not our journey and any worries or thoughts in that direction might lead us into danger. Our main purpose is to get across. That's where the real journey will begin.'

Mog grunted. A few moments later they reached the other side and Yaloa dismounted, climbed to shore and turned to help Mog. Their feet were dry and Yaloa knew better than to dwell on the reasons behind such details and his thoughts turned to the open road in front of them. Should he take that direction to reach the Star People? His spirit helper should be here to tell him.

A swoop of wings caught his attention and Eagle landed gracefully in front of them, towering over them both. All doubts vanished and with a signal to Mog the pair climbed on Eagle's back and clung to his silken feathers as he rose into the sky, soaring to the great expanse among the bright stars and the light of the moon.

Eagle raced across the cosmos, the stars blurring into wide streaks. Suddenly, Eagle plunged headlong, throwing Yaloa's heart into his throat and a deep pressure against his chest. Eagle continued downward, until it seemed as if Yaloa could stand it no longer and he and Mog would be hurled into the void below. A moment later Eagle ceased diving and leveled off. Looking below, Yaloa could see they glided over a large, white expanse that was dotted with dark specks. The specks eventually shaped themselves into horses that galloped across a dusty plain. Eagle followed them on their journey until a large body of water halted their progress.

'The sea.'

It was Mog who spoke. Yaloa had never seen the sea and he scanned the moving water water that churned and rolled spume and wave and marveled. He licked his lips, tasting the salt that gathered on them, sniffed it in the air. It was nothing like the small rivers and lakes of his experience. Before he could reflect any more, Eagle soared down towards the sea and plunged into it, breaking the surface to the depths below.

A large fish swam towards them, his silver scales aglow.

'King Salmon?' asked Mog. 'Keeper of Wisdom.' There was no need to ask, Tlachtga's tale-telling had them both well versed by now.

Salmon led them through the dark water soundlessly, his scales flashing from some unseen light. On they traveled, feeling no sense of the water, seeing only King Salmon leading them forward. With a flick of his tail, he was gone and Eagle headed upwards, ascending slowly, the darkness swirling around them. The water burst open above them and they moved through its opening and headed into the sky. Eagle flapped its great wings, scattering droplets in long swooping motions. Once again they soared over land, leaving the water and the darkness behind, meeting instead a bright whiteness. Moments later, Eagle came to rest upon a white plain, a whiteness that stretched cold, bright. Snow.

Yaloa and Mog stepped from Eagle onto a surface that was packed hard as ice. In the distance Yaloa could see a white mountain, its peak disappearing in cold misty cloud. To Yaloa's right was a large outcropping of tall pine trees, their branches swaying slightly in the wind. He heard an owl hoot. An animal burst from the trees and loped across the plain towards them. Yaloa strained to make out its shape, but it reached their side in lightning speed, so his first clear view of it came as it lunged at Mog, a great snarling dog. Mog fell back to the ground, teeth and fur flashing at him as Yaloa's shouts rang out behind him.

Yaloa grabbed the dog and pulled it away from Mog. The dog turned to Yaloa, snarling and snapping its great jaws as it struggled in Yaloa's grip. It was a strange dance, the two of them gripping each other, wrestling vigorously.

'Use your knife!' shouted Mog.

Yaloa ignored his words and continued in his bare-handed life and death struggle with the dog. The dog pulled Yaloa to the ground and his head banged against the hardened snow. He lay there, motionless losing consciousness, the dog poised above him, ready for the kill.

Mog rolled over and grabbed the knife from Yaloa's side. The dog snapped at Mog's hand just as Yaloa reached up and grabbed the dog by the throat, pulling it away from Mog. His grip was strong and firm. He threw the dog to the ground and rolled on top of it. After a brief moment, he grabbed the dog's snout, bunched his hand into a fist and punched the dog in the head, knocking it senseless.

Yaloa rose slowly, his chest heaving and his breath blowing a mist in the cold. He leaned over the dog and examined the ground beside it. His hand closed around a small object. A tooth. It would do to keep something as powerful as this.

Without a word, he turned to Mog and helped him up and walked over towards the trees, where a small group of people was emerging. A man drew away from the group and came up to Yaloa and Mog. He held a rattle in one hand. On his tunic was emblazoned a stylized eagle.

'My brother,' said the man. He handed Yaloa the eagle feather and retreated slowly back into the woods.

Mog made a move to follow them, but Yaloa put a restraining hand on his arm.

'You must not follow the Star People. They have spoken.' Behind him, Eagle cawed. The meeting was over. Time to return.

Tlachtga sounded the rapid call-back beat, her heart following its rhythm in her anxiety over the two men. The beat slowed to loud, forceful strikes, then ended with a loud bang. She'd thought she'd lost them both when their rattles had stopped and their breath disappeared. The moments had stretched painfully until the rattles began to shake and their chests rose and fell in their normal pace.

Yaloa sat before her, still and silent. Beside him, Mog opened his eyes and started flexing his muscles. They both looked drained. Yaloa's eyes, smudged and weary, struggled to focus. He glanced briefly at Tlachtga and tried to smile, and then looked at the group behind her, searching it carefully. Mog looked over at him, his face puzzled and concerned, while he rubbed his hands up and down his bare arms. One of the elders moved to their side, handing Yaloa a horn cup filled with a restorative drink. Yaloa took it and drank deeply, before handing it over to Mog. Tlachtga watched Yaloa, forcing herself to remain in her place and respect the ritual, her worries running rampant through her mind. She saw him sway, her resolve fled and she rushed to his side, reaching him in time to catch him in her arms.

He came around shortly, but Tlachtga was still concerned. She mixed her own special draft and helped him drink it down and had him lay down on Mog's pallet for a restorative sleep. Later, when Yaloa was in a deep sleep on Mog's pallet, Tlachtga talked quietly with Mog, the small fire outside providing the only light in the dwelling.

When Tlachtga finished her description of the events she had witnessed, she looked at Mog expectantly. He sighed. She knew he was tired, but she needed to know what had happened. Now, while it was fresh in his mind, before they related the journey to the elders.

'It was a powerful experience, Daughter. One I will never forget,' he said, and told her what he'd seen.

TLACHTGA STROKED MEDB'S HEAD, feeling the sun's warmth across the white spot along Medb's forehead. She pressed her large belly against the horse's side, feeling Medb ripple in response. The motion was soothing, easing some of her ache. Two moons had passed since she had been able to mount Medb, so the contact she made now was the closest she came to riding. Tlachtga buried her head deeply in the horse's mane, inhaling her scent and taking comfort.

The sun was strong on her back, inviting her to think of a cool walk along the stream. She might even dangle her feet and gain some relief from carrying the extra weight. Perhaps, if she leaned back a little, she might even see her feet, a rare treat of late. Tlachtga placed her hand on her swollen belly, a motion she had repeated several times since waking. Many suns had passed since the baby had dropped its position and she was growing increasingly uncomfortable.

Tlachtga lumbered slowly through the camp, oblivious of the small group of women digging roots in the small plot.

'That babe is keeping you moving?' someone shouted to her.

Tlachtga looked over and saw Kayáani with Qaltsixkli, Buan's new wife, accompanied by Kayáani's cousin. The three of them waved to her. Kayáani's own small daughter lay on the blanket beside the plot, her limbs waving in the sunlight.

Tlachtga patted her belly. 'This one will be a good runner, I think. He is taking me for a walk, right now.'

'Oh, do not worry,' said Qaltsixkli laughing. 'It will not be long before the babe will be walking on its own.'

Tlachtga smiled, and with a wave she moved on. Qaltsixkli was such a sweet woman, and in the short space since her marriage to Buan, Tlachtga had come to feel that she had found a real sister. She had treasured this new relationship, especially during the past few moons with Yaloa and Mog still away on their quest for horses. Their continued absence caused her much anxiety. They should have returned during the Moon of the Running Hare. They were now in the Moon of the First Frost, nearly two moons later.

She wanted Yaloa to be here for the babe's arrival. She needed him to be here. Tlachtga forced down her worries, slowed the steps that had quickened with her racing thoughts. She tried to take comfort in Teslintoo's pronounced courtesy, evident since Yaloa had announced the impending journey. There was no reason, but her own instinct that made her distrust Teslintoo's changed behavior and her insistence she help with Tlachtga's birthing. Refusing Teslintoo's assistance would bring shame on both of them. She could only pray that Yaloa and Mog would return in time to be present for the birth.

The stream was in her sight now and she shifted her weight slightly. A pain seized her belly, shooting down her side. It subsided after a few moments and tears filled her eyes. She walked a little and felt a rush of wetness down her legs. Not yet, she thought, not yet. Her mind shouted *Yaloa*, reaching out with an intensity and urgency that she felt certain he would hear. She tried to focus on the walking, breathing in slow, calming rhythms as she made her way back to the camp.

By the time Tlachtga arrived at her dwelling she was sweating hard. The thick felt flap that covered the entrance blurred and then doubled. Searching for support, she grasped the wood frame that shaped the entrance. Two more pains had already clutched at her body since the time she had turned back. She heard a shout and turned to see Buan and Qaltsixkli at her side.

'Tlachtga, are you well?' asked Buan with alarm.

'Is it the babe, is it time?' said Qaltsixkli. Tlachtga just nodded, unable to speak. Qaltsixkli put her arm around Tlachtga's shoulder, leading her into the dwelling while she instructed Buan in a low voice over her shoulder. She settled Tlachtga on her pallet, folding a fur robe into a pad for her head, and moved over to pour Tlachtga a drink of water from the earthen jug.

'There is time yet before it comes, Tlachtga. Drink some,' said Qaltsixkli, kneeling by her side. 'Try and rest in the meantime.'

Teslintoo entered then, a leather bag under her arm. She moved over to Tlachtga's other side and knelt down beside her. Putting her hands to Tlachtga's belly, she examined different areas, pressing slightly in various positions, asking Tlachtga questions in a curt, officious tone. Tlachtga tried to answer, but a contraction seized her again, making it impossible to speak.

Her breath shortened to rapid pants, until the pain eased. Qaltsixkli helped her remove her trousers and raised her tunic for a closer examination. Teslintoo barked instructions to Qaltsixkli to retrieve the prepared rush matting and spread it out on the floor beside the pallet while Teslintoo mixed herbs from her bag in a cup of water. She held the cup for Tlachtga, watching as she drank it down. With Qaltsixkli's help, Teslintoo moved

Tlachtga into position on the rush matting. Tlachtga looked over her shoulder, her eyes catching the leather bag, Teslintoo's painted symbol now in view on its side. She could just make it out. It was a dog. She gasped, clutching her belly, a deep contraction, responding to her alarm.

'The babe's head is not in the right position,' Teslintoo was saying. 'You must do as I tell you, when I tell you.'

A searing pain tore through Tlachtga, blocking out everything around her. Teslintoo spoke to her sharply again and Tlachtga tried to listen, her mind filled with fear and desperate longing for Yaloa. She panted in short sharp breaths, her body contorting in agony.

CHAPTER THIRTEEN

Bríd woke with a jolt and clutched her stomach as a searing pain tore her inside. Was it the pain that had woken her? She rubbed her stomach and looked at the clock. Mother of God, she was so late. For all her tiredness, the meal last night had lasted longer than she would have wished and she'd been late getting to bed. Her sleep was troubled with confusing images of those three people—Mog, Tlachtga and Yaloa. It was the thought of Yaloa that caused the heat to flood her body. The memory of embracing Yaloa, making love with Yaloa, and feeling his child grow within her. Surely, it was just the restaurant food that had given her this lingering sense of birth pangs.

Her breath came in short pants as she got out of bed and pushed herself towards the bathroom, careful of her tender abdomen. She splashed water on her face and took a gulp of the water bottle by the sink. The mirror revealed her pasty face and shadowed eyes. She went over to the toilet and sat on the lid, her face down between her knees. Gradually, her breathing slowed and the pains subsided. What an awful start to the day.

. . .

They all sat around the small office, every extra space given over to the chairs that seated those who attended the meeting. Dr Lei, if it weren't for the small spectacles slipping down his nose, could pass for an inscrutable Buddha as he listened intently to John's impassioned plea for his help. Jin was positioned between the two, his face impassive and his arms folded across his chest. Dr Chou was beside Bríd, sniffing occasionally and lending a word or two of clarification when it was needed. But for all John's words and Dr Chou's assistance, Bríd had no idea what Dr Lei was thinking. And she could sense John was just as baffled as she.

John had said little to her the previous night when they were at dinner, and had carefully chosen to sit next to Dr Chou and opposite Jin at the restaurant. He did glance her way occasionally, but she could neither read his expression nor interpret the few vague words he directed to her. Despite the fact that he'd virtually ignored her all night, she still found herself praying he would succeed today.

John took a file out of his case and pulled a batch of printed images from it. One by one, he handed the images across to Dr Lei, explaining the initial layout of the chamber, the mummy's positioning, the clothes he wore and, finally, the artefacts buried with him.

Jin followed the explanation, his eyes narrowing slightly as he watched Dr Lei review each image carefully. When Dr Lei had finished he handed them back to John.

'May I have a look?' asked Jin.

John hesitated a moment and then handed Jin the file.

Jin flipped through the images and glanced up at John. 'You managed to recover the images you lost?'

'Sorry, no,' he answered. 'These I printed out before they were lost. Luckily.'

'You lost some images?' asked Dr Lei.

John nodded casually. 'Somehow they were deleted. Someone's oversight, I presume. But we do have these prints. And of course the orignals.' He gave a wan smile.

John was clearly lying and Bríd could only suppose it was because he didn't want anyone else to know he had a backup on a memory stick.

'The images are startling,' said Dr Lei. 'The condition of preservation, the quality of the clothes and artefacts, all point to a significant find. You are to be congratulated, Dr Sheldon.'

'Thank you,' said John. 'Can you see now why we would ask your support in trying to convince the authorities to change their minds about closing down the site so soon?'

'Oh, I can see, all right,' said Dr Lei. 'But that does not mean I can prevail upon them to change their minds.'

'But what if, as I said, we agreed to re-inter the mummy when we're done?' asked John.

Dr Lei shook his head gently. 'I do not know, Dr Sheldon. I suppose I could approach them with this offer. But you must see my position. We are a small museum, really. We have little funding and no real authority or influence.'

'I see,' said John. He glanced over at Bríd, his face tense. 'There's something more. Something that might help to persuade them.' He shuffled through the photos Jin had placed on his lap and pulled out one. 'Look at this one.' He handed it to Dr Lei. 'Study that headpiece. Look at the style of carving. It's not like the carving on the cart.' He pulled out another print. 'Look at that knife, the workmanship on the handle. That's different, too.'

Dr Lei looked up from the photos. 'Yes,' he said slowly. 'I see what you mean.'

'It's Asian, isn't it?' asked John.

'Possibly. Possibly,' answered Dr Lei.

Dr Chou leaned forward. 'Can I see those?'

'Of course.' Dr Lei handed Dr Chou the prints.

'You understand I would have to consult with some others to be sure,' said Dr Lei. 'But you might be right. The authorities might let you continue if you establish an early Asian link. I will see what I can do.'

John's face relaxed slightly. 'I appreciate whatever help you can give. But we haven't much time. They want us to start clearing the site the day after tomorrow.'

Dr Lei acknowledged his thanks with a nod and rose. 'So, we have no time to lose. I will get to it straightaway. But before I do, I thought, as you are here, you and your university colleague might want to see some of the other artefacts recently recovered from the general region in which you are working.' He nodded to Jin and Dr Chou. 'You gentlemen, I know, have already viewed these articles, but you are welcome to come, too.'

'No,' said Jin before Dr Chou could answer. 'We'll remain here until you return.'

Dr Chou started to object, but changed his mind and nodded his agreement in the end.

Dr Lei ushered them down the corridor, through rooms filled to the brim with disused display cases and numbered storage boxes. He told them that the large amount of items they had stored there allowed little room for any real exhibits, except in a few areas. Bríd glanced at the precariously balanced boxes shoved against walls and under cases and wondered how they tracked any of their items in such conditions.

Eventually, they came to a room off a larger exhibit area. The air was cooler in here, the humidity levels more balanced. Dr Lei switched on the light and closed the door behind him. Shelves lined one side of the room opposite a small examination table. Dr Lei retrieved a box from the shelves and placed it on the table.

'There,' he said. 'I think you will find the items in there of interest.'

'Thank you, Dr Lei,' said John. 'Thank you for everything.'

'You are welcome,' said Dr Lei. He placed his hand on John's shoulders. 'You must take care, John. These are difficult waters you have sailed into. There is much at stake. I advise you to trust no one. I can say no more than that.'

John stood silently, clearly too surprised by his words to do anything but nod.

'Now, my friend, I must go and fill my role as a dutiful government servant. But rest assured, I will do what I can.' With a brief nod to Bríd he left the room, shutting the door after him.

'What did he mean, do you think?' asked Bríd.

'I'm not sure. But he's right. We should be careful.'

'There's something going on, isn't there? Why did you lie about the prints?'

John looked gave her a careful look. 'Like Dr Lei said, trust no one.'

'You don't trust Jin? But why?'

'I don't know Jin. I'd never heard of him before this dig. Sure, he went to Stanford, his credentials in the field seem sound enough, but no one I know has worked with him. Not in my area, anyway. When I asked him about it, he said his earlier work was in ancient Southeast Asian sites, and his papers were mostly published in China in Chinese. Why is he suddenly interested in western China? Areas that at one time were under Muslim influence?'

'I'm not from your field,' said Bríd quietly.

'That's different. I asked for you. I knew your background.'

'You asked for me?'

His eyes darkened and he sighed. 'When Paul broke his leg and I needed a replacement, I asked for you. I knew you hadn't any dig lined up for the summer and I thought it was about time you got some real field experience, not just day trips to sites in progress.'

She could hardly take in his words. 'You knew about the extent of my fieldwork?'

John gave a little laugh. 'Don't look so panicked. You're a bright student, Bríd. Many in the department have been keeping their eye on you. We've high hopes for your career and, well, this past year or so, we've noticed you've been a little distracted. Not as committed as we would want. I thought field experience might help bring it back.'

She looked down at the table, the box still unopened before her. What could she say to that? Was he really interested in her academic performance? But surely that was her supervisor's role, not his. Why had he taken such an interest?

'Why don't we look at these items?' said John. He pulled on the gloves lying beside the box and removed the lid.

Silently, Bríd followed suit with the other pair of gloves and watched him take out the items one by one and lay them carefully on the table. When he'd finished they silently surveyed the group. An indigo wool hat shaped like a tam o'shanter lay next to a mud-colored hood, whose curiously curved end suggested Greek or Anatolian connections. Beside the hats was a pair of beautifully carved wooden combs. Bríd picked them up and admired their perfect, smooth teeth, so evenly rounded they could be modern. She showed them to John and their heads bent close as they admired the delicate workmanship.

She picked up a pair of mottled grey drinking horns, the surface polished to a silky finish. Behind her, John murmured a short explanation about its origins and use, his breath a light waft on her neck. She bent over, put down the horns, and picked up a piece of textile, conscious of the nubby texture through the thin surgical gloves. She resisted the urge to press it to her cheek, to inhale any lingering traces of lanolin that would remind her of the sheep at home. She put it back and held up another, more elaborate piece of cloth. Her fingers stilled, then trembled slightly as she recognized the pattern. It was plaid—the one in which Tlachtga's tunic was woven. She looked closer and touched the lines of crossing weave that formed the distinctive plaid pattern she'd seen only yesterday. Bríd forced herself to breathe deeply, fighting the dizziness that suddenly washed over her. She closed her eyes for a moment, and when she opened them, she could see Mog, Yaloa and Tlachtga seated on the ground.

Mog wore the eagle headpiece, the hide around his shoulder, and his eyes were shut. Yaloa sat bare-chested beside him, his hair hanging loose and a rattle lying in his lap. Yaloa drank from a cup, passed it to Mog and placed something in his mouth. He took up his rattle and began to shake it. Drumming sounded. Tlachtga sat opposite the two, striking a stick against a skin drum held in her other hand, as though it were a bodhran. The beating drum echoed in Bríd's head and the constant rhythm sent her mind spiraling off into an unknown space, into darkness.

She regained consciousness to find John rubbing her wrists and softly calling her name. She looked into John's eyes, her head cradled in his arm.

'Bríd,' he said, his voice full of worry. 'Are you all right?'

She moaned softly, the drumming still echoing faintly in her head. She rubbed her brow gently. 'I'm okay, don't worry.'

'What happened? One minute you were standing there looking at plaid cloth and the next thing you were falling to the ground.' He pursed his lips. 'Was it another episode?'

She nodded. She started to speak, but John put his finger to her lips. 'Don't say anything yet. Give yourself a minute.' He helped her rise and put her on a small stool pulled from under the table. With a firm hand he pressed her head between her knees while he rubbed her back gently, forcing the blood back up to her head.

After a few moments she lifted her head and sighed. How should she tell John that the person they had discovered was indeed a holy man, a shaman in his culture? A shaman, that someone of John's culture wouldn't dare disturb. There could be no doubt, not after what she'd just witnessed. And it wasn't just Mog, but Yaloa, too. Clearly the pair of them had been about to embark on a kind of shamanic journeying. What would he think of it now, providing he believed her, took her word for it? Did she really want to confuse him more? She looked up at John and tried to decide.

'There. The color's come back into your face and you're breathing has improved.' He frowned slightly. 'These episodes are occurring more often now. It worries me.'

Bríd nodded, grateful for the conversation's direction. 'They are, I know. But I think it's when I come into contact with something directly related to these three.'

'Three?'

'Mog, Yaloa and Tlachtga.'

'Yes,' said John. 'I remember now you said those were their names. But what connection was there this time?'

'It was the plaid. I'm sure of it. I was studying it closely and I realized I'd seen it on Tlachtga yesterday. By the stream.'

John nodded slowly. 'And what happened after that?'

Bríd bit her lip. Wildly, she searched her mind for something plausible to tell him, but her mind came up blank. 'Well,' she began. 'I heard drumming. At least I think it was drumming. All three were there.' She looked over at the table and scanned it for clues about what to say.

The door opened and Dr Lei entered.

'I'm sorry, John,' he said. 'But we have to lock up now for the mid-day break. You're welcome to come back this afternoon and continue here, though.'

'Thanks, Dr Lei,' said John. 'We might do that, depending on your own progress with the authorities. Have you had any luck yet?'

Dr Lei shook his head. 'Not so far. I have tried a few times, but the man I need to speak to has been in meetings all morning, but he has not phoned back yet. I have left several messages.' He gave John a reassuring smile. 'Do not worry. I shall not give up.'

'Thanks,' said John. 'I appreciate it.'

After the contents were replaced in the box and the lid secured, Bríd followed John and Dr Lei out of the room and back through the maze of corridors and rooms to his office. Once inside the office Bríd saw it was empty.

'Where are Dr Chou and Jin? Have they left already?

'I believe so,' said Dr Lei. 'I was called away and one of the staff said they had gone.' He gave a wan smile. 'Perhaps they were hungry.'

John frowned and slung his bag over his shoulder. 'That's a little strange. But maybe we'll catch up with them at the restaurant down the road.'

'I am certain you will.'

Bríd picked up her own bag, and after brief goodbyes to Dr Lei, the pair left the office and made their way to the exit. Bríd could sense John's puzzlement, as she was herself. It was strange that Jin and Dr Chou had left without them.

Once on the street, Bríd and John looked around and located the nearest restaurant. It was across the street and down about 100 meters.

'Let me just try to phone Bob on the satellite phone a minute,' said John. 'I want to let him know how things stand.'

Bríd and John moved against the wall, out of the way of the passing crowds that jostled along in both directions. John pulled out the phone and began making the call while Bríd took in the scene around her. Undeniably, a mix of cultures and races flooded this city. White features blended with Asian and even traces of African, to provide such a variety among the sea of faces that could provide DNA studies for decades. The clothes also reflected the mixed backgrounds. There were innumerable combinations and colors of dress that blended eastern ethnic patterns and styles with western, creating vibrant and unique results.

'Excuse me. Dr Sheldon?'

Bríd and John turned to see two Chinese men in uniform standing next to them.

'Yes,' said John. 'I'm Dr Sheldon.'

'Can you and your companion please come with us?' said the taller of the two. He gestured to the car paused in the street, the driver still behind the wheel.

'What's this about?' asked John.

'Please, if you and your companion would just step in the vehicle.'

Bríd followed a reluctant John to the car and got into the back, her heart racing. The car took off at a great speed, shoving her against the seat, wedged as she was between John and the shorter of the policemen. What could the police possibly want with them? They'd done nothing wrong. Was it something to do with the dig? Maybe they wanted to talk to John directly about his request for an extension. But would the police be involved in something like that? Possibly.

'Can you at least tell me what this is about?' asked John.

'All in good time, Dr Sheldon,' said the tall policeman seated up front.

'But are you arresting us? Have we done something wrong?' John demanded, his voice rising slightly.

'Just a minor complication,' said the same policeman. 'We will soon have it straightened out. You will bear with us please.'

His English was precise and carefully spoken. Bríd studied the back of his precisely barbered head in an attempt to fathom why they were in this car, heading at breakneck speed to who knew where. John meanwhile pestered them about what was going on, until he was finally told to be silent.

After about ten minutes, they pulled up at a modern building and they were ushered from the car inside. With a policeman on either side and the tall one leading the way, Bríd and John were escorted down a corridor and into a side room. It was empty of any furniture except a table and three chairs.

The tall policeman gestured to the chairs. 'Please. Sit down.'

John glanced at Bríd and gave a small, resigned nod. The two sat down, placing their bags on the floor next to them.

'If you would be so kind as to hand me those?' The tall policeman gestured to their bags.

John's eyes narrowed. 'What do you want with them? They contain our personal belongings and some work papers.'

'Please. Just do as I say.'

Cautiously Bríd picked up her bag and handed it over, John following suit. What could they possibly find of interest in her belongings? She listed in her mind the passport, purse, phone, camera, pen, notepad, sunscreen, headache tablets, and other items that she'd crammed in the bag this morning.

Her heart racing, Bríd watched as one by one similar items were removed from John's bag. Finally, they pulled out his file filled with the prints from the dig. The tall policeman picked up the file and opened it. One by one, he removed the prints of the artefacts and placed them on the table, all of them at different angles and different ranges, the images clear and unmistakable. None of them contained images of the mummy.

Bríd glanced over at John. Except for a slight flicker in his eyes, he remained impassive, saying nothing. Clearly someone had removed images of the mummy from the file. Again. The question was, who? The only people that could have had access to the file were Dr Chou, Jin and the museum staff. Unless someone came into the office when no one was around. In that case, it could be anyone.

It was her turn for a bag search. Slowly, one by one, they pulled out the familiar items and placed them on the table. After her larger belongings were unpacked, they reached inside her bag and removed a small metal brooch. Backed only by a sharp pin, it was circular, with swirling etched designs. Bríd had never seen it before in her life.

'That's not mine,' she said.

The tall policeman smiled grimly, his eyes hard. 'Yes. Exactly. But the question is, how did it come to be in your bag?'

Bríd's heart began to race. 'No, you don't understand. I didn't put it in there. I don't know how it came to be in there.'

'She didn't put it in her bag,' said John, his voice firm. He reached across and gave her hand a squeeze. 'Why on earth would she put that pin in her bag?'

'I've no need to explain to you, Dr Sheldon, what these ancient pieces are worth on the black market.'

'That's ridiculous,' said John. His eyes narrowed. 'What made you check our bags, anyway?'

'We had information this morning that an item was missing from the museum. We naturally needed to question everyone who had been there.'

'But when was the item last seen? I mean, how did they notice it was missing?' Bríd was genuinely puzzled. It was all wrong. With such haphazard storage methods, how would they know when a single small item the size of a brooch was missing? None of it made sense, except that someone had placed that brooch in her bag.

The tall policeman stood. 'I'm afraid, Miss—' he looked down at his notes—'O'Leary, we'll have to detain you for further questioning.'

'What?' said John. 'Look, there's been some kind of mistake here, surely you can see that. I'm certain we can clear it up easily.'

'I...I don't know what more I can say to explain,' said Bríd, her voice shaky. What could she tell them to defend herself? 'I really don't know how the brooch got in my bag. Someone must have put it there.'

'Nevertheless, we will go through your movements in the museum from your arrival to your departure.' The tall policemen barked orders at the other policeman by the door. 'Dr Sheldon, we will have to question you separately, if you would kindly go with my officer.' The other policeman grabbed John by his arm and hoisted him out of his chair.

John gave Bríd an encouraging look. 'Don't worry, Bríd. It'll be all right.' Then he disappeared out the door.

Bríd sat in stunned silence. This had all happened so fast. She could easily explain her movements that morning, but she only had John to corroborate them. Would they believe John? And who would have put the item in her bag? It was obviously done when she was out of Dr Lei's office looking at the artefacts in the other room. Anyone in the museum could have gone in there, presumably. But why would they want to plant that brooch in her bag and call the police? Was this somehow linked with the missing prints? Her mind raced with possibilities.

CHAPTER FOURTEEN

CHINA C. 1500 BCE

'Mother, Mother, look at me!'

Tlachtga turned and looked at her son mounted on his small horse under Yaloa's guiding hand. Teaching riding skills was now second nature to him and he did it well, but she couldn't help but smile as she watched him solemnly lecture the son he doted on. Mog was nearly as bad in the way he paid Kee so much attention.

Kee's brown hair flashed red lights in the sun, a testament to his ancestry. In all else, though, he favored his father. In the four summers since the difficult birth, Kee had grown strong and agile and she was glad of it, but she still worried.

Tlachtga gave them a wave and walked towards them.

'Father says I am learning so quickly that soon I shall be able to ride Fand on my own!' He bounced in his seat with excitement, nearly slipping.

'Whoa, be careful, my son.' Yaloa grabbed his arm and righted him. He patted Kee on the shoulder and grinned over at Tlachtga.

'We still need a little practice, I think, before that happens,' said Yaloa.

'Well you two should come now. It is nearly time for the feast,' said Tlachtga, suppressing a laugh at her son's expense. 'I think you have done enough training for this day.'

Kee's face fell. 'Come now, you know you will enjoy the feast.' She laughed in earnest now, watching her son war with his desires. 'I will see you back there,' she told them.

Tlachtga turned and made her way over to their dwelling, leaving Yaloa and Kee to see to Medb before they all went to the feast area.

'How goes the master horseman?' Buan said to her, seeing her pass. He was just coming out of his dwelling, his little daughter Lóol yawning sleepily in his arms. His delight in teasing Kee had not faded with the birth of Lóol three moons ago, though he hated to leave her company. Tlachtga guessed Qaltsixkli must be helping over at the feast area still, while their daughter napped under Buan's watch.

'The horseman is in need of mastering a few more things.' Tlachtga laughed, moving towards him. 'There is no doubt he enjoys it, though. He wanted to continue riding instead of going to the feast. And you know how much he loves his food.' Tlachtga chucked Lóol on the cheek, making the little baby smile, her brilliant blue eyes shining in the light. There was no doubt those eyes were as blue as the nesting birds she'd seen in spring.

'Are you going over to the feast now?' Buan asked.

'Not just yet,' she answered. 'I have to get a few things first.'

Buan nodded and they parted company and headed toward the feasting area.

It was a special harvest feast, a rare occasion and celebrated despite the recent paltry harvests. The hunt had been good, but that had been more luck and mobility than any special bounty. The horses had made the difference. Their holding pen now housed ten horses, including Segda, Medb and their colt, Fand.

In the four springs since Mog and Yaloa had returned with the horses, Mog, Buan and Yaloa had worked hard to train them and teach the tribe members to ride. Even a few of the women had made time to learn, showing their support for Yaloa's hopes and plans. Qaltsixkli and surprisingly, Kayáani, were among the women who practiced daily with the men.

Yaloa's sister was not among those who demonstrated support for Yaloa's plans. Teslintoo had never flaunted her dissent openly, but Tlachtga could hear it in the tone of voice and the manner in which she phrased her questions. There was a small group of dissenters who were against the long journey, and Tlachtga would not be at all surprised if Teslintoo was at its root. The dissenting group was the reason Yaloa continued to delay the journey, but he hoped that the increasing drought and scarcity of food would help them see there was no choice but to leave. Yaloa's message from the Star People told him that. They had to travel East, to the sea and beyond. No one knew how far that was. No one, bar Mog, Buan and Tlachtga, had ever seen the sea.

YALOA SMILED at the colorful array of food, deliberately setting aside his worries so he could enjoy this time of celebration. The feast was spread out in the ceremonial clearing on blankets and it nearly filled the large space. Everyone had contributed and the result was a riot of color and a variety of delicious spicy odors. Beans, stewed meats, fish, millet and root vegetables marinated in herbs and goat's milk were only some of the things on offer. Stacks of flatbread lay beside plates heaped with goat cheese. Loud chatter and laughter filled the air, while everyone loaded their earthen bowls and took seats in clusters at the edge of the blankets.

He piled his own bowl high with his selections and moved

over to sit beside Tlachtga, who was filling Kee's bowl from her own. She smiled up at him in greeting. Yaloa returned the smile and made himself comfortable. He looked over at his son fondly. Kee was already chattering away to Mog about his horse training, his animated voice audible to many others. There was no doubt he captured attention. Everyone around him was responding to his tale, his dark eyes lively and twinkling and the hint of a dimple in his cheek deepened under the wide, joyous grin. Yaloa could see he had the makings of a good leader, though perhaps not the temperament for a shaman. It was still early, time would tell.

Kee held his hand up high, demonstrating the height of the jump he was certain he could make with the horse. It warmed Yaloa's heart to see so many smile at him indulgently until he caught his sister's sour expression. There was little doubt in his mind that Teslintoo disliked Kee intensely, though others might not suspect it. At the moment she sat apart from them, her husband sitting uncomfortably beside her. Yaloa smiled at her and she nodded civilly to him.

Teslintoo had not been the same since he and Mog had journeyed to the Star People, all those many seasons ago. From that point on she'd become withdrawn around him, keeping her own counsel on most things. This change made him uneasy and led him to wonder again about the wild dog he'd fought on that soul journey. When he saw it lunge at Mog, Yalao's first instinct was to pull it off and try to kill it. Then, when he caught a glimpse of its eyes, dark and angry, he was shocked to realize that it was Teslintoo in her spirit form. Desperate, he tried to call out to her in his mind, but the dog would not answer. Their struggle continued, Yaloa fighting to disable the dog rather than kill it, should his guess be right. Finally, he managed to knock the dog senseless, his fist meeting its snout with a force that dislodged the dog's tooth. Yaloa had spotted the tooth as he bent over the motionless dog and carefully picked it up. It wasn't an ordinary one. It was a tooth won in the spirit world and therefore it carried much power. The power of Dog. If the dog was indeed Teslintoo, then Yaloa now carried a part of her spirit and she could not harm those of his blood.

Yaloa had tried to find some way to examine his sister, to find evidence that would support his suspicions in the days immediately following the ritual, but she had avoided him. If her face was bruised, he could not tell, and he knew she had skills to limit its traces and heal it quickly. Her smiles never showed teeth, and he wasn't able to find just cause to ask her to open her mouth. Any questions he put to her she answered vaguely. Part of him didn't want to confirm his suspicions, so he avoided any outright accusations. And he admitted to himself that didn't want to make an enemy of his own sister. He loved her.

It was also difficult to for him to believe that she might harm Tlachtga or their son, though he was always cautious when he dealt with Teslintoo. As long as he had the tooth, he reasoned, he knew they would be safe. Besides, he still had hopes he could win her cooperation with the coming journey. Up to now she had avoided all tasks associated with the preparations, though she never voiced her objections, as far as he could tell. But as a medicine woman, people noticed her actions, and the group who didn't want to leave the area held fast to their convictions. They, too, withheld their assistance, which extended the preparation time for departure.

Yaloa pushed aside these thoughts and tried to focus on Kee's tale.

'That was quite a day with Medb,' said Buan, laughing. He had come over to sit beside Mog during the tale. 'Surely Medb runs away when she sees you coming. You give her such a workout, she must hobble back to the pen.'

"Oh no, Uncle," said Kee. "Medb likes it. She comes over to

me before I call."

'Ah, she most likely is looking for the treat tucked into your waist pouch,' said Buan, nodding solemnly.

'No, no, Uncle,' said Kee. 'She likes it. I promise you.' Kee looked at Buan closely. 'Oh, you are teasing me again.' He giggled.

Buan threw back his head and roared. Everyone else in the group followed suit, their amusement fed by Kee's good-hearted response.

'Your uncle has not learned the weakness of his own position when he comments about horse riding,' said Mog. He raised his finger and tapped his head. 'Yes, I remember many times when no treat, no matter how large, would have persuaded Medb to allow Buan to mount.' Across from him, Tlachtga giggled. 'Now I seem to recall—' Mog began.

'No one really wants to hear that old story,' Buan said, cutting him off. 'I would much rather hear a tale from Tlachtga. Would you give us one with your harp?'

Tlachtga laughed. Everyone around her voiced their encouragement, Yaloa included. He always loved to hear her perform.

'I fear it is more a distraction you are looking for, Buan, rather than a tale,' said Tlachtga. She rose and left the group to fetch her harp.

'Father, do you think Mother will tell the tale of the fish?' asked Kee eagerly.

Yaloa grinned wryly. 'Salmon,' he corrected. He knew Tlachtga would be disappointed if Kee didn't call the fish by its right name. She spent much time telling Kee the stories, but he didn't always remember the fine details. Yaloa knew Tlachtga tried to patient, tried to conceal her need to have him know as much about her heritage as she could impart.

Tlachtga returned, her harp under her arm. Yaloa settled himself more comfortably, preparing for an enjoyable time. She chose the tale of *Greine* bringing the sun. Yaloa had heard her tell it many times before, but somehow, with each telling Tlachtga brought a freshness to it that made him feel it was his first hearing.

The harp's sweet tones washed over Yaloa, easing his muscles and soothing his mind. The tale opened softly, telling the time of *Greine's* own birth, a small bit of star fire in the sky. Then the tale laughed and bounced with *Greine's* growth until, fully matured, she stood strong and bold, ready to outwit *Fire God*. *Fire God* concealed his light, revealing it only at his own whim. The music grew bold, with little tones cunningly inserted. *Greine* met with *Fire God* during a great storm. She worked on his vanity and promised him the more powerful fire of a lightning bolt, in return for a ball of his fire. The harp showed *Greine's* hidden laughter as she stood there, a lightning bolt in her hand. *Fire God* handed her the large ball of fire and as *Greine* moved to pass him the bolt, she threw it into the ground, its power disappearing into the earth. Before *Fire God* could move to her, *Greine* took the large ball of fire and hurled it into the sky, disappearing after it.

The strings sounded loud and joyous, declaring the triumph of *Greine's* cunning. Engrossed in the tale, Yaloa hadn't noticed the sky had darkened considerably. By the tale's close, though it was clear the light was failing, the day's span was nowhere near finished. Yaloa scanned the sky, but could not see a trace of cloud. He looked at the sun. A dark and round object was passing in front of the sun, obscuring its light. He looked around at the gathering, observing the murmurs and shifting limbs.

"Everyone will go to their dwellings. Quickly," Yaloa ordered in a strong, firm tone. "I will seek answers from the spirits." He looked over at Tlachtga, saw her concern, and motioned her to take Kee inside.

The ceremonial ground was cleared in a few moments, the

bowls and platters of half-eaten food and the partially filled cups the evidence of a hasty departure. Mog remained and stood beside Yaloa, his head raised to the sky, his arms reaching outward. His lips moved, mouthing words of invocation. *Greine* was a sun spirit specially connected with Mog. Perhaps he could help make the sun return. Yaloa closed his eyes and tried to reach out with his own spirit and help Mog in any way he could.

The pair stood there, motionless, for a long time. Yaloa's spirit reached out, but he couldn't go far. At every turn he seemed to be blocked by a dark curtain he found impossible to turn aside. He heard Mog gasp. Yaloa opened his eyes and saw Mog pass his hand over his eyes.

'What is it?' asked Yaloa. He touched Mog's arm and Mog looked down at him, his eyes unfocused.

'I am fine, my son,' said Mog. 'It is only now that my light comes to me now from within, where my sight is now seated.'

'You cannot see?' asked Yaloa in disbelief. Mog shook his head.

'But I feel the return of the sun's warmth,' he said. "It has come back?'

Yaloa looked up at the sky. The sun was there again, whole and bright, and the dark object was gone. 'Yes,' he answered. 'It has returned. Your prayers and power have succeeded. But you have paid a terrible price.'

'What price?' asked Tlachtga, arriving at their side, Kee in tow.

Yaloa frowned at her, wishing she had remained inside until he had told her it was safe to venture out. He couldn't be too angry, though, because he knew her concern for them both had brought her back as soon as she could judge it safe for Kee. Now she would learn all too soon what he would have liked have had more time to prepare her for.

She stared at Mog. 'Can you not see me, Father?' she asked.

Mog put his arms around her, drawing her close. 'Do not worry, Daughter,' he said, stroking her head. 'I am still here. Although I may not see the common things, I can still see within. *Greine's* power still burns bright within and now becomes a full part of my being. The wheel of light has turned and it surely shows that there will be a dark time, but the light will return to us.'

Silent tears trickled down Tlachtga's face as she struggled to accept his words. Yaloa squeezed her arm in support. Kee crowded close to them.

'What is wrong?' he asked, trying to make sense of their words. 'Mother, Father, Grandfather, what did that darkness mean? Have you ever seen anything like it before? Everyone is saying it is a sign. Is it a sign? What sign is it? What was it?'

Tlachtga laughed weakly and reached down to pull her son up into her arms, hugged him close and kissed him on the cheek. Kee wriggled in her arms, embarrassed under such affection he thought fit only for babes.

'You are right, my son,' answered Yaloa. 'It is truly a wondrous thing that has occurred. I have never seen this happen, nor has your mother, or even your grandfather. We must not treat it lightly.'

Kee's eyes widened in amazement. 'Even Grandfather has never seen such a thing?' He looked over at his grandfather. 'Grandfather, why do your eyes look so funny?' he asked.

Mog reached over to pat Kee's hand, feeling his way along Tlachtga's arm. 'Ah, Grandson, *Greine* has now put the light inside of me, so I can see all that is within,' he said. 'Alas, though, I can no longer see the outside world.'

'You cannot see outside? You cannot see me?' Kee asked, puzzled. 'But you can see inside yourself? Why would *Greine* do that? Because you are special?'

'You have the right of it, Son,' answered Yaloa in Mog's stead.

'It is a very special thing to be able to see within yourself. Many people cannot do this at all. Your grandfather can now see many places for us, places we cannot look. Places that will show him things to help us when we begin our journey.'

Gutao came up to Yaloa's side, leaned over and murmured to him in an urgent tone. It seemed Teslintoo had taken this opportunity to give vent to her feelings. She was blaming Mog and the plans to leave as the cause of the temporary loss of light. It was a warning.

Yaloa sighed. This was not a welcome turn of events and he knew he would have to nip it off in the bud. He didn't want her words to spread ill will and panic. Straightening his shoulders, Yaloa headed towards Teslintoo's dwelling.

He found her sifting through her bags of medicines, muttering. He was glad to find that she was alone.

'Sister,' he said. 'I would speak with you a moment.'

She looked up from her work and narrowed her eyes. 'Of course, Brother.' She indicated the rug near. 'Please sit down and I will get you a drink.'

'No. I only came for a moment.' Yaloa knew she wouldn't like his refusal of her hospitality that was clearly bad manners, but that was part of the point he wanted to make.

'As you wish,' she said. 'What is it you wanted to say to me?' Her tone was cool.

Yaloa spoke to her directly. He didn't want her to mistake his meaning. 'You must cease your talk against this journey. It is causing dissension and uncertainty among our people and that will not help them for the time to come.'

'I speak as I find, Brother,' Teslintoo said, her voice rising. 'And I find that my brother can no longer see clearly since the arrival of those foreigners. His vision is clouded by lust and promises.'

'I would say that your own vision is clouded by emotions

that do not serve you well,' said Yaloa. He kept his voice firm with effort, determined not to let her words anger him.

'I am not the only one who sees these things! There are others who agree with me,' said Teslintoo her voice nearly at shouting level.

'A few who have succumbed to your poisoned words?' Yaloa bit back the rest of the thoughts that came to his mind. He sought calm and tried to remember the love and close relationship they once had. 'Sister, please. I do not wish to exchange angry words with you that go nowhere. You are too dear to me. Our parents would not wish for us to behave badly towards each other.'

Teslintoo's face softened a little. 'Yes, our parents would wish us to be close. To work together as one to do what is best for the people. Can you not see that the woman you have taken as your wife is dividing us? She is the real cause of the dissention among our tribe.'

All calm vanished and his anger rose so much he could barely hold himself back. 'Cease these words at once! I will not have you now or ever saying such lies to me or anyone. Do you understand?'

The edge in his voice was so sharp his sister flinched and stared wildly at him.

'Do you understand!'

She nodded slowly, her face contorting against the tears, anger and hate that filled her face.

'I would not have us angry with each other, Sister,' Yaloa said, his voice softer. 'But you must accept that my wife and her father will remain here, with our son. That will not change.'

Teslintoo narrowed her eyes and cocked her head, her lips moving slightly. 'Yes, Brother,' she said finally. 'I see.'

Yaloa nodded and bade his sister goodbye, but he couldn't help but wonder exactly what she did see.

CHAPTER FIFTEEN

Tlachtga stood in the cool dry wind of the Harvest Season's end, watching Kee lead Mog to Medb's side. She had just saddled Medb for Mog and Kee's daily ritual. Medb, as gentle with Mog as she was with Kee, would amble along with Mog mounted on her back and Kee leading her with a rope. They took the same course every day, allowing Mog to venture further than he might on his own. Tlachtga knew Mog also enjoyed this time alone with his grandson. Tlachtga smiled as Kee watched Mog mount, his little frame ready to assist Mog if needed. Kee carried out his task solemnly, the weight of his role filling him with a sense of importance.

In the many moons since his blindness, Mog had adapted well, but Tlachtga knew he missed his easy mobility. He still carved a little, using a slow whittling approach, guiding the knife carefully with the edge of his fingers. The leatherwork and harness-making he had passed over to Yaloa. Yaloa had learned the skill quickly, guided when necessary by Buan.

Kee's desire to assist his grandfather was unexpected. He had taken it upon himself to guide Mog through the camp, leading him carefully around obstacles and over the brush, to visit the horse training site, or anywhere else he might wish. Kee described all the activities they watched, developing an eye for detail that Mog carefully directed. And Mog was careful to require Kee's service only at certain times of the day, so his grandson would still feel free to play and enjoy the company of others in the usual way.

Besides being a physical reminder of the day the sun left, Mog's blindness also stirred some uneasiness among those who were reluctant to leave the region for a new home. Since that day, though Teslintoo kept her comments out of Tlachtga's hearing, Tlachtga held no doubts about her strong influence over the uneasy group. Still, Yaloa worked hard to move their plans forward and win the dissenters' support.

Tlachtga looked over at Mog now and suppressed the frustration she felt every time she thought about these dissenters who didn't understand or appreciate how much bringing back the sun had cost her father. She watched Kee chattering to Mog, his hand tugging the leading rein to signal Medb to move forward.

They ambled on in their usual manner, heading towards the stream to sit and fish for a while. Mog usually told Kee stories to pass the time and also teach him something of Mog's people. They had been following this pattern most days since the beginning of Planting Season, at the Moon of the Mountain Flowers. Now Kee helped him with the stories, adding things he left out and answering questions Mog posed about its meaning. Tlachtga had laughed when Mog told her of this.

'What are you smiling about?' asked Yaloa, coming up alongside of her. He put his arm around her waist, a visible sign of public affection rarely displayed by his people.

'Our son,' she answered. She leaned into his embrace, grateful for his comfort over the thoughts she hadn't spoken.

'Ah, yes,' said Yaloa. He nodded towards the retreating figures. 'He has a captive audience for his ready tongue.'

'It is more likely the other way around,' laughed Tlachtga. She looked directly at him, still taking great pleasure in his face, treasuring the deep sense of joy at being with him. 'He is a good son,' she told Yaloa, knowing she also included him in the statement.

'He has a very good mother to thank.' Yaloa, squeezed her again. The two turned back to their dwelling, Tlachtga questioning him about the cart construction Buan was working on in the clearing a short distance away. She knew Yaloa admired Buan's carpentry, as did Gutao, who assisted Buan as much as possible to learn the fine points of the craft.

Shouts rang out. Turning, Tlachtga saw Kee running towards them.

'Mother, Mother! Come quickly! It is Grandfather. Medb has thrown him and he is badly hurt!'

Tlachtga ran towards her son while Yaloa called out for Buan. She caught up with Kee, found out where Mog had fallen and took off again as soon as he told her. She arrived at the spot, her heart in her throat, and found Mog bleeding and unconscious, but still alive.

Choking back her tears, she knelt beside him and examined his body carefully for injuries. His limbs seemed whole, but the blood coming from the gashes at his side and the back of his head worried her deeply. She took the sash from around his waist, ripped it in half and made a simple bandage for his head and then his side. Yaloa and Buan arrived just as she completed her work. Under her instructions they fashioned a seat with their arms and carried Mog between them, taking care about his wounds. During the seemingly endless journey back to camp, Tlachtga watched Mog closely. His face became increasingly pasty and the moans he uttered at each jolting movement faded to a feeble sound.

Eventually, they arrived at the camp and carried Mog inside his tent. Tlachtga ran to gather her herbs and bag of medicines from her own dwelling. When she returned, Yaloa helped her remove the temporary dressings and strip off Mog's tunic and Buan set a leather pail of water at her side, as instructed.

Carefully, she began washing the wounds, first the gash at Mog's side and then one at the back of his head. She worked tenderly but expertly, her fingers probing the extent of the wounds. The gash at his side still bled freely. She wrapped it up again temporarily and then turned to her herb bag, selecting the ones needed. She moistened the herbs with some water and kneaded them with her finger to release their potency and form a paste. She took a large leaf from her bag and put the paste on it to make a compress, then pressed it against Mog's side wound, holding it firmly in place. After a few moments, she asked Yaloa to take her place while she prepared the next step to close the wound.

The dwelling flap was pulled aside and Teslintoo entered. 'I hear your father is badly injured and I have come to offer my services,' she said woodenly.

Yaloa nodded to Teslintoo, and before Tlachtga could say a word, he motioned her to take his place. Tlachtga suppressed her irritation, turning her attention to the task ahead. She took a special thin bone needle from her medicine bag, along with a small cloth packet of long horse hairs. She pulled a hair loose from the tiny bundle and threaded it through the needle, whispering a short invocation.

'I am sorry, Father,' Tlachtga said softly, leaning over Mog's side. 'This will hurt.'

Mog's eyes fluttered slightly at her words. Tlachtga paused a moment, then withdrew a single leaf from a small dark leather packet, oiled and worn with much handling. She crushed the leaf between her fingers and she placed it inside Mog's mouth at his gums. Working quickly and carefully, she sewed the wound shut with horse hair, reapplying the compress and the bandage to hold it in place. The sewing seemed to have halted the bleeding. That task completed to her satisfaction, she turned to re-examine the gash at his head. The bleeding had stopped, but she could feel a slight swelling near the base of his skull that worried her. Sighing, Tlachtga pulled up a blanket to cover Mog, praying the swelling was not pressing inward. That would be something that could not be helped. She'd done everything she could do for him physically.

'I thank you for your assistance,' Tlachtga said to Teslintoo while she collected her medicines. 'Now I think my father must rest and I shall stay here beside him. There is no need for you to remain.'

Teslintoo narrowed her eyes, staring up at Tlachtga, then nodded and left without further word. Tlachtga sighed and turned to her father again, noticing the fluttering pulse at his neck and the milk-white pallor of his skin. His body was still, the heavy drugged sleep overtaking him to give him rest from the pain.

Tlachtga bit her lip, gathering her resolve and steeling herself for the steps she was going to take. This course of action was generally not approved and she had done this only once before. That time had also been for her father and she had succeeded. Now, the situation was even more perilous, the journey filled with more risks, but she would do it.

She went over to the bag containing Mog's regalia. Carefully, she removed his bull's hide and eagle headpiece and placed them on Mog. He didn't stir, the drug leaving him oblivious to her actions. Tears filled Tlachtga's eyes and obscured her vision as she removed her harp from its wrappings and placed it on the cloth-covered ground beside her. She took out her own sacred bag and removed a pot of blue paste, an etched silver bowl, and a long peaked felt hat, so tall it nearly exceeded her own height. She poured water into the bowl, its inside winking at her through the swirling ripples as she poured. The water slowed into a silent pool, until it showed only a clear reflection of her face. Taking the pot of paste, she traced blue circles on her forehead, a deliberate ritual repeated three times for each circle. Sounds, deep, rich and long, issued from her chest. She reached for the hat and carefully placed it on her head, its wide brim extending further than her shoulders, its point rising up towards the heavens. She placed the harp in her lap, plucked a string over and over while she intoned the sound with her voice. The intonation blended with the harp, creating a mix of vibrations that worked through her, lifting her soul up into the cosmos in a desperate search for Mog.

TLACHTGA OPENED HER EYES. She looked down at Mog and saw his white and still face. His lips were tinged with blue and the flesh on his body lay flaccid under its own weight. There had been only the slimmest chance that she could have stopped his soul from departing his body this time, but she'd had to try. And she had failed. His soul had left with a purpose that couldn't be halted.

Tlachtga closed her eyes again. Her mouth opened to begin the *Caoine*, the loud wailing lament that would bid Mog goodbye, release his spirit and send his soul on to its next path. She rocked slowly back and forth, her wail setting the rhythm for her motion. A voice joined hers, its deep sounds giving an undertone of support. She opened her eyes and saw Buan kneeling at Mog's feet, his position a reflection of her own. Behind him, Yaloa and Kee sat with their legs crossed, their faces filled with pain and grief. Tears coursed down Tlatchtga's cheeks but she was determined to continue the rituals.

Tlachtga loosed her hair from its ties and it fell about her, cloaking her heavily, like the grief that settled in her heart. She removed the knife at her belt and sliced away at her hair, rending large chunks of it from her head. She continued on, cutting and slicing, until her hair lay in a pile in front of her, and her head was covered only in short curls. Silently, she handed the knife to Buan. He took it from her, loosed his hair and began to cut it. After he had finished, his head covered only in a finger-length stubble, he cut a small lock from Mog's head and handed it to Tlachtga. She tucked this small bit of Mog, his remaining medicine, into the pouch at her waist.

The two of them gathered the pile of hair, a weave of reds and browns, and carried it outside to the hearth fire. With Yaloa and Kee standing behind them, they threw the hair into the fire, intoning the chants, the words an invocation of blessing, a prayer for the safe passage of a soul. The group silently watched the hair curl and fizzle in the flames as it turned into swirl of smoke that drifted up slowly, disappearing into the sky.

TEARS RAN down Tlachtga's blackened face as she watched them lower Mog's body into the chamber. Buan had suggested this special burial method as a way to honor her father's status. It was not their usual custom, but the large stone cairns used by her people for burial were not available. Yaloa was in agreement, wanting to help in any way possible. So Yaloa, Buan, Gutao and some others had created the chamber during the past few days while she carefully prepared Mog's body and arranged for the feast to follow his interment. The men had dug a deep pit, lined it with logs and mud bricks, leaving space for all the things Mog needed for his journey to the Otherworld.

Tlachtga had wrapped him in his bull hide and put his carved eagle headdress on him. The men had dismantled the cart that had brought them here and laid it at the bottom of the chamber to serve as a platform for Mog's body, a vehicle to speed him on his journey.

Tlachtga looked down into the deep hole, Yaloa, Buan and Kee already there, circling her father's body. Helping hands lowered Tlachtga down in the chamber and she sank slowly into the dark space, the odor of cool, damp earth greeting her, pulling her into her own darkness. Yaloa leaned over and placed a small twig of journeying medicine across Mog's chest. She fought the knot that tightend around her chest and the spinning lights in her eyes. Her tasks were not complete. Carefully she reached over with the rushes in her hand and lit them from Buan's already smoking bundle. The rushes flared bright, blinding her momentarily, then settled into a slow smoking torch. She took a deep breath, started the invocation and moved slowly around Mog's body in a sunwise direction, circling three times.

YALOA WATCHED the group sitting across from him, chuckling at Buan's words. Beside him, he noticed Tlachtga attempting a smile. Buan raised his hand, holding back their laughter, and began to relate Mog's life, citing all his accomplishments. The tale grew, each embellishment becoming more and more outlandish, until Mog's life became larger than life. The group nodded and drank deeply from their cups, the fermented milk drink pushing away the awkwardness following the burial. Yaloa tried to suppress the memory of Tlachtga's terrible grief, dark and black as the ashes smeared on her face. It had cut him deeply to see her suffer so. He felt responsible.

While Tlachtga had tended Mog's wounds, he had gone out

to look for Medb. He'd been concerned for her safety, but he also wanted to understand what had caused her to suddenly buck and throw Mog to the ground, knocking him senseless. He'd found Medb a short while later, making her way slowly to the pen. Her limbs were trembling slightly and the saddle hung precariously at her side. Yaloa had gone over to her, murmured soothing words and stroked her nose. After a few moments, her trembling had subsided and she'd nudged his hand for a treat. Slowly, he'd removed the saddle and placed it on the ground. She nudged him again and he put his hand on her neck and crooned to her softly while his hands travelled down her legs, along her sides and across her back, his fingers probing for signs of injury.

When he'd reached the middle of her back, Medb had flinched under his touch. He'd stopped and bent closer to examine the area. It was red and raw, and in the middle, a spot encrusted with blood. Yaloa picked up the saddle, his mind racing, and ran his fingers along the underside, until he located the offending object. It was a large thorn, embedded so the sharp point faced downward, to work its way deep into Medb's skin under Mog's weight.

Thinking back on it now, Yaloa almost wished he hadn't found anything at all, that he could still consider it might have been an accident, that his suspicions didn't lead him to his own sister.

CHAPTER SIXTEEN

PRESENT DAY CHINA

Bríd stared at the hairline crack in the table before her. She'd followed its trail for the last hour, as she waited alone in the room that been her home for the last six hours. Only it wasn't her home. Again, she fought the trembling that threatened to overwhelm her. What would happen? What could they possibly do to her? She swallowed the bile that rose to her throat. She'd only had a glass of water since they left the museum this morning. And now it was evening.

After hours of repeating her story over and over and disclaiming any knowledge of the pin's theft, her questioners had left abruptly. Not once did they explain what might happen, what she could expect. They'd met her requests for a phone call with indeterminate grunts and ignored her demand for the presence of an Irish government representative, something that came to her just before they left.

What was happening with John? Were they still questioning him? Surely they could see that she and John were telling the truth. She bit her nail. Why was someone trying to discredit them? Her mind had played on that this last hour. It must be the dig. She knew that both Lu and Chang took a dim view of their work. They were certainly at the site when the images were deleted. Could they have arranged to remove the prints from John's folder and plant the brooch in her bag? But no, how would they have known John had printed extra images? If they had known that before John had left the site, they would have taken them and concluded that John had backed them up on a memory stick. Yet John still had them on his memory stick.

Something else was bothering her besides that.

The door opened. The tall policeman entered. Behind him she glimpsed a familiar face. Her heart lifted momentarily. It was Jin. Had he convinced them of her innocence? Or was it something else? Something that in the long hours locked in this room she'd begun to suspect.

The two men began an exchange in Chinese. Jin looked over at her, his eyes cold and remote. Bríd's heart sank. Still, she felt she should try.

'Jin, could you please explain that I would never have taken that brooch? That I was with either you, Dr Chou and Dr Lei, or with John the entire time I was in the museum.'

Jin directed his look back to the tall policeman. 'I'm afraid I can't vouch for Miss O'Leary,' he said. 'It's a shame that given such opportunities to study and examine our precious heritage that someone like her would then commit such a grievous offence.'

'Are you saying that I took it?' said Bríd. She made a great effort to keep her voice from trembling. 'How can you say that? You know it's impossible. I wouldn't do such a thing.'

The policeman showed no reaction to Jin's remarks while he studied Bríd's face. Her hands grew clammy and she could feel the color draining from her face. With Jin so condemning, who would believe her?

'Even though Dr Sheldon might corroborate her story, there is nothing to say they both weren't involved in the theft,' said Jin.

'Yes, Colonel,' said the policeman. 'Thank you. I can see that.'

Bríd reeled in shock as Jin took a seat in front of her. Why did the policeman call him Colonel? Who was he, really?

'Now Miss O'Leary,' said Jin in a sharp tone. 'I want you to know this is a very grave offence you've committed. Thefts of items of national heritage are taken seriously. Lengthy imprisonment is not out of the question, no matter the diplomatic efforts by your countrymen.'

Bríd stared at him hard. What was he trying to say? Was he threatening her? 'But I didn't do it. How can I make you see that?' Bríd was near to tears. Jin was obviously a government officer of some kind and he seemed to be determined to scare her. It was working. If they didn't believe her, or John, there was no one else who could help her now.

The door opened again and a young policeman entered. He saluted the other policeman and bowed to Jin, before speaking. When he finished Jin barked a question, clearly angry. The young man stammered an answer. He handed a piece of paper to the other policeman and Jin grabbed it from his hand, scanning the sheet quickly. He shoved the paper back into the policeman's hands and rose then strode out of the room.

After a few moments of silence, the tall policeman turned to Bríd. 'It seems there has been a mistake. A museum staff member has just relayed to Dr Lei that he had brought the brooch with some other items into Dr Lei's office earlier, to consult with him about it and laid the piece on the table near your bag. The staff member said he then must have inadvertently knocked the brooch into your bag. He did not realize that is what happened until he had heard about the details of the arrest.'

Bríd blinked, trying to make sense of the feeble story. She looked at the policeman's skeptical expression and realized he'd little faith in it too. But did that matter? Would they release her now?

'So, it seems, Miss O'Leary, I am to let you and your colleague go.' He smiled grimly. 'I would, however, caution you. The government is insistent that you close down the expedition immediately and you and the rest of those involved leave the country as soon as possible. You are no longer welcome.'

Bríd nodded dumbly through his speech, her breath held and her hands clenched under the table. She could hardly believe his words. Was she safe now? Would they let her go?

The door opened again and a different policeman appeared with her bag. Behind him was John, looking drawn and pale, his face filled with worry. When he caught sight of her, his eyes lit up briefly and he smiled. She rose and started towards the door.

The tall policeman grabbed her arm. 'Wait, Miss O'Leary,' he said. 'I need you to sign a few papers, before you leave.' He nodded to John. 'And you, Dr Sheldon.'

Escorted by their now familiar questioner and another policeman, they walked down the corridor to a small office by the front door where the policeman presented Bríd and John with a pen and some papers in Chinese. He indicated where they should sign.

John looked down at the paper skeptically. 'What does it say?'

'It's just a statement acknowledging that you will leave immediately and that you will not apply to return to China for at least ten years.'

John looked up his face grim. 'Ten years?'

'Ten years.'

John stared at the paper for a moment, then slowly picked up the pen and began to write his name. Bríd bit her lip, her heart reaching out to him. She knew what a blow it was to John's research, his career and all the work he'd put in the past years.

John passed the pen to her and she made her own wobbly attempt at signing her name through the tears that blurred her eyes. She felt his arm go around her and she leaned into him as they both made their way out of the building and onto the street, now cloaked in darkness. She sat in silent grief, gripping John's hand, as they rode back to the hotel in a taxi he'd hailed outside the police station, too cautious now to say or do anything until they were alone.

When they were back in the hotel John went with her to her room. Once inside she fell apart and John pulled her into to his arms and mumurmured words of comfort. She started to shake and the tears coursed down her cheeks. After a few moments he picked up a bottle of water and offered it to her.

'Drink this,' he said. 'I wish it were something stronger, but it'll help a little.'

She gulped down the water gratefully. It did go a little way towards making her feel better, but it also made her acutely aware of the gnawing hunger pangs in her stomach. As if to emphasize it, her stomach rumbled.

John laughed. 'Well, at least something is still working energetically.'

Bríd answered with feeble laugh of her own. 'It's been a while since I ate. They didn't give me anything at the police headquarters.'

'No, I didn't get anything either.' John rose. 'I'll just call Bob a minute and tell him what's happened. Then we'll go get something to eat, okay?'

Bríd nodded. John pulled the satellite phone out of his bag and went over to the window. After a few minutes of conversation with Bob, he came back over to her, his face drawn into a frown.

'I told Bob everything. He seemed okay about it. Said we had enough research and material at this point to keep us going for a good few years. He seems to think by that time the authorities here will have calmed down enough and let us back in again.' John shook his head. 'He also said that Scott's sick.'

'Sick?' said Bríd.

John nodded. 'Some stomach bug. Sounds pretty bad. He's running a fever and vomiting all the time. It's laid him up in bed. Bob says it's nothing to worry about but he's out of commission for a few days at least.'

'My God. It does sound serious. Will Bob be able to manage things there with just Miffy?' She could picture how much help Miffy would be. But at least it wasn't her, alone in the lab with Bob.

'He said not to worry or rush back. He has it all under control.' John stood silently beside her, deep in thought. Then he sighed and looked down at her. 'Well, shall we find something to eat?'

LATER, in a small, unpretentious restaurant in a side street, Bríd finally found herself relaxing. Maybe it was the potent local beer which they both decided they deserved, the steaming dishes that they ate ravenously, or the noisy happy atmosphere that seemed so normal and assuring that made her finally unwind. She could even laugh when John made a small joke about one of the dishes he'd tasted, her face flushing with the heat and enjoyment.

John reached out for her hand and looked into her eyes. 'It's good to see you laugh again.'

Bríd smiled slightly. 'Four hours ago I wouldn't have believed I would be sitting here laughing.' She shuddered. 'God knows what would have happened if they decided I was guilty. We were guilty. I was imagining all sorts of things. Jin said I could be imprisoned for stealing a piece of Chinese heritage.'

John's eyes darkened. 'That bastard. He's behind it. I'm sure of it.'

'He was there at the police station. He questioned me,' said Bríd.

'He did?'

Bríd nodded. 'The others called him "Colonel" and deferred to him. Then he started telling me the charges were serious and I could be imprisoned.'

'Well that confirms it. I knew all along the bastard was up to something. He turns up out of nowhere and becomes Dr Chou's assistant. When I asked Dr Chou about it, he only said that he came recommended by a colleague of his in Beijing.'

'So, he didn't know him before the dig.'

John shook his head. 'Never met him before, though he said his credentials were sound. But it still didn't sound right to me. Despite Jin's pretended interest, he didn't seem to have taken time to fully ground himself in the work.' He paused, reflecting. 'Then when the images were first deleted, I really became suspicious. He was the only one really who had the opportunity. I left him alone for a few minutes that time when I went out to you.'

Bríd nodded, the incident coming back to her. It was just after she'd been at the lab with Bob and he'd kissed her neck. She reddened at the memory.

'I was only out there a few minutes, but the computer was already on, so it wouldn't take long to do it,' John continued. 'Then, when the police looked through the file and the prints were missing, that's when I was sure it had to be him.'

'Of course. How could I be so stupid? But why would he do it?'

'What did he say to you? Theft of national heritage?' John smiled grimly. 'He's working for the government and they obviously don't want any of it getting away. They couldn't take the chance of just visible officials like Chang and Lu, persistent though they were. No, they decided to put someone on the inside. Someone who would be in on the daily decision-making in the team. Someone we wouldn't suspect.'

'Do you think Dr Chou knew?' asked Bríd.

'I'm sure Dr Chou knew. He would be familiar with the other Chinese scholars in his field of work and know that Jin was not genuine.'

'That's terrible,' said Bríd.

'Don't be too hard on him,' said John. 'I doubt he had much choice.'

Bríd nodded slowly. 'I'm sure you're right. But where does all this leave us now? Do you think Bob is right? Given a few years the government will let you back in?'

'I'm not sure I buy that. They haven't been very keen on what we found this time, no matter what happened or didn't happen today. It's unlikely they'll be anxious for me to uncover more of the same.' He shook his head in resignation. 'No, unless I could guarantee that my work wouldn't uncover anything that countered their idea of history, I don't think I'll be able to come here again. And I can't guarantee anything.'

Bríd touched his arm. 'John, I'm so sorry. I know how much effort you've put into your work.'

'It's pretty much over for me,' said John. 'My hope of tenure is gone. I'll have to start looking around for another post as soon as I get back, I'm sure.'

'But surely with Bob's support you have some hope?'

John snorted. 'I think as soon Bob gets back and realizes the extent of the damage, he'll be disassociating himself as much as possible.'

'Is there no one else you can turn to?'

John gave her a wan smile. 'No. Not really. I'm hardly the most dynamic and winning colleague in the department. But thanks for your sympathy. It means a lot.'

'But where would you go?' She lowered her voice. 'You wouldn't go too far away, would you?'

'I don't know where I would end up.' John sighed. 'I don't know. Maybe it's all for the best. This dig has uncovered more questions than answers.' His eyes clouded over. 'I don't know if I really want to go on digging up the past. Digging up artefacts, human remains. Sam said it would come to no good and it looks as though he was right. What am I trying to prove, really?'

Bríd studied his face, the pain and sorrow so evident now she could almost touch it. What could she say to comfort him, to give him hope? Should she tell him to give up his research, to find something else to give his life meaning, when she herself had only just realized that she couldn't give up her music, no matter what pain it had been a part of?

'Do you still love the research, the thrill of new discoveries?' she asked. 'That's what makes anthropologists and archaeologists succeed, isn't it?' As she spoke the words she realized it really wasn't true for her. What she loved was the piecing together of the evidence, the formation of new stories. She stared at John. 'It's the story for you, isn't it?' said Bríd slowly. 'It must be. The way you make them come alive, drawing in the listener. It's like no one else I've ever heard.'

John stared silently across the table at her. 'You should hear Sam, then.'

'Sam tells stories?'

'He's the clan's history keeper.'

JOHN SAID little as they walked back to the hotel and went upstairs to their rooms. Once outside her door he cupped his hand under her chin, leaned down and kissed her gently.

'Thanks,' he said.

'For what?'

'For being you. For being here, with me.' He brushed a stay curl from her face. 'For being so beautiful.'

He studied her, his face so close to her own, his eyes dark and smoky, his hand lingering on her cheek. She lifted her chin and pressed her mouth on his, a light, teasing touch that would go no further, except that he responded and she couldn't help herself. The kiss deepened as he wrapped his arms aro+und her. A kiss that stirred her, took her breath away and pulled at her deep inside.

John moved away. Bríd moaned slightly, unwilling to break the embrace. He stroked her head gently. 'Let's do this right, okay?' He took the key from her hand and opened the door. Once inside he led her over to the bed. He removed her blouse and ran his hand along the side of her face and down along the breast bone, underneath her bra to the soft skin of her breast. She sighed and surrendered to the moment.

Later, when they'd finished making love and he held her in his arms, he picked up her wrist and traced the circles tattooed there. She shivered.

'When did you do this, Bríd? I don't remember it there before.'

'Just after Gran died.'

'Is that when you cut your hair?'

She nodded and sighed. 'It seemed boldy symbolic at the time.'

'Grief,' he said.

She nodded, unable to speak. 'But the circles. There is something more there about the circles.'

He put a finger to her mouth. 'Sh-h-sh. There is no need for words.' He leaned over and kissed her long and hard. She slipped her arms around him, the tattooed circles pressed against his back.

CHAPTER SEVENTEEN
CHINA C. 1500 BCE

Fand tugged against Yaloa's guiding hand, showing just the slightest amount of stubbornness in an effort to prove he was only going through the exercises repeatedly because he chose to. Yaloa smiled, keeping his hand firm. Fand wasn't much different with his usual rider, Kee.

Kee stood a short distance away and watched his father run Fand through his paces, cloaking his anxious wait for Yaloa's approval under a studied attempt at nonchalance. The exercise complete, Yaloa led Fand over to Kee, deciding to put his son out of his misery.

'You have done a fine job with Fand,' he said, reaching Kee's side. Kee's face brightened, relief and pride washing over him with such force Yaloa almost laughed. Keeping a neutral expression Yaloa added, 'I think you stand a fair chance in tomorrow's horse skills competition.'

'Really, Father?' Kee said, his face alive with excitement.

Yaloa nodded. Kee's chest swelled, nearly bursting with pride at the compliment. With the great effort evident on his face, Kee tried to bring his emotions into a more dignified realm.

It was hopeless. Yaloa dared not laugh, though. He dismounted instead and handed the reins to his son.

'Why don't you give Fand a rub down and see that he gets some well-earned food,' said Yaloa. Kee nodded and scurried off with his horse, barely able to refrain from skipping. Yaloa could hear him talking excitedly to Fand about tomorrow's event.

Watching Kee's head nestled close to Fand's side, Yaloa shook his head. The sun was so bright Fand's roan-colored coat showed amber and even the red lights in Kee's hair were in evidence. His son was in his sixth summer and stood taller than most of his age. When he was mounted, he looked larger than life, his skill and grace on the horse so natural, Yaloa knew he'd been born to it. Yaloa wished Mog could have witnessed Kee's gift mature.

Yaloa thought back on the past season since Mog's death. He'd missed him almost every day, the impact of his wise counsel, his skills and his good humor fully realized in its absence. He knew Tlachtga suffered more than anyone else, though. Her grief was deep-seated, derived from a connection so strong, he knew she still felt its strength, even in her father's passing on. Her eyes, still hollowed and greyed, had only recently reflected the smiles of her mouth, giving Yaloa cause to hope she might be starting to heal. His other hope lay in the babe she carried inside her these six moons or more. Its growing liveliness drew her attention, and seemed to lift her spirits as she thought ahead to the future. Yaloa smiled, thinking of the babe. They were all looking forward to another child.

He saw Tlachtga walking towards him, graceful and lithe, despite the swollen belly. Her hair was a brilliant crown of riotous curls that reached her shoulders and framed her face, still milk-white and smooth. Her beauty never ceased to stop his breath, her smile pull at his heart. She was his omen of fortune.

With her by his side he could never feel anything but certain joy at their future.

'How is Fand? Is he ready for the competition?' asked Tlachtga when she arrived at Yaloa's side.

'You are really asking me if Kee is prepared,' Yaloa teased her. 'Do not worry. He will make his mother proud, and show that he is a son blessed with her skill. And all will wonder if his mother's smile has wrapped itself fully around her head. No one will know where it begins and ends.'

Tlachtga laughed and gave him a little shove. 'Do not tease me so. You deserve much credit for Kee's skill and Fand's easy handling. He is truly a fine horse.'

Yaloa put his arm around Tlachtga. Together they headed back towards the camp. 'I sent Kee to tend to Fand," he said. "He has taken on Fand's care very well.'

'Ah, that is because he sees it not as a series of chores, but the care of a friend,' said Tlachtga.

'Still, I think he shows a good sense of responsibility,' said Yaloa. 'He seems more than ready for his naming ceremony. We should hold it soon.'

Tlachtga nodded and smiled. 'He will be pleased. He has been hinting at it for almost a moon.'

'The time seems right, now,' said Yaloa. 'He is just in his sixth summer. Tomorrow will be a good demonstration of his readiness.' Yaloa paused a little. 'He should have his naming before the birth of the babe.'

He left the other thought unspoken. Yaloa wanted the naming done before they began their long journey east. He had let it be known they would begin the long trek just after Tlachgta gave birth. He had delayed it longer than he should, his suspicions about his sister making him reluctant to push the completion of all the preparations. But since Mog's death, Teslintoo had become more subdued, almost darkly silent. Yaloa had watched her carefully as she went about her daily activities, and he noticed whom she talked with, and what she said. Occasionally, Yaloa would even take out the tooth from the small pouch he kept around his neck, reassuring himself of its presence, its protection. He had no proof, in fact he wasn't even certain of her guilt, all he had were suspicions.

Nearing the camp, Yaloa gave Tlachtga a light squeeze of assurance, assurance that was more for him than his wife. Perhaps he had been wrong. Perhaps the danger was now past. He could only hope so, because the preparations were complete and once they began the journey it wouldn't be easy to keep a close watch on Teslintoo.

YALOA STUDIED Kee as he trotted out into the clearing mounted on Fand, the two of them arrayed with as much flamboyance and flourish as Buan and Kee could muster. Buan had helped Kee groom Fand all morning. They had combed his mane and tail and braided colored yarns into the horse hair. They had tied yarn to the saddle, setting off the bright appliques on the felt underblanket.

Kee had also woven the yarn into his own hair, flashes of blue and red that hung long to the middle of his back. He had on his best tunic, a red and indigo plaid, and his dark trousers were tucked into his best black leather boots with red applique stitching. Yaloa smiled. It was quite a show. His son already had a sense of dramatic impact, creating an image bigger than life.

At the moment, as Kee went through the first part of the exercise, he lived up to the image, Fand circling and weaving deftly in the required directions. He had not placed a wrong foot and had kept within the bounds, completing the course at a rapid pace. Yaloa grunted his satisfaction, and reached to squeeze Tlachtga's hand. They stood together, one set of parents among many whose children were performing here today. The adult competition would take place later, its course more difficult, requiring a faster pace. But Kee was among the best here at this course, Yaloa had no doubt.

Breaking from the course, Kee urged Fand into a gallop, racing towards a small stone pillar, some long forgotten marker, to retrieve the felt cap perched on its top. Kee neared the marker, the gaily colored yarn a whirlwind waving from all angles from his head, the saddle, and Fand. Reaching the pillar, Kee leaned down, and with a graceful sweep of his hand, removed the cap from the pillar and placed it on his head. Still riding at a fast clip, Kee circled the pillar then headed back towards the clearing, loud whoops and hollers of appreciation greeting his return.

Tlachtga and Yaloa joined the shouts of support for their son as he circled the clearing one last time, his face beaming with pride and joy. His course completed, Kee led Fand out of the circle, his head held high, his chest expanding as wide as possible. The yarn strands from his head and the horse fluttered softly in the wind, as if already proclaiming him the winner. Reaching Yaloa's side, he dismounted with a small bounce. Yaloa clapped him on the back and praised the ride.

'That was perfect, Son,' Yaloa said. 'You have proven your skill this day.'

'Thank you, Father,' said Kee. He was breathless, but his eyes sparkled with sheer joy. Tlachtga came up behind him and swept him up in a big hug.

'That was truly magnificent, my son!' she cried. 'You showed real skill. We are very proud.'

Kee's face reddened with pride and embarrassment. He tried to withdraw himself from her embrace in attempt to maintain a more mature appearance, but Tlachtga was firm in her hold. Eventually, she loosened her arms, laughing at his struggle, and allowed him to withdraw. He gave her an apologetic grin and turned to pat Fand whose sides heaved under his recent exertion, assuring him of their success after such a perfect performance.

Buan, Qaltsixkli and Lóol arrived and crowded around Kee, giving their praise. He accepted their compliments with grace and answered their questions politely. Yaloa smiled, watching his son follow the forms of courtesy, everything correct and formal, yet still injecting a note of personal warmth to make the words more welcome.

'Cousin, oh Cousin,' said Lóol, tugging excitedly at his trousers. 'You were flying!'

Kee squatted down to bring his face level with Lool's. 'I was indeed, Little One. Fand and I became a bird, feeling the wind in our wings, hunting for prey.' He put his hands outward and balanced them up and down, as if he was coasting along.

'A bird with very colorful plumage,' teased Buan. 'One that any prey could see as far away as a day's ride. Making you a very hungry bird.'

'Oh, don't mind him,' Qaltsixkli said. 'He is just jealous he could not put on such a fine show as you did. It was splendid, Nephew.'

The crowd fell silent, ending the exchange. It was time for the next competitor. Ahgishana, Teslintoo's daughter, rode out into the circle. She was dressed in a bright colored tunic and sash, a defiant splash of color in the face of her mother's disapproval. Yaloa had at last overruled Teslintoo's objections to Ahgishana's eager desire to train after watching her gaze longingly every day at the others learning horse riding. Once she was permitted to learn, she'd worked hard, quickly becoming skilled under Yaloa's firm guidance.

He watched her now as she circled the clearing, noting approvingly that she sat her mount well, and her focus had improved much in the past few months. He looked over at

Teslintoo, standing at a distance, her lips pursed, her body taut. Qalaktc and their son, Yakwun, stood closer to the circle, watching Ahgishana intently, smiles of encouragement on their faces. Yakwun had ridden earlier and had acquitted himself well. Yaloa hoped Qalaktc's proud smile at his son's performance had helped make up for his mother's sour demeanor and lack of acknowledgement.

The two of them followed Ahgishana's progress as she circled around the clearing one last time. Having completed that part of the exercise, she turned her horse and galloped off towards the pillar to remove the cap, perched once again on the top. She gathered speed, racing her horse towards her goal. Arriving at the pillar, slowing only a little, Ahgishana pulled the horse around and reached down for the cap. As she rose up into the saddle, the cap in her hand, her foot slipped on the wooden stirrup, pushing her leg up and causing her to lose her balance.

Yaloa watched in speechless horror as Ahgishana tumbled off her horse, hitting her head directly on the pillar point, before landing on the ground. A deadly silence fell upon the crowd and everyone stood motionless, too stunned to move. A moment later, shouts broke out, the crowd suddenly came alive and raced madly towards the still shape that lay in the distance.

Teslintoo arrived before anyone else, though Yaloa was close on her heels. She knelt beside her daughter's motionless form and called her name in loud, pleading tones. While Teslintoo vigorously rubbed her daughter's wrists, still calling to her, Yaloa noticed a small trickle of blood at her ear. He looked over at Qalaktc, who stared fearfully at the tiny red pool beside Ahgishana. Yaloa knelt beside his sister, and began to examine Ahgishana's limbs, torso and head for injuries, carefully working around his sister's kneeling form.

He didn't feel any broken bones, there was no swelling around her head, or anywhere else that he could detect, yet she remained unconscious. He rose again and asked Qalaktc to help him carry Ahgishana back to their dwelling.

They carried Ahgishana between them. Their progress was slow, hampered by Ahgishana's unconscious form and Teslintoo holding her daughter's hand and calling her name. The crowd trailed behind them, a somber and silent procession, Teslintoo's pleading voice the only sound to fill the air. Yaloa felt Tlachtga at his side and turned to see her with Kee close behind. Her face was drawn with worry and she looked fearfully at Teslintoo. Yaloa gave her a reassuring glance, trying to convey optimism for her and everyone else. Hope and prayer was what they needed. Tlachtga clutched her silver disc and he knew she was summoning all the healing power she could for their niece. Yaloa hoped it would be enough.

Ahgishana was still unconscious when they arrived at Qalaktc's and Teslintoo's dwelling. As Yaloa laid her gently on a pallet, he noticed her face had taken on a healthier color. Perhaps all would be well. She stirred slightly, a slight moan escaping her throat. Teslintoo had wasted no time to resume her vigil at her daughter's side and cried out now at this hopeful sign. Yaloa stood back from the two of them and turned to see Tlachtga enter. She moved over to him, a question on her face. He smiled a little and gave a small hopeful nod.

'Is she conscious yet?' asked Tlachtga in a low voice.

'She has just stirred a little,' Yaloa replied, matching her low tone. 'It looks promising. There are no limbs broken, nor any swellings or cuts that I could find. Just a small amount of blood that came from her ears.'

Teslintoo looked up from her place beside her daughter and saw Tlachtga. Her eyes narrowed, becoming small flints of fire as she pulled her mouth back against her teeth.

'You!' she snarled with vitriolic force. 'This is all your doing! Why did you ever come here? You have brought nothing but trouble since you came! The land has dried up, the game has become scarce. The herds can fit into one enclosure now." Teslintoo spat out her words with paralytic force. 'This has all happened since you brought this ill luck with you! You and your horse ideas. It is nothing but dangerous play. We cannot see the land, or move properly on back of those beasts. It is an unnatural thing that you have us doing and now it has taken my daughter!'

Yaloa saw Tlachtga flinch under Teslintoo's powerful anger, the color draining her face, her eyes becoming wide and hollowed. She opened her own mouth then closed it. He knew she understood it was pointless to try and reason with Teslintoo. Caught up in her fear and concern for her child, she was beyond any rational thought at the moment. Yaloa drew her into the comfort of his arm and squeezed her gently, trying to convey some reassurance.

He turned to say some calming words to Teslintoo, still kneeling at her daughter's side. Qalaktc was beside them both now, attempting to calm his wife, rubbing her arm, brushing away the tears that coursed down her cheeks. At that moment Ahgishana's eyes fluttered and her head moved slightly. Teslintoo gasped and called to her daughter again, her tears flowing faster and stronger. She kissed her daughter's forehead, cheeks and chin. Ahgishana's eyes opened slowly and focused on her mother's face.

'Mother,' she said in a puzzled voice. 'Your mouth shapes words, but not sound.'

Her brow creased slightly, trying to work out the puzzle. Her eyes became fearful as her words took on the full force of their meaning. 'Mother,' she said in panic. 'I cannot hear my own words.... I can hear nothing!' Her voice broke and she started sobbing. Teslintoo tried to calm her by stroking her forehead and hands and looked up at Yaloa frantically.

'What is wrong?' she asked him. 'What can I do to help my daughter?'

Yaloa looked briefly at Tlachtga, concern flitting across his face. It might be something simple. Perhaps it would pass in a few moments. He crouched beside Teslintoo, taking her hands and looking into her eyes.

'We will make her a soothing brew,' he said as calmly and firmly as he could. 'You get the water ready and I will go fetch some special herbs. It may be, with some rest, she will be fine. She would also feel better, I think, if you bathed her head.' He patted her hands and she nodded to him.

Yaloa rose again, moving quietly to the door where Tlachtga waited. Together they left the tent, their thoughts unspoken but understood. They walked in silence for a while, turning the events over in their minds. Once they were some distance from the dwelling, Yaloa put his question to Tlachtga.

'What do you think, then?' he asked.

'It is difficult to say,' answered Tlachtga. 'She may still be feeling the effects of the fall. If she gets some rest, keeps quiet and still, all may be well. But I do not like the blood. That is not a good sign. It may be that she will never hear again. But let us give it some time.'

'I feared as much,' said Yaloa. It was only an outside chance that Tlachtga might know some remedy or incident that would have contradicted that fear. 'I think Teslintoo knows this, too. But we must, as you say, hope that rest and quiet will set things to right.'

'I will give you the herbs for the drink that will soothe and quiet her,' said Tlachtga. 'It is best you give it to her. I think if I bring it myself Teslintoo will object to it.'

'You are right, and I am sorry for it,' said Yaloa. 'She is distraught and does not know what she is saying at the moment.

Still, it is best we do not anger her too much. Tell me how to prepare the drink and I will see that she gets it.'

Tlachtga smiled weakly. With meticulous detail she explained the drink's preparation to Yaloa as they came up to their dwelling. She retrieved the pouch of herbs in the storage place inside, selected the ones she needed, and handed it to him.

'I will remain here and wait for Kee,' she said. 'He is helping Buan and the others with the horses. While I wait, I will send up prayers to *Brija* for her healing.' She kissed Yaloa as she pressed the herbs into his hands. Her eyes were clouded with tears. Yaloa caressed her face.

'It will be fine, Beloved,' he reassured her. Giving her a firm kiss, he turned and started to retrace his steps, his strides purposeful and long. He hoped his words proved true and tried to set aside his worries about the impact this accident might have on their travel plans. They had to leave, there really was no choice. And they couldn't put it off much longer.

CHAPTER EIGHTEEN

Yaloa leaned over and corrected Ahgishana's fingers and gave her a reassuring pat. 'You are doing well,' he signed to her. He turned to his son. 'What did I just say?'

'She is doing well,' Kee said earnestly. 'And me, am I doing well?'

'Sign that to me and I will tell you,' Yaloa signed to him. He grinned over at Ahgishana. 'Kee is afraid he will not keep up with your skill,' he signed and mouthed the words at the same time.

Tlachtga laughed at them as she took a seat beside Yaloa. He knew she found sitting for long periods increasingly difficult under the bulk of her pregnancy. That was one of the reasons he had agreed to help teach his niece a new way to communicate. It had been Tlachtga's idea, suggested in the face of Teslintoo's smothering desire to be her daughter's ears; walking constantly by her side and attempting to anticipate every thought and need. It was understandable, when all hope of her daughter's hearing returning faded with each passing day. It was frustrating for a young girl like his niece, though, who'd finally resorted to various tricks to have time by herself. But she was doing well now, after several meetings to learn the language.

Tlachtga signed a question to Ahgishana. 'Do you think Kee is ready to have his name day in a moon's time?'

'I am ready, Mother,' Kee said. He signed hurriedly to Ahgishana. 'Please tell her that I am ready.'

Ahgishana giggled and nodded. It was good to have a sweet sound come from her mouth. Yaloa had talked with Tlachgta about the possibility of getting Ahgishanou to speak more, before she lost that ability. For now they left her to make her decision about it.

'He should be ready,' Ahgishana signed. 'Though I still think he throws like a girl.'

'What?' said Kee. He gave her a small shove. 'I am no girl. Take that back.'

Yaloa laughed and patted his son's head. 'Perhaps if you answered her calmly and in sign language, she might think you are less like a girl.'

The dwelling flap opened and Teslintoo entered. She scanned the area, her face a mixture of worry, anger and hurt. Startled, her daughter gaped at her, a guilty look on her face.

'Come in, Sister,' said Yaloa. He kept his voice deliberately calm. 'Join us here. We were just talking about Kee's naming day.'

She rushed over to kneel over by her daughter, took up her hands and kissed her forehead. 'Oh my dear one, I'm so glad you are safe.' She turned to Yaloa. 'Talk? And I suppose my daughter had to sit there, isolated from your conversation while you chattered away, never thinking she might want a drink or a bite to eat?

Tlachtga glanced at Yaloa, amused frustration on her face. She shook her head slightly. Yaloa sighed. 'We weren't neglecting your daughter at all. She is well looked after, I can assure you. We were, in fact, teaching her a way to talk with us.'

'Talk? How dare you speak about that after what you've done to her?'

Yaloa took a deep breath and tried again. 'My niece has a quick mind and has soon grasped the Trader signing as a means to speak with us. She can understand it very well now and we use that to speak to her. She is also learning to read lips.'

Ahgishana tugged her mother's sleeve. 'Do not worry, Mother. It is so,' she signed to her.

Teslintoo looked at her, tears filling her eyes. She sniffed hard. 'You want to do this?' she signed slowly.

Ahgishana nodded, her face beaming. Teslintoo looked over at her brother. 'Very well. I can see that you have convinced her this is the path for her, but I will take over her teaching.'

Yaloa gave a resigned nod. He knew that her grasp of the language wasn't as good as his own, but he thought it best to leave it for now. 'Of course,' he said. 'She will learn well with you as her teacher.'

Tʟᴀᴄʜᴛɢᴀ sʜɪғᴛᴇᴅ her weight clumsily against the fur bolster, finding comfort difficult with an active child in her ungainly stomach. Searching for distraction, she looked over where Yaloa and Kee worked busily on a leather belt, putting last minute touches on its elaborate decorations. She smiled at them, knowing their effort was driven more from a need for filling time before Kee's naming ceremony that day, than artistic design.

Yaloa looked up from his work and caught Tlachtga's smile. 'I think we have covered every spare space in this belt now,' he said, grinning back at her.

Kee paused at his father's words and leaned back on his heels. 'Yes,' he said, admiring the belt. 'Is it not magnificent?'

He held the belt up for them to see. Both parents smiled broadly at him. There were swirls and patterned notches etched in a lively manner all over the wide band.

'You don't think it's overdone, do you?' he asked, cocking his head as he examined the belt himself.

'I'm sure it will look splendid,' said Tlachtga. 'No one will be able to miss the wonderful skill that has gone into its crafting. It is fine work, indeed.'

Satisfied, Kee took a small cloth and began to polish it lightly, brushing off the last traces of dirt and leather bits.

Tlachtga smiled again, thinking how her father would have enjoyed this moment. She fought the tears that still pricked her eyes whenever she thought of him and sought instead the thick cloak of warmth that signaled his presence to her. Her babe kicked in response. The babe could feel it, too.

The door flap was pulled aside and Ahgishana entered. She stood straight and tall, her long black hair flowing loose and thick about her round face and lively eyes. Her wide mouth smiled at them now and she waved her hand in greeting, clutching a small bag in the other hand.

Tlachtga waved back and pointed to the blanket. 'Welcome to our dwelling,' she mouthed. 'Come in and sit.'

She entered and said carefully, 'I have brought a gift for Kee, for his naming.'

Kee came over to her, took the gift and signed his gratitude. 'I thank you, Cousin,' he said to her, his lips in her line of vision. 'You are very generous.' Kee signed rapidly to Ahgishana, pausing only to unwrap the cloth that held the gift. He withdrew a brightly woven head band woven in an intricate depiction of an eagle in flight, the wings appearing to float along the surface. Kee cried in appreciation, then looked up.

'It is beautiful, Cousin,' he mouthed to her. He signed the magic it conveyed to him and her face broke out in a large smile.

'A fine gift for a naming day,' Yaloa said, gently touching her arm. He signed his admiration for her gift, telling her she possessed her mother's skill at weaving. Ahgishana shook her head modestly, but her eyes sparkled with pride.

Tlachtga felt glow of pleasure at such an exchange. People had been coming with gifts all morning, but this was special. This evening, during the feast, it would be their turn to give gifts. Gifts for everyone that helped them with Kee, which was virtually the whole of the tribe. But they had a special gift waiting for Ahgishana. It was a new felt saddle cloth. This was Yaloa's idea to help her resume horse riding. Ahgishana had expressed an interest in riding again, but she feared her mother's objections. The saddle cloth was Yaloa's way of telling Teslintoo it was time to let her ride again.

Kee sat down with his cousin, while Yaloa gathered up the tools they had been using and left to return them to Buan. Tlachtga resumed her mending, some half-hearted sewing she had picked up to pass the time. Soon she would retrieve the special outfit she had made for Kee, the folds padded with cloth against creasing, herbs spread in the seams to keep it fresh. The tunic was an intricate plaid of the indigo blue and moss green of her father's special colors. She had labored over it during the spring mornings when the light was strong and Kee was off with the horses. Kayáani and Qaltsixkli had helped a little, Kayáani concealing it in her own dwelling when it became too large to hide at home. It was stored at Kayáani's now.

Kayáani had grown to be a real friend to her, like Qaltsixkli; the two as different as night and day, but just as close. Kayáani's daughter, Kiyanee, had just had her own naming and wore it proudly. Her name meant 'Mountain Flower,' a fact she reminded all with the flower she wore constantly in her hair. She had her mother's temper and always found a moment to taunt Kee with her newly acquired status, calling him 'Baby

Bird,' whenever she crossed his path, and Kiyanee seemed to find many ways to do that.

'Hello, the hearth,' cried Kayáani from outside. 'It is your cousin, come to call.'

Tlachtga smiled, thinking her musings must have summoned Kayáani. 'You are welcome to our hearth,' she answered. 'Please come in and share our hospitality.'

Kayáani entered bearing a large bundle. Kiyanee followed close behind, a smaller bundle in her hand. Kiyanee looked over at Kee and Ahgishana, signed hello to Ahgishana and stuck out her tongue to Kee.

'Greetings, Baby Bird,' Kiyanee said. 'We have come to give you a gift for you naming.'

Kee stood up quickly, his head coming well above Kiyanee's. He stuck out his own tongue in reply. 'Greetings, Ugly Weed.'

Ahgishana giggled, needing no translation for the well worn joke between those two. The pair glared at each other momentarily until Kiyanee remembered her manners and handed him the bundle.

'Here is your naming gift,' she said. 'Though I am sure someone as rude as you does not deserve it.'

'Such gracious giving deserves gracious thanks,' said Kee, wrinkling his nose at her. He opened the gift eagerly. It was a finely carved adult spoon with a deep bowl, big enough for scooping large portions from the pot.

'My father carved it,' said Kiyanee proudly. 'I helped with the design and rubbing the oil seasoning into the wood.'

'It is a fine bit of carving,' said Tlachtga. 'I can see its smoothness from here.' She smiled over at Kayáani, who had taken a seat beside her. Kayáani placed her large bundle beside Tlachtga.

'I brought over everything for you, to save you the journey,' Kayáani told her. 'You will have enough to do today and you must save your strength.' She patted Tlachtga's belly lightly. Kayáani was also carrying a child, but she was many moons away from delivery. She had lost a child a few seasons before, early in the pregnancy, but this time she had advanced further and felt fit and healthy.

Tlachtga unfolded the bundle, checking carefully that everything was in place, unharmed by bugs or any other destructive element. The folds were still carefully in place, the herbs unmoved and no other sign of harm present. She smiled contentedly. All was ready for the ceremony.

Tlachtga dipped her finger into her pot for one last scoop of ochre paint. With a light touch she extended the line of the swirl around Kee's eye to bring it along his cheekbone and up to his nose. She stood back a short distance to survey her work. The sun burst across Kee's forehead and along his cheeks, a stunning display of ochre and blue paint paste. Just above the design he had tied Ahgishana's headband, so the eagle now flew above the sun, soaring high in the sky. It was a fitting and splendid display.

Satisfied, Tlachtga gave Kee a nod and turned him towards Yaloa for inspection. Hearing a growl from Kee's stomach, she smiled. A whole day without food was a long time for her son, and she knew he would be eating enough for two at the feast this evening.

'How does it look, Father?' asked Kee anxiously.

Yaloa nodded his approval. 'Very impressive,' he said. 'There is no doubt you are a young man now, no longer a little boy.'

At his father's words, Kee drew himself up to his full height, expanding his chest under the tunic that hung loosely across his chest. It would not be long before he outgrew it, Tlachtga observed with a wry grin. Still, he looked splendid. Yaloa withdrew a small bundle from his waist and handed it to his son.

'I have saved this for you until now,' he told him. 'Your mother and I made it especially for this day.'

Kee looked down at the bundle in his hand. With slow reverence he unfolded the cloth to reveal a knife, shiny and new, its blade a mottled reflection of the joy on Kee's face.

'This is a very special gift,' he cried. He turned the knife over in his hand, running his finger along the blade, testing its edge. 'It is magnificent. I am honored.'

His joy was such that he allowed Tlachtga to kiss his cheek and she hugged him lightly while she did. She might not get the chance again and she wanted to make the most of it. Her son was no longer a babe to cling to his mother's side and he wasn't likely to forget that. Tlachtga lifted her head from her son, hearing the drums starting in the distance.

'It is time now,' she said. 'The ceremony is starting.'

Yaloa gathered up his drum and the tools for Kee's naming tattoo. The tattoo would be linked to Kee's new name, a name that had two parts—a public name and a secret spirit name, used only in the spirit world. His mother gave him the secret name, for it came through the womb, given to her by his power spirit while she nourished his soul. It was the link with the Otherworld.

The three of them walked to the ceremonial clearing, Tlachtga clutching her harp under her arm. She would be including some of her own rituals in this naming ceremony, invoking *Brija* to help her pass on his spirit name. She felt the harp's familiar wood shape and found some calm for the small knot of anxiety in her stomach. Everything must go well, for Kee's sake. Quietly, she mouthed a prayer.

They reached the clearing, the evening light casting faint shadows with the pale orange glow of the setting sun. It was the time between day and night, the special time for spirits. A pale moon, full and large, was mounting the sky already. It was the

Berry Picking Moon, ready to shine on this auspicious event. The crowd, patiently awaiting their arrival, parted for them to enter. Tlachtga saw Buan's familiar face smiling next to Qaltsixkli and their daughter, Lóol. They looked at her reassuringly. She moved past them and followed her family to the center of the clearing. The drumming stopped.

'Greetings, People of this Land!' he cried. He turned to face the mountains, their flame color brilliant in the fading sun. 'Welcome, Spirits of this Land. We the People ask you to join our circle this day's end and night's beginning.'

The gathered people repeated his invocation in a simple one-word statement, a time worn ritual condensed to a single, powerful call.

'This ceremony marks respect for the spirits that protect this child until he is strong enough to resist the calls back to the Otherworld, The Land of the Dead. It is also a celebration of the tribe, giving hope for the future. It is the second one this moon, a happy thought for all of us.'

Yaloa concluded his speech and stepped back. Yakwun entered the circle, made his way to the center, beside Yaloa, licking his lips nervously. He took a deep breath and began to recite the ancestry of Yaloa's Eagle clan. He had prepared for this recitation for many seasons, listening carefully every time his mother or Yaloa explained it. It was an honor for him to recite the ancestry at Kee's naming, and Tlachtga knew Yakwun wanted it to be perfect.

Yakwun crossed his arms to indicate he'd finished. He grinned broadly, proud that he'd completed the ancestry without any mistake in sequence or name. He glanced at his parents, saw pride mirrored in their faces, and left the center to the sound of the beating drums. It was Buan's turn next. He made his way to the center, holding his own drum. He smiled at Tlachtga and gave Kee a wink. Tlachtga suppressed a tiny sigh and a giggle. She could only imagine how Buan would explain her heritage.

'Ah, now,' said Buan, his deep, rich voice resonating loudly. 'I am here to tell you of Tlachtga's ancestry. It is an ancestry that goes back a long way, like the esteemed ancestry of our leader, Yaloa.' Buan pounded the drum once, giving his statement emphasis. Tlachtga knew he was only warming up.

'Yes, an ancestry that goes into the mists of time—living with the gods themselves. The spirits that were present in the old land. The spirit of the sea, *Ma Na Nan,* the spirit of the sun *Greine*, and many other spirits of that place.' Tlachtga reddened, not daring to look at anyone, but hearing the small gasps of amazement coming from the group. She fought the urge to reach out and punch him at his exaggerations. Still, it was the way of her people, to give her stature, and she knew he meant well.

Buan finished after a while, the crowd staring at him in awe-filled silence. Tlachtga had no doubt where her son found his gift for flourish and show. It was a fine performance. Buan walked from the circle and Yaloa stepped forward again, a wide grin on his face. He had appreciated the entertainment at least.

He cleared his throat and took on a solemn demeanor. 'I ask you, The People, to open up your circle, and welcome the spirits present for the naming of this boy.' He held his arms open wide as everyone murmured the words of welcome. He took up his rattle from his belt and began to shake it.

Tlachtga stepped forward beside him and braced her harp against her round belly. She plucked two strings on the harp, intoning its sound at the back of her throat, and down into her chest. She sang out her invocation, rolling the words and tone round and round, first in a circle and then a downward spiral, ending on a low tone. She put down the harp, lifted her arms outward and began to chant. A chant of the animals, the sky, the earth, the rivers and sea, invoking light and dark, and the voices of the Otherworld that gave memory to the times that were. She invoked *Brija*. And the Lady came.

Tlachtga turned to her son, her body filling with the light and energy she knew so well, and placed her hand on his forehead. She leaned down, speaking to him softly in her own language, a language he knew through the telling of the tales.

'I am your Mother. You are my Son,' she told him. 'The spirits gave me your name, long ago, and now I give it to you. This name will bless you and keep you as you follow your path. It will call your spirits to guide you.' She paused and saw the Lady now before her, pulling her and her son into the Lady's force.

'You are the name of the lands,' Tlachtga continued. 'The lands that will call you, the lands that will be for the People. Their hope. You are *Cumma Dorib*, the Keeper of the Fire. In *Brija's* name I give this secret name, this true name, to you. She clutched her son's arms lightly to give him a kiss. As she pulled back, she caught her wrist on the knife at his belt. The knife she had fashioned. She looked down at her arm and saw tiny beads of blood forming. A large rushing noise filled her head and through the roar, the Lady spoke to her. *You have done well, my Daughter. You have completed your destiny.*

Tlachtga gasped, not certain she heard correctly. Kee looked up at her questioningly, and she smiled down at him. She stepped back carefully and let the ceremony continue, fighting off the slight faintness.

Yaloa drew his son to the light of the fire and removed the pouch from his waist that held the tattoo tools. Singers began a chant, invoking the blessing on the tattoo Yaloa inscribed. With precision and care, Yaloa worked three stylized hills against a bed of flames on his son's arm. This was the design they had agreed upon to follow Tlachtga's cryptic instructions.

When he completed the design, his son whispered to him briefly and he nodded. Yaloa took up his son's wrist and worked sun tattoos on each of them. Tears filled Tlachtga's eyes. She didn't know her son had planned this. The designs finally finished, Yaloa turned his son away from the fire, to face the crowd. The drums beat attention.

'I present Muach to the People,' said Yaloa, announcing his public name. The crowd roared, shouting back a welcome.

This action felt so right to her, filling her with such joy. She looked down at her own wrists, smiling at the tattoos she carried of her people, and wiped away the small trace of blood that remained from the earlier scratch.

CHAPTER NINETEEN

Tlachtga inhaled the dusty smells of late summer, the dry brush, the hot baked earth. Sighing, she put aside the tunic she was mending, unable to concentrate. Earlier, she had attempted to distract herself by watching the horse training. Yaloa and most of the men were fitting horses to carts, getting more of them used to the harness and pulling weight, or exercising the remaining horses to prepare them for the long journey ahead. Some of the women were helping, too. They had over twenty-five horses now. Tlachtga hoped it would be enough.

Tlachtga lumbered to her feet, groaning at the shifting weight. The babe had recently dropped and she found it difficult to sit. She stretched her back, trying to give it some ease, and decided on a short stroll. Walking around the camp, she noticed the silence. Most people were over at the practice grounds, the area where she'd first trained Yaloa to ride. It seemed such a long time ago, a whole lifetime. She patted her swollen belly. A response, sudden and drenching, rushed down her legs and into her boots. Staring at the wetness spreading along her trousers, Tlachtga didn't notice Teslintoo come along side of her.

'Your time has come,' Teslintoo stated.

Tlachtga knitted her brow and smiled uncertainly. 'My water has broken, but I have not felt any pains yet.'

Teslintoo grunted. 'We should prepare, though,' she said in clipped tone. 'Return to your dwelling. I will get my things.'

Tlachtga looked helplessly after Teslintoo's retreating figure. In one big rush, her old fears returned, choking her, cutting off her breath. Above all, she wished Yaloa was here, but she was reluctant to ask Teslintoo to get him. It was against all custom, and last time it was only Yaloa's insistence that had succeeded. A pain seized her unawares, and temporarily drove all thought from her mind. When it passed, she made her way back to her dwelling.

Teslintoo entered a short while later, her bag of medicines in her hand. Tlachtga leaned against the main support pole and suffered another contraction.

When it had eased, she felt Teslintoo take her hand, the skin dry and papery against Tlachtga's sweating palms. Teslintoo led her over to the pallet.

'I want to examine you now,' said Teslintoo. 'Ensure that everything progresses well.' She helped Tlachtga remove her boots and strip off her damp trousers and dried Tlachtga's legs and thighs carefully with a cloth before she began the examination. Tlachtga could hear her muttering as she pressed her fingers and palms along Tlachtga's belly at different angles and then along the birth entry. After a while Teslintoo leaned back on her heels, the exam complete.

'The babe is well positioned,' she said in a neutral tone. 'And it has begun its journey into this world. But I think it will be some time yet before he arrives. Meanwhile, I want you to go outside and walk slowly around the dwelling, to keep the babe moving. I will make the birthing drink and other preparations.'

Tlachtga nodded, feeling a small bit of gladness that she

would be out of Teslintoo's hands for a short while at least. Perhaps Yaloa would return by the time the babe was ready to appear. She rose laboriously, and with Teslintoo's assistance, put on her other pair of trousers and boots. The dry cloth felt good against her skin.

Tlachtga made her way outside and circled her dwelling, skirting the cook fire, the grinding pit and all the other little obstacles that surrounded their home. After a while these points became markers in her loop that she counted each time until eventually she struggled to move her legs forward. She had lost track of time, knowing only that her contractions seized her more often than not and she was exhausted. She stumbled into her dwelling.

'I cannot do this any longer,' she said in a voice that barely carried. 'I must rest.'

Teslintoo looked up from rush matting she'd laid down since Tlachtga left. Beside her lay bowls, cloths, her knife and a small bundle of herbs. She stirred a drink held in a cup.

'Yes, I suppose you may stop walking,' she said. 'Drink this birthing brew before you get into position. You will need its strength.' Teslintoo rose and handed Tlachtga the cup. She took it, and leaning against the center post, she drank it down. Teslintoo gave her a satisfied smile and led her over to the rushes and helped her remove her trousers and boots before settling her into position. She lifted Tlachtga's tunic and felt her stomach, the pelvic area and the birth entry again. Her finger probed carefully inside Tlachtga, testing the birth's progress. Withdrawing her fingers, Teslintoo dipped them in the bowl of salve she had prepared. She probed further this time, her fingers and hands greased against resistance.

A searing pain ripped through Tlachtga's stomach and down into her belly. Black spots danced in front of her eyes. She retched and leaned over on her side, her stomach heaving, but only a small amount of fluid came out. Teslintoo stuck a bowl under her chin to catch the rest.

'Do not worry,' Teslintoo assured her. 'It is the strength of the contractions that cause you to react so.'

The pain subsided and Tlachtga leaned back gratefully against the large bolster Teslintoo had placed on the rush matting. Tlachtga closed her eyes, feeling suddenly lethargic, her limbs a dead weight. A moment later she forced open her eyes and looked down at Teslintoo working busily at her womb. Tlachtga could hardly feel Teslintoo's fingers now. In the distance, she heard a familiar voice. Yaloa came over and knelt by her side, clutching her hand. A dull roar in her ears kept her from hearing what he said. Vaguely she became aware of the wetness between her legs and she thought perhaps the babe had finally appeared. With an effort she raised her head, looked down and watched a dark pool of liquid pour from her, spreading wider and wider.

YALOA SEARCHED THE NIGHT SKY. It seemed the best place to look for Tlachtga, away from the site where her life's blood had drained from birthing their son. He attempted to wipe those last moments from his mind, the memory of his desperate efforts to staunch the flow of blood, the rags and cloths he'd applied over and over, only to come away soaked. He'd paused when the babe slipped out of Tlachtga, arriving blue and still, covered in birth fluid and blood.

Teslintoo cleaned its nose and mouth and tried to start its breath while Yaloa attempted once more to halt the flow of blood from his wife. Helpless, he watched his Tlachtga's body become still, her chest motionless under the tunic that was hitched up around her belly, a belly that was no longer swollen with life. He leaned over, kissed her pale, blue lips and stroked her hair. Even then, it shone a brilliant red under the sweat and tangles.

'It is no use, Brother,' said Teslintoo. 'The child is dead.' She held out the small body to him, the tiny limbs and amber-haired head matted with blood. The eyes were shut against the world, the lips closed, never to utter a cry. Yaloa had stared at the baby, unable to comprehend such a loss.

He'd risen abruptly and strode out of the dwelling in an effort to put space between him and the terrible scene behind him. He walked blindly, unaware of his surroundings, until he found himself well out of site of the camp, here by the stream, with his back on the ground staring up at the sky.

Now the sky was alive with stars, signaling the night's progress. He knew he should go back, see to Muach. For the moment, though, he could only think of keeping vigil here. To search the sky for some sign, some indication that Tlachtga had begun her journey. His mind could comprehend nothing beyond that thought. His eyes ached with unshed tears, and his stomach burned. Somewhere inside, only half of him remained. That part now screamed with the pain of separation.

Yaloa sat up slowly and ran his hand through his hair. His fingers snagged on a knot and he ripped through it, taking a small clump of hair with him. He stared at the bits in his hand, remembering the ritual for Mog. Yaloa reached for the knife at his waist and grabbed a section of his hair. With swift, angry motions he sawed away at it, shoving the knife back and forth with force. The hair gave away in his hand and he tossed it on the ground. Grabbing another large chunk he hacked away again, repeating the motion over and over, until most of his hair lay in front of him.

He gathered up the hair into his hand, then plucked a strong blade of grass and tied it around the bundle of hair, muttering a prayer, one of Tlachtga's. He remained silent a few moments and stared at the bundle, the sky lightening around him. Sighing, Yaloa rose slowly and replaced his knife at his waist. The light had reached the distant mountains and he knew he could delay his return no longer.

As he neared his dwelling, the camp silent in the dawn light, he saw his son sitting cross-legged beside the doorway, fingering his carved belt. Muach's face was streaked with dried tears and dirt, creating a pattern of darkened shadows. He looked up at Yaloa's approach, started to rise, his eyes searching and questioning. A moment later he resumed his seat and frowned down at the belt.

Part of Yaloa found it difficult to rouse himself to embrace his son's grief and apply the needed healing words and actions. His son could never understand Yaloa's feeling of utter emptiness, a permanent vacuum inside that would never again be filled. But Muach had his own hole that needed tending and Yaloa had to help him. He sat down beside his son.

'Sometimes we lose what is most precious to us before we are ready to lose it,' he told Muach.

'Too many times,' muttered Muach.

'True,' said Yaloa. 'And sometimes we are never ready to lose that which is most precious. I am not ready to lose my wife, and you are not ready to lose your mother.' He fell silent for a few moments, letting his words sink in. Muach remained silent, stabbing the ground in front of him with his small knife.

'While we are not ready to lose them,' continued Yaloa, 'we must help them, especially if they were not ready to leave. This we must do for your mother. We must help her soul onto the next world. She needs us to do this.'

Muach paused in his digging and stared up at his father. His face was drawn and filled with grief. A moment later it cleared slightly at the thought of this purpose.

'Yes, of course, we must help her. This is an important duty. She needs us.' He paused. 'How are we to help?'

'The first thing we must do is give her strength for the journey. We must send her our prayers, the strength of our bodies, and our wisdom. This we do through the hair from our heads.' He pointed to his head. 'You see I have cut my hair?' Yaloa opened his hand and showed Muach the bundle of hair. He motioned to the knife in Muach's hand. 'Now you must cut your hair, too.'

Slowly, under Yaloa's watchful eye, Muach sliced away at his hair, his chin held erect, the fine hair giving way under his resolute force. Yaloa intoned the prayers softly, setting them both in a dreamlike state while Muach completed his task.

When it was done, Muach collected up the hair and Yaloa handed him a blade of grass he had plucked before the journey back. He rose, motioning Muach to follow and they headed to the hearth fire, its embers glowing red in the pale light. Staring at the glow, he realized Tlachtga would never tend the hearth fire again, never perform the banking ritual before sleeping. The force of her loss hit him hard, a blow deep in his stomach, knocking out his breath. He moaned low and Muach reached for his arm, understanding the thought that had seized Yaloa. Feeling his son's touch, Yaloa steadied himself. He looked down at his son.

'Now, we must put this hair in the fire,' he told Muach. 'So that it can transform into smoke, rise to the sky and reach your mother's soul as it travels to the Otherworld. This will give her strength on the first part of her journey.'

Yaloa dropped his bundle of hair in the fire and watched it curl and crackle, burning away to smoke. He began the low chant again, while Muach released his own bundle into the fire to create the smoke that would join the other spirals that drifted up into the sky. Muach added his own chants to his father's, picking up the simple tones and sounds that gave it shape. When the last bit of hair had disappeared, Yaloa looked down at his son.

'It is time to begin the other preparations,' said Yaloa.

With Muach close behind him, Yaloa made his way inside his home, so much of it the same since he had seen it last. He forced himself to look at the pallet, to see what his heart wanted to deny. Tlachtga lay there, her skin as pale as the moon, her bright hair spread out around her. The women had washed her, combed her hair and wrapped her in a blanket along with their stillborn son. Buan sat beside her, his face awash in grief, his head just stubble, hair that had only just recovered its length from its earlier ritualized cutting, now gone. That was too much loss for one person. Over to the side, Qaltsixkli worked silently pounding the herbs, grains and dyes that would be used to prepare Tlachtga for her journey.

Yaloa's throat clenched and he tried to swallow. He wasn't ready to go to her yet, feel her cold hands and see her unmoving lips. In a low voice he asked Buan to join him outside with Muach. The three left the dwelling and went over to squat by the hearth fire. With as much calm as he could manage, Yaloa outlined his thoughts about Tlachtga and the babe's burial. Buan nodded slowly while he spoke, his solemn expression broken only by a weak and painful smile. Beside him Muach gave silent assent to his father's statements with one firm nod of his head.

YALOA STOOD SILENTLY, Buan by his side, a lit rush in his hand, and Muach in front. Soot blackened their faces, their hands, and matted their hair, the odor competing with the smell of the warm earth that filled Yaloa's nostrils. It was not yet the Moon of the Summer Flowers.

Soon they would leave, before the winter set in and the game was hard to come by. The journey seemed an overwhelming task, one that would take him further and further from those he loved. More than he had counted upon. He glanced at Buan. Buan had told him today that he was planning to take his small family and return to his own people. Qaltsixkli, knowing his losses drove him to recover his blood ties, had agreed to go with him.

Too many loved ones gone. How could this have happened? His heart and mind wrestled with each other, his old suspicions rising again, yet finding no fertile ground to plant truth. There was no evidence, no proof to say his sister had been the cause. Surely the tooth would have protected them if she had killed his wife. Just the same, he would watch his son closely and keep his sister at a distance. Others would notice, of course, but that might not be a bad thing, for they would silently follow suit. He would do all he could to protect his son.

Drums sounded over his head, calling him back to the present, the heavy beat matching the weight of his heart. Buan, Muach and he were the only ones down in the burial chamber, besides the bodies of his wife and son. The three of them would perform the rituals in the cramped space carved out beside Mog's tomb. The grave had been constructed in a matter of days, the wall to Mog's chamber used to support one side. It seemed only right and proper to place Tlachtga next to her father as she went on her journey. With Buan's aid, Yaloa had followed all the customs of Tlachtga's people, doing all he could to assure her soul a successful journey.

He stared down at his son's head, reluctant to begin the part of the ritual that would end with a final parting from Tlachtga. Buan touched his arm gently. Yaloa sighed and nodded his assent. Carefully, Buan separated the burning rush into three sections, handing off one to Yaloa, then another to Muach.

Slowly they moved around the cart platform that held the bodies, circling sunwise once, twice, three times.

The three of them completed the third turn, Buan ending at Tlachtga's head. Yaloa moved to Tlachtga's feet, Muach coming up beside him. He allowed himself to look at her, drink in her view one last time. Against custom, Yaloa had dressed her himself, donning her wedding garments, weaving flowers in her hair. The curls reached just below her shoulders in a riotous color of flames. The babe lay next to her, wrapped in the cloth from the tunic of Muach's naming ceremony. Muach himself had insisted upon it, and Yaloa knew Tlachtga would approve. It was as if Muach was sending his own signals to his spirit helpers to aid this young soul on its journey. With such help there was no danger his soul would get lost.

Yaloa had already carefully placed the harp under her arm, the strings trembling slightly at the motion. The sound receded slowly in the chamber and still echoed in Yaloa's head. The echo would never leave him, he knew, and even now it shaped the tone of his chant. The chant filled his whole body. He lost sight of the view before him as he felt himself rising upwards, spiraling away. His hand reached out. A whisper of a touch brushed him, the beloved voice sighing around him. A drum beat sounded heavy and sharp, calling him away, insistent and severe. Slowly and reluctantly he opened his eyes and saw his son beating the drum, his face filled with alarm.

Buan looked at him, a question in his face, and Yaloa looked away. Swallowing hard, he found his voice again and resumed the chant, his eyes open, focused on his son's head. Buan sprinkled water on the bodies from the bowl at Tlachtga's head, then reached for the smaller bowl filled with earth. His fingers grabbed a small clump of the dirt, scattering it lightly across Tlachtga's chest. Taking up each bowl, he handed them to Yaloa. When Yaloa had repeated the motions, he handed the bowls to

Muach, who followed suit, his hands trembling slightly as he let go the water droplets.

The ritual complete, Buan and Muach stepped away from the platform and made their way over to the opening that led to the other chamber and the way above. They left Yaloa to have the last few moments alone with his wife and child, before they sealed the chamber.

Yaloa moved to Tlachtga's side and took up her hand. He withdrew the small pouch at his waist and folded her fingers around it. Perhaps this pouch would ensure her soul's journey. A journey that must be completed in order for the soul to return once more. A soul he would never stop searching out, because he knew there would come a day when they would be together once more. Yaloa leaned down and kissed her lips one last time.

'Until we are together again,' he said. He moved his hand to rest briefly on his babes's head and left.

CHAPTER TWENTY
PRESENT DAY CHINA

Bríd woke up with a start, her heart racing. The moonlight poured in through the gap in the curtains, illuminating John's face beside her. Was it the moon that had woken her? Her heart slowed to a more even tempo until she began to recall the dream. It was so vivid, it had immersed her so deeply, it lingered still, and now created a fresh wave of grief. They were both dead. Tlachgta and her newborn child. The loss was so great.

Beside her John stirred. 'Is something wrong?' he asked.

She tried to turn her face away so that he couldn't see she was crying. How could she explain all that she felt at the moment? But John reached out and turned her face toward him.

'What's the matter? What happened?' He sat up in the bed and pulled her towards him. 'You're not upset about what happened last night, are you?'

Bríd gave a shaky laugh. 'Not at all,' she said. 'No, it's nothing to do with that.' Last night had been wonderful and healing. She sighed at the memory, relishing his arms around her now. The touch of his bare skin on hers still had the power to arouse her.

'Then what is it?'

'It's the dream I had.' She looked up at him, not certain she wanted to remember all she'd seen and felt.

'It was bad?' John began to rub her arm in comfort.

'Not exactly bad,' Bríd said. 'No, it was upsetting, at the end.' She paused and eventually decided to tell him everything she'd seen. When she recounted Tlachtga's death, the tears flowed.

'Ssshhh,' said John and he kissed her head. 'It's all right now.'

'Oh, it was so sad,' said Bríd. 'Yaloa and their son were devastated. The care and ritual they gave to her when they interred her was so moving.'

'What did they do?' John asked in a low voice. He stroked her head gently while she slowly described the ritual she'd witnessed; the carefully dressed hair, her wedding clothes, the harp and the actual ceremony Yaloa had performed for her journey to the Otherworld.

When she finished she looked up into his eyes, so like Yaloa's, and allowed the tears to spill over to her cheeks. 'He loved her,' she said simply. 'And she him.'

John's eyes darkened. 'I see that now.' He kissed her softly, still stroking her hair.

They lay that way for a while and Bríd allowed his soothing touch to ease the grief she felt deep inside. The knot that had been twisted and hard since Gran's death and Ciarán's betrayal somehow loosened under the fresh weight of these other deaths and John's comfort. She could feel her breathing easing into a slower, sleepier pace as she drifted off into her thoughts.

Suddenly she jolted into wakefulness. 'John, the chamber!'

'What about the chamber?'

'Not Mog's, hers. Tlachtga's.'

John gave her a puzzled look.

'Don't you see? She was interred in a chamber, like Mog. And the chamber was right next to his. Is right next to his.' She pulled up and away from him. 'John, it's still there, I'm sure of it.'

John nodded slowly, taking in her words. 'You could be right,' he said.

'I know I'm right,' she insisted.

'Let's say you are right. It's too late to do anything about it now.'

'Is it? If we go now, get there early in the morning, we may still have time to at least confirm it.'

'Confirm it?'

'Confirm all that's been happening to me. That I haven't been imagining it.'

John put his hand to her face, cupping her chin. 'Bríd, I do believe you. I don't think you're making it up.'

The tears welled up in her eyes again. 'But don't you see? I need to know. I have to find out if it's all true. It's a story, John. But is it the right story?' Her voice became almost a whisper. 'And is it part of my story?'

John gave her a long, hard look then kissed her. 'Okay, we'll give it a shot.' He looked at the clock and threw back the duvet. 'If we're going to get there at first light, we'd better move.'

Bríd gazed out of the window into the darkness. Ahead, the road stretched endlessly before them, a vast and much travelled distance that in centuries past had carried spices, silks and other exotic treasures.

They hadn't said much to each other since they'd begun the journey back to the site, the night stillness soon overtaking them when they left the city. The silence was comfortable and Bríd allowed her mind to wander over the days' events. Could so much have happened in so short a time? She found it hard to believe.

She could never have imagined that coming on a dig in China could be fraught with so many political undercurrents and dangers. It was naive of her, she could see that now. The only danger she'd foreseen had been from Bob and that, as it turned out, was easily handled. Well, easily enough with John's help, as she recalled his protective request that she switch jobs with Jin. And Jin, how could she have been so fooled by him, how could all of them have been so fooled? She could have been imprisoned. And John. If it weren't for Dr Lei, they both could be facing lengthy prison sentences. It was a chilling thought. As it was, John had enough to deal with when he returned home.

She looked across at him, a shaggy lock hanging over his tired but still handsome face, visible in the moonlight. If his career at Penn hadn't been finished would they still have made love, she wondered. Or would his scruples still have held firm, even in the face of all they'd been through? She didn't think so. At least it didn't seem like it all those hours ago when he gently removed her clothes, kissed and caressed her in all the remote corners of her body, slowly making love to her until she lost all sense of time. That sense of deep surrender, that strong connection, had continued throughout her dreaming and was still with her now, even stronger.

It was the dream that made her sure. The dream confirmed there was something more between them. She knew it. She could feel it in her. Bríd touched the medallion under her shirt. It had been with her all night, around her neck. Her grandmother would understand. Gran had spoken of just such a love in her own stories of her great aunt. A love of an exotic man across the ocean. Dark like her.

Would the chamber be there? It must be. She was sure of it. Then she would know. Know it was her story, a story that tied her to this place, a story she thought tied her to John. She gripped the medallion hard. Tlachtga had worn a silver medallion around her neck. Bríd had seen it in the dream. Tlachtga had called it a disc and it was part of her ritual wear. Was it similar to her own? This was the real key, she thought. If she could see Tlachgta's disc, compare to her own, she would know, then.

'How are you feeling?' asked John.

She reached over and laid her hand on top of his. 'Okay,' she said. 'And thank you.'

'For what?'

'For doing this, for being you.' She smiled.

He squeezed her hand and smiled. After a few moments he spoke, his tone serious. 'There is still that bit in me that wants to know more. Though it's pointless, in terms of publishable research and theories, furthering my career, or even proving anything about clan history, I would like to know more, if I could, about these people that were here.'

Bríd nodded, understanding perfectly. After a few moments she finally voiced the thought that had been dogging her the whole night. 'I just hope we're in time. And they haven't covered over the chamber yet.'

'I hope so, too,' said John.

WHEN THEY PULLED into the site, the light was just breaking over the horizon, casting deep shadows across the silent grounds. There was no sign of movement in any of the tents, the dining area, or either of the trailers. Bríd's breath caught as she noticed the small digger parked beside the lab.

'Look,' she said and pointed to the digger.

John nodded. 'I saw that. They must have brought that yesterday. But what on Earth for? It seems overkill just to move the layer of dirt that covered the willows and skins that formed the top of the chamber.'

'I don't know,' she said. 'I just hope they haven't used it yet.'

John said nothing as he switched off the engine and the two of them got out of the car and made their way over to the chamber opening. To Bríd's relief, the chamber was still open, its hole yawning widely before her. She gave a sigh of relief.

'Right. I'll get a few picks from the office and we'll get started,' said John quietly. 'With any luck the wall won't be thick between the two chambers and it won't take long.'

'I don't think it is,' said Bríd softly. She blushed deep red. 'At least I think that's what I dreamt.'

John gave her an odd look then went to the office. He returned a few minutes later with two picks and two sets of gloves. 'Better put these on first,' he said, handing her the gloves.

When they were ready, the two climbed down the little ladder now leaning against the side. Once inside John turned to Bríd. 'Which side? North or south?'

Bríd closed her eyes for a minute, trying to recall. 'South, I think. Yes, south.'

John nodded, moved over to the wall and handed her a pick. Together they established a rhythm hacking away at the wall of the chamber. Sooner than she expected, they'd made a hole big enough to crawl through. She peered inside into the darkness trying to see.

'It's no good, Bríd. We need a flashlight.' He handed her the keys. 'Here, go inside the lab and get the flashlight there on the table right by the door. I'll stay here and clear away more of this wall.'

Bríd climbed out of the chamber and made her way to the lab. She fumbled with the key as she tried to turn it in the lock only to realize that the door was open. Who'd left it unlocked? Mystified, she opened the door and found Bob standing in front of a rectangular box, hammer in hand. Beside him stood Miffy.

'Bríd!' said Bob. 'What are you doing back so soon?'

Bríd flushed. 'We decided not to spend the night there in the end. We wanted to get back and help.' She looked around the room, taking in the crates and boxes that surrounded Miffy and Bob, their packaging spilling out onto the tables that supported them. Her heart sank. Would she get a chance to look inside the chamber if they were here in the lab and nearly finished the packing? 'You're working late,' Bríd said. 'Or is it working early?'

Bob looked a little flustered and Miffy shifted uncomfortably. 'That's right. We've been at it all night to try and wrap this up in time.' He pointed to the boxes. 'Most of the artefacts are packed.'

'Oh,' said Bríd. Bob seemed anxious, almost nervous. 'How's Scott?'

'Scott?' asked Bob in a bewildered tone. 'Oh. Right. Scott's doing okay. A little better. I just checked on him. He's sleeping at the moment.'

Bríd eyed the rectangular box. 'Where's the mummy? The chamber is still empty and I don't see him here.'

Bob rested his hand on the box. It was about six foot long and thee foot across and so much like a coffin she didn't need his answer.

'I decided to put the mummy in the box before we interred it,' Bob said in an even tone. 'It's the least we could do to protect it.'

The door opened and John entered. He looked around the room. 'What's going on?'

'Bob says he and Miffy have been working all night packing up the artefacts,' said Bríd. 'They've also made a coffin for the mummy before they re-inter him in the chamber.'

'A coffin?' John's eyes narrowed as he moved over to the box, running his fingers along its edge. 'Why would you do that, Bob? Why would you make a box that looks more like a shipping crate than a coffin to re-inter the mummy? Just what are you up to?'

'You can see this situation has become impossible, here,' said Bob in a reasoning tone. 'It will be ages before they let us back in here to do any more digging. What are we supposed to do in the mean time? How do we keep the academic hounds from our door? They won't care that the Chinese are being unreasonable. So what can we do? It's too late to try another discipline, especially if we're tainted.' He held up his hands. 'There's no money or glory in just teaching, John. You know that.' Bob gave a cajoling smile. 'There are other ways to win money, if not glory. Private ways.'

'You mean a private sale?' asked John.

'Exactly,' said Bob. 'A sale to a private collector, an individual with great means and discretion. And no one ever need know. The authorities here will think the mummy is back in the ground and we'll have made a tidy sum. It's perfect, John, perfect.'

'You're crazy,' said John. 'It'll never work.'

'Of course it will,' said Bob. 'How would anyone know?'

'Chang and Lu will know for a start.' John pointed to the box. 'How are you going to slip that box past them?'

'Chang left yesterday, when they delivered the digger. The digger, John. The digger is for us to bulldoze the chamber, John. They want nothing remaining. They don't care about the mummy except that it should be wiped out of existence.'

'What about Lu, though?'

'Lu is fast asleep.' Bob smiled in satisfaction. 'I made sure of that. I drugged his coffee last night. A hefty dose. By the time he wakes up the chamber will be filled in, the mummy collected and no one will be the wiser.'

'Someone's coming to collect the mummy?'

'It's all arranged,' said Bob. 'They're coming in an hour, with a truck. They'll transfer it to a warehouse where they make freezers and it will be whisked off inside one.' He grinned. 'Quite clever, isn't it?'

'It's crazy, not clever,' said John. 'What are you thinking? You'll never get away with it.'

'Think of the money,' said Bob. 'It's a lot of money. I'd split it with you.' He glanced over at Bríd. 'And her, too.'

'Money,' said John, his anger building. 'Money and fame. That's the bottom line with you, isn't it? It's not about the scholarship, the mutual support of colleagues. Just comes down to money and fame.' He looked at Miffy. 'That's what impresses the ladies though, isn't it? And you can't resist. Always pawing them, pressuring them to go to bed with you so you can flaunt your latest young thing in front of the others. It's disgusting. And now you've gone too far.' John shook his head. 'Sorry. I won't be a party to your little plan.'

'Nor me,' said Bríd. She'd listened in horror to Bob's idea and presumption that it would be easily accomplished. It seemed no better than scattering Mog's remains across the desert. At least he would be part of the earth and sky and near to his last home, instead of in some private climate-controlled viewing chamber preserved as a rare object to be displayed for a privileged few, without a care to any sacredness. She didn't know what she would have done if John had accepted Bob's offer.

Bríd gasped as Bob reached into his pocket and pulled out a gun. 'You've made your choice then,' said Bob. 'Pity. I really would have rather had you on my side.'

'Bob!' Miffy stepped away from him. 'Are you nuts? What are you going to do with that gun?'

'Shut up, Miffy, and just do as I say.' He picked up some rope from a packing case and threw it over to her. 'Tie their hands.'

Miffy stared at him for a few seconds before she picked up the rope. She went over first to Bríd and then John and tied their wrists behind them. When she'd finished, Bob pointed to the cloths on the table. 'Now gag them.' Miffy did as she was told, her eyes frightened and lips trembling.

With that task completed, Bob opened the door and shoved John and Bríd towards it. 'Now move. Both of you.' He motioned to Miffy. 'Stay here with the artefacts until I come and get you.'

Bríd followed John out of the lab. Bob shoved them along towards the chamber opening, stopping beside the ladder.

'Climb down, both of you,' he said.

Bríd did as she was told, trying to still her shaking legs and maintain her balance as she climbed slowly down the ladder, one rung at a time, leaning forward towards the ladder, her hands tied behind her. When she reached the ground she looked up and watched John's careful descent. Seconds after taking his place by her side Bob, pulled up the ladder.

'I'm sorry, John,' he said. 'I don't want to do this, but you leave me no choice. You and Bríd will just have to have "an accident." The chamber will collapse while you re-inter the mummy. I'll be very upset. Especially in the light of the way the Chinese treated you. Who knows? If I threaten to complain loud enough, they might be willing to strike a deal about further research?' Bob gave a hearty laugh. 'Now that would be the perfect irony, wouldn't it, John?'

John stared up at Bob and shook his head. Bríd huddled against the wall, the fear growing. Bob's face disappeared from the opening's edge and she could hear his retreating footsteps. John came over to her and told her to turn around so her back faced his. She could feel his fingers working on her knots. The knots were large, clumsily tied, and soon she could feel them loosening. With a final tug, her hands were free and she turned to work on John's, pulling fiercely on the rope. Seconds later he, too, was free.

He tore off his gag. 'Quick,' he said. 'Get inside the other chamber, while I try and scale this wall.'

Bríd looked dubiously at the bricked wall. There were very few places a foot could pitch. 'Do you think you can?'

'I have to try. There's no other way. I have to get to Bob before he starts filling in the chamber.'

In the distance she could hear a heavy engine start up. Already!

'Quick now!' said John. 'Into the chamber, we haven't much time.'

Without another word she scrambled through the hole to the other side as the menacing sound of the engine drew nearer. Its tone changed to a higher pitch. She imagined the bucket lifting and scooping up earth. Had John managed to reach the edge yet? Would he get there in time? She felt helpless, trapped. What if he failed? She'd be in here, by herself. She strained to see in the darkness around her. How long could she last in this chamber, with no water, food and what's more, very little air?

The sound of falling earth and a billow of dust broke into her thoughts. John. Where was he? She screamed his name. More earth and dust greeted her cries. She moved back towards the opening, clawing through the rubble and dirt that now reached the lip of the opening. The light from above revealed a hand. 'John!' she cried. She pulled at the hand, tugging it closer to her. She crawled through the hole and madly started clawing the dirt away until she uncovered his arm and then the rest of him, working against the time until the next load of dirt was dumped. She reached his head and brushed away the dirt. She leaned close and felt a faint hint of breath on her cheek. Sobs wracked her body, hindering her progress, but still she worked, clearing away the debris until she could pull him through the hole into Tlachtga's chamber.

Once on the other side, she cradled his head in her lap and called his name, the tears running down her face. 'John, oh please. Please. Don't leave me.' Her breathing was labored, the stress and emotion of the last few minutes overwhelming her. She brushed the remaining dirt from his face and bent down to kiss him as another burst of dust came in on them. John began to cough. His eyes fluttered and then opened.

'Oh Jesus, thank heaven you're all right,' said Bríd.

'I'm still here,' said John, his voice raspy. Slowly, amid Bríd's protests, he got up. She could make out his figure in the weak light that still filtered in through the hole. How much time they had before another load of dirt obliterated all the light was anyone's guess.

'Are you hurt?' asked Bríd. She stood up beside him and touched his arm.

He rubbed his head gently. 'No, I don't think so,' he said. 'The force of the earth knocked me off the wall and I hit my head. It put me out for a while, that's all.'

'Any dizziness, nausea?' Bríd tried to remember what she could about concussion.

'No, no. I'm okay,' he said. 'That's the least of our worries. We need to find a way to get out of here. Maybe there's something in this chamber that can help.' He looked through his pockets and finally pulled out the matches he'd picked up at the hotel. He struck one, its initial flare throwing distorted shadows against the wall. Holding it high, he moved towards the center of the small chamber, towards the figure lying on her platform. Bríd came up beside him, all thought of their purpose vanished in the awe of what lay before her.

She was beautiful, her hair still spread out like rays of the sun, the flowers weaving their way among the curling locks and the harp in her arms. Next to her was the child, still newborn in size, its tilted eyes and high cheekbones clearly evident.

Bríd grabbed John's arm. 'My God,' she said. 'It's Tlachtga.'

A large boom sounded as the wall began to collapse and mud bricks tumbled around them. Bríd tried to move away from the falling debris, but then darkness engulfed her.

CHAPTER TWENTY-ONE

Bríd opened her eyes and blinked against the lights above her. In the distance she could hear footsteps. She looked around her. She was lying in a bed in a drably painted room that contained only a small wooden chest beside her metal-framed bed. Hospital? She lifted her head and a wave of nausea overtook her, so she leaned back against her pillows again. No sense in tempting fate and trying to get up to summon someone. She moved her limbs. At least she could detect nothing was broken and there were no IV drips attached to her arms.

She closed her eyes and tried to push away the thoughts that crowded her mind. Was John all right? What had happened with Bob and Miffy? Had they gotten away? She could still taste the fear and the pain from from a tumbling brick that reminded her how close she'd come to death when she took refuge in Tlachtga's chamber.

Bríd's eyes misted at the thought of Tlachtga. She wished she could have spent more time with her, and the baby, too. She looked so beautiful there, holding her harp, the flowers dressing her red hair, her clothes so lovingly arranged. Yaloa's presence was so evident in all that care for detail. She'd wanted answers when she so foolheartedly pressed John to drive back early and look for that chamber. What if she hadn't insisted they go back early? Bob would have spirited away the mummy before they'd have arrived and no one the wiser. He'd have returned to the university and taken up his teaching. That couldn't be the case now, if she was still alive and able to explain the situation. And John, if he was alive. She fought back tears. He was of course, he was. She took some deep breaths, calmed herself and hummed a tune in her head.

'BRÍD?' a voice whispered.

She opened her eyes and with some effort focused on the face before her. Scott. 'Hello,' she said.

'You don't know how relieved I am to see you,' he said.

She smiled and looked beyond him. He was alone.

'Where's John?' she asked. 'Is he all right?'

He shifted his eyes. 'John's fine. He only had some bruising, nothing much. He stopped in to see you earlier, but you were still unconscious.'

'Where is he now?'

'He had to go back to the site with the government officials. He told me to stay here with you.'

She digested this piece of news and fought the disappointment that rushed in. 'What about the others? What about Miffy and Bob?'

'They're both in custody at the moment. Miffy's family is flying over. I'm sure they'll pull a few strings. Since she roused me in time to stop Bob from filling in the chamber, instead of going along with Bob's plan, they may go easy on her. I don't think there are any strings that can be pulled for Bob.' He frowned. 'It will be prision for him, no doubt about that.'

'He deserves it. He tried to kill us.'

Scott nodded. 'I know, the bastard. I'm sorry about that.'

'It's not your fault.'

'If only I hadn't taken that stuff Bob gave me, I could have stopped it all.'

'He planned it, Scott. Of course he made sure you took that so-called medicine. And Jin Lu. He was just as much of a bastard, pretending to be on our side, one of us. He got John and I arrested, you know.'

'I know. John filled me in. Jin worked for the authorities in a special unit, it seemed. He was made a part of the team to keep a closer eye on us than the other officials.'

'What about the mummy, though?' She was careful to make it singular.

He shook his head frowning. 'I don't know. The authorities have taken it into custody. Hopefully it will end up at the museum here in Ürümchi and not bulldozed back in its grave.'

'And all the artifacts as well.'

'I think there's a better chance they would be preserved in the museum. There's nothing specifically Caucasian about them.'

She nodded and closed her eyes against the tears that suddenly welled.

Scott leaned over and patted her hand. 'I've tired you. I'll go now, but I promise I'll come again as soon as I can.'

When he left a tear trickled down her face. It was the thought of Mog lying in the museum with everyone crowded around him. Mog separated from Tlachtga. Perhaps it would be better if he was put back in his burial chamber.

But where did that leave her? Or John, for that matter? The answers she'd sought in the chamber, were they still important? What she'd found was not what she'd expected. There was no disc around Tlachtga's neck, no connection to her remote Irish descendants. What she found was a red-headed woman with a mixed race child. A woman so dearly loved Bríd had been almost able to touch its strength in the chamber. It was a love that transcended the many centuries that had passed between Tlachtga's life and her own. A love that filled her with awe and made her glad that it would not be disassembled, documented and analyzed for the world. The chamber was gone now, in any case. Crushed under the collapsing wall when they dug out her and John.

'Miss O'Leary.'

She turned her head and saw an Asian nurse at the door. 'These men are here to see you.'

Bríd looked beyond the nurse to the two uniformed men she indicated. She didn't recognize them, but it was obvious they were police. The authorities hadn't wasted any time. The nurse entered and came to her bedside.

'If you're up to it, they would like to ask you a few questions.'

The men came up beside her. 'It would be best if you could answer them now.'

Best for whom, she wondered. She nodded.

The questions came at her in a precise manner, one after the other. Why had she returned to the dig so quickly after her release? What had she seen when she arrived? What happened between her and Dr Kirby? What was John's part in all of this? On and on they went and she repeated the facts over and over. It was clear to her that they felt John was implicated in some way. But she stuck to her assertions and explained everything in detail, so that eventually they seem convinced.

'That will do for now,' one of them said, shutting his notebook. 'We may have to come back again, though. Tomorrow. The doctor says you will be released tomorrow, if there are no further complications. And then you will go home.'

'Home tomorrow?' It seemed so quick on the one hand. But

she was anxious to go home, away from this place. Away from China.

'You will be escorted to the airport.'

'But what about my things?'

'We've asked one of your colleagues to bring them here for you.'

'Dr Sheldon?'

'I am afraid that is not possible. Dr Sheldon is needed for our inquiries at the moment.'

Bríd closed her eyes, trying to fight the frustration and disappointment. Would she be able to speak to John at all before she left? It didn't seem like it. She would have to wait until she got home. Home. Home to Ireland, to *Gort na Carrig*. She couldn't imagine going to Philadelphia just yet. She wanted to think and there seemed no better place than the farm.

SHE KNELT DOWN by the well and scooped up some water in her hand, intoning a little prayer that came to her. She sipped the water, then crossed herself. How many times had she come here with her grandmother? But this time, this time it seemed more than just a special visit with Gran, walking with her as she did the rounds then coming to pray at the well for an ailing friend or relative.

Now she was the one who was ailing. What was she to do? Where were all her plans now? Her dissertation, her hopes for a teaching position in Ireland and pursuing her music. Where were they? How much did she want that, now? She had no huge ambitions, that much she knew. The music would always be part of her life, but how much, and where? And how did John factor in her life? Did he blame her for nearly getting them killed?

She'd tried to call the satellite phone from the airport, but had no reply. When she'd first arrived home just a few days ago, she'd tried to phone the department at the university, but they said he wasn't there and they didn't know when to expect him back.

A moment later, as if summoned, a text came through to her phone. She opened the text and read it. *I'm sorry I've been out of touch. We need to talk. I'll explain everything then. John.*

She stared at the message, trying to read the answers to all her questions in the few words that were there. What did it all mean? There was nothing in the message that gave her any idea what was going through John's mind. In frustration she picked up the phone and typed in a reply. *Yes.We have to talk, soon. Phone me. Bríd.*

She watched the message go and sent with it all the urgency she could muster. She hated the thought that her life hung in the balance. In fact, why should it? She took a deep breath and stared back at the water, trying to reclaim the calm she'd felt earlier. For a long while she watched the ripples stirred up by the slight breeze that played around her and wobbled the image that stared back. She gasped. For a moment, just a brief moment, it was as though she was looking at Tlachtga. Perhaps it was the poor light, or the water's movement in the well, but there was something there, something in the eyes or the mouth that seemed more than her own image.

It was then it came to her. All the pieces of the story that she knew of Tlachtga. Of Mog. It was an Irish story, she was sure of it. Hadn't she known it deep inside her? But this time she could prove it. At least to herself.

After finally locating the book, she pulled it off the shelf, took it over to a table and sat down. The university library was fairly quiet this time of the day in the middle of the summer.

There were just some remote sounds of construction outside and a few lowered voices of students talking at the next table.

It took her a while, but she finally found it. Though she had expected it to be here, the passage still caused her to gasp out loud when she read it. Mog Roith was one of Cormac's druids involved in the final battle against Munster. Mog, who was a powerful druid, lost an eye in the Alps and the other while stopping the course of the sun for two days. He could also fly through the air like a bird to oversee his enemy's deeds. Exactly like a shaman, thought Bríd with a shaky laugh.

Bríd read on. Mog had a son Buan and a daughter Tlachgta. Tlachtga, with Mog's help, made the rolling wheel for Trian, created the Stone in Forcathu and the Pillar Stone in Cnamchaill. It apparently killed all who touched it, blinded all who saw it and deafened those who heard it.

She read on about Tlachgta. She was a dark goddess who was a touchstone of wisdom and could kindle fire from apparent deadness. She bore three sons: Dorib, Cumma and Muach (the name of three regions in Ireland) and died giving birth to the last one.

Bríd sat in stunned silence. Though she was vaguely familiar with bits of the legend, when she read it now and connected it to the events and people she'd become linked with in China, it took on a whole different perspective. Stripped of archetypes and legendary status they became richer, but no less awesome in her mind.

Bríd turned the page, looking to read on. But instead of text she saw an image. An image of three interlocking circles. Bríd didn't need to read the caption. She knew whose symbol it was. Her wrists itched. She stared at the image, her mind not really ready to accept it. Not just yet.

· · ·

IT WAS ONLY LATER, in the quiet of the farm, that she sat outside in the early evening light and pulled out the photocopy of the book's image. Slowly she removed the medallion from around her neck and turned it over. There, in the fading sunlight, she could just about make out the faint etching, once so very deep, of three interlocking circles. She knew now why there was no disc around Tlachtga's neck in the chamber. Because it was in her hand now. Passed down in her family somehow. Her family stretched all the way back through time to Tlachtga. Tlachtga was part of her. It hardly seemed possible, but deep in her heart she'd been certain all along. Just as she was certain that John was connected to Yaloa. Would that matter to him, now? Bríd sighed. No, it was probably too late for that.

THE PUB SEEMED crowded for a weekday until Bríd remembered she'd seen the big coach at the back. The room wasn't that large, with the fireplace opposite the door, away from the bar. Old photos of the village and music events long past lined the walls, making little space for the dart board on the other side of the room. The newly tiled floors made for easy cleaning, as did the decor, but the character lost from the old wood tables and slate Bríd still lamented.

As Bríd entered she recognized many local faces, though. They smiled and nodded to her as she passed them on the way to the bar, exchanging a word or two as though it'd only been a few days since she'd last been in. Áine, the landlady, came over to her to serve. Áine had a word for everyone, her heart as generous as her bosom, though she'd never miss a trick.

'Bríd. How are you? Any news?' she asked in Irish. 'Besides your hair?' She grinned and started to pull a glass for Bríd. 'You've not put your head in the door what a good while.'

'Nothing strange,' she answered, her own Irish automatic. 'I've finished early out in China, that's all.'

'Was it China you were headed? I'd heard something of the sort. On a dig? And how was it?'

'Just another hole in the ground in the end,' said Bríd.

'Speaking of holes, there's been quite a hole here without yourself playing in the session. But there's one starting up now. Have you brought your fiddle?'

Bríd shook her head. 'It's back home.'

'Ah well, never mind. The boys are over in the corner and they'd be glad to have you, anyway. Jimmy's got his whistles there with his concertina, I'm sure you could borrow one. And Sean's just come in with his fiddle. I think there's a flute player and a couple of box players coming later on, so.'

Bríd smiled at this easy welcome, took her pint and made her way to 'the boys.' Well into their sixties and accomplished musicians in their own right, 'the boys,' were the local farmers and mechanics. Through many decades the pair had been coming to this pub every week for music sessions. They were often joined by other musicians, self-taught or otherwise, who came to exchange tunes, have fun and enjoy some good *craic*. Bríd had known Jimmy and Sean since she could remember.

She sat down, glad she could just enjoy the music. Glad also they wouldn't ask her about her dissertation, her academic plans, her experiences in China.

After a few greetings and a passing remark on her hair, Jimmy passed her a whistle. 'Any new tunes?' he asked

His shock of white hair hung in its usually unruly manner into his twinkling blue eyes. Tobacco stained his white mustache a yellowish hue. He smiled at her, revealing his gold tooth, the only straight one among the others that pushed for space. Sean, balding and wearing dark-rimmed glasses, with his reed-thin frame, was the Jack Sprat of the pair. He sat opposite Jimmy.

Bríd took the whistle and smiled. 'Do you have this one?' she asked them both.

She started off on a lively jig, *Last Tango in Paris,* that she'd learned the year before from a fiddler in Philadelphia, who'd had it from someone in New York. After the first round they joined her, Sean on his fiddle and then Jimmy on the concertina. It was a quirky tune that suited the light lyrical qualities of the whistle. Her breath filled the slender metal pipe and flowed out the holes, an endless action in a tune this fast. The long expenditure of air left her body in unconscious repetition, her fingers fluttering over the holes, dancing their own dance. Each action was its own meditation, its own creation of wonder that formed an audible beauty. All these things—the sight, the feel and the sound of created music—were magic for her. This was what mattered.

Bríd became aware of the room, the chatter of voices and clanking of glasses now replaced by tapping feet, clapping hands and a few whoops and hollers. The three of them, in their own silent communication (a wink and slight nod), blasted off into a local jig that seemed to naturally follow the new tune. They finished the piece with a flourish, amid shouts and claps of appreciation. After a few minutes, Sean launched into a Seamus Ennis tune, a favorite reel that always kept Bríd on her toes, but she loved just the same. Toward the end of it, flushed and laughing, she paused and Sean took over with his concertina slipping and sliding the notes in a jazzy style.

Sean leaned over to her. 'Meet Dizzy O'Gillespie,' he said.

Bríd laughed and elbowed Sean, a reprimand of no impact, but good fun. She hugged this feeling of simple joy closely around her. It felt good to laugh, free of thoughts and anxieties. Just pure fun.

Behind her, hands came forward and plunked a Guinness down in front of Jimmy and another beside her half-filled glass.

'I'll be back in minute with your Guinness there, Sean.'

Bríd froze when she heard that familiar voice. Smoky and rich, baritone highlights amid full bass voice, it caressed words, intoned them with soft silky textures. She stared at her glass, trying to still her racing heart. How the bloody hell did Ciarán know she was here? She looked over at Sean and Jimmy, who busily studied the heads of their pints. She sighed. Did it really matter? She supposed any one of the villagers could have spotted her car outside Gran's house, put two and two together, and phoned Ciarán. Áine's heart could stretch to this, too.

As Bríd glanced around she saw that Ciarán had placed his flute case by the empty chair next to hers. It was his usual place, left vacant, perhaps intentionally. Ciarán set his pint and Sean's down on the table, then eased his lanky frame on the chair with liquid grace, born of much practice.

'You boys keeping well, then?' Ciarán asked.

After nods and raised glasses for thanks, Sean and Jimmy drank deeply. Ciarán turned to Bríd as he picked up the flute case and opened it. 'Jesus, Bríd, the hair. Did you have a spell at a convent?' He removed the flute halves, placed the case under his chair.

She didn't bother answering him and watched him assemble the flute, blow across the mouth piece and adjust the tuning in a soft, sensuous motion that Bríd used to think revealed a sensitive heart. His touch was deft and sure, running his fingers along the holes, or his hands across the cleft in her shoulder. She met his eyes.

'I'm keeping well,' she said. 'And yourself?'

'Oh, grand, I'd say. I've had a few gigs in Dublin. Amazing, they were.' He gave her a crooked smile. 'It's not like playing with you, though. That was special.'

A silent groan filled her. What did he think he was playing at, trying on his crooked smile, soft-eyed look with her, like she was some ingénue girl.

'Well now, a shame it is, but I'm certain you'll find another just as special,' she said. 'Were there problems with Siobhán?'

Ciarán concentrated on tuning his flute a moment, sounding a note and then twisting the two halves slightly before putting it up to his mouth to sound another note. He turned back to her with a wide smile.

'Ah, yes, well now,' he finally answered. 'Once the recording deal fell through she seemed to find herself caught up with another musician. A box player.' He grinned at the others. 'Shall we have a tune, then?'

Ciarán put his flute to his chin and jumped into a lively reel, *Dogs Among the Bushes.* Sean and Jimmy struggled to keep neutral faces as they put down their pints and joined in. Bríd rolled her eyes and followed suit. After a few moments, she lost herself in the music, threading through tunes. When they'd finished, Sean and Jimmy could still barely contain good humored smirks despite their efforts to hide them behind their pint glasses. Bríd found she could gloat openly while Ciarán studiously avoided any glances.

'Give us a song, Bríd!'

She smiled at the request, thought a moment, then decided to sing a quirky tune. No laments. No man gone to war, sea or seed, leaving his woman. No woman leaving, for money or death. She would sing *Táimse 'gus Máire,* a local song of a married couple.

'Well done, Bríd,' shouted Áine, from over at the bar. Her voice, bar seasoned and forceful, rang out clearly. 'Now how about singing one of my favorites for me, *Taimse 'im Choladh*?'

Bríd's eyes prickled sharply. She was surprised at the intensity of her reaction. A deep, dark longing, dizzying in its strength, surged up inside her, taking her unaware. The song was a vision poem, describing a man asleep and asking not to be disturbed because he's having a dream of a beautiful woman. The woman is Ireland. Slow and evocative, it was a tune sometimes played at funerals. And now, the thought of the words, and its many meanings and settings was almost too much for her. Gran, Mog, Tlachtga and John came to her mind. With a great effort, she pushed aside her thoughts and let the music fill her head.

She closed her eyes and began the song, her notes fine and long. Phrases fell from her lips, the pain and separation, isolation and desertion. These phrases, deep and resonant at the back of her throat, pulled longer, richer tones from her. The words rested inside her, stored in her heart, while a hand touched hers lightly. She opened her eyes. A silence, hushed and still, was suddenly broken by the first clap and a loud whistle.

She searched the crowd for the familiar face, the music still echoing in her head. That he could reach her here, now, took her breath away. Suddenly, the room felt airless and overheated with the press of too many bodies.

Bríd took several deep breaths, rose and walked over to the bar on the excuse she wanted to get a glass of water and some nuts. If she ate something, she reasoned, she wouldn't have to sing or talk much for little while and she might even be able to escape out the door for some air. She reached the bar, her journey broken many times for handshakes, pats, and a few words here and there. It was a journey made with motions and words that seemed to come from somewhere else and not her own body or mind. Áine took her order and returned with it quickly.

'*Bhí se go halainn*, Bríd,' she said. 'I don't think I ever heard it sung so well.'

Bríd smiled. 'I'm glad you thought so.' Áine's attention had already moved to the next customer. Relieved, Bríd edged away from the bar towards the door and slipped out.

Once outside, Bríd inhaled deeply and savored the relative quiet, only slightly disturbed by the muffled sounds of music and conversation that leaked out of the pub. It was a clear night, filled with shimmering stars and a half moon that cast shadows all around her. She took a sip of her water, put it down on the ground and opened her nuts. She munched thoughtfully, the salty spicy taste surprising her mouth, causing her to smile. She'd forgotten how good they tasted.

She looked around. At the end of the building two teenagers leaned against the wall. The boy had his back to Bríd. Bríd found herself drawn into watching them, the language of their bodies speaking awkward volumes. The girl tilted her head and pushed her hips forward, away from the wall in an unconscious gesture. The boy raked his hair with his hand and shifted his posture to a hand on the wall—a pose that could seem more aloof, but could also move his arm closer to her shoulder. Their murmured conversation rose and fell in an intimate cadence. A timeless ritual that could challenge the idea of self.

It seemed to her that her idea of herself had changed dramatically in the past month. She had left Ireland thinking that all the ties and connections that mattered in her life had been severed, gone forever. Now she realized that she'd had ties that stretched back generations, thousands of years, and they still held firm, supporting her, shaping her. And her ties with Gran had never broken, those connections were still there. She touched the medallion that rested on her chest. This was who she was. No matter what happened or what path she chose in life, she, Bríd, was the descendant of Tlachtga. Somehow, somewhere, whether through Buan or through Muach, she was here now.

She realized that before she had felt locked up, stuck in a box that had become small. Too small. She suddenly remembered the tale of Raven releasing the sun, moon and stars, bringing light into the world. Only Raven, through his transformation, was able to perform such magic, such a bold, creative act.

'Ah, the sweetness of young love.'

Startled by Ciarán's voice, she knocked the glass by her feet and it spilled over, the liquid running in rivulets to her feet. She reached down quickly, a muffled curse on her breath, and managed to salvage some of her drink. Standing back up, she took a sip.

'I didn't hear you come out,' said Bríd. 'You gave me a fright.' She looked over at Ciarán. His dark curly hair hung in its usual disarray, his clothes a mirror of it. It all combined to suggest a charming innocence. The shirt, only half-tucked, invited total forgiveness, as did the dark-lashed eyes, flashing humor and the hint of a plea.

Ciarán, dropped a casual hand to her shoulder. 'Sorry,' he said. 'I wanted to make sure you hadn't gone home yet. I was hoping I could get you to come in and play some more tunes with us. Sure, the evening's just begun.'

'I'll be in for a little more. I was just getting some air.' She leaned back against the wall.

'Reliving some of our youth, too?' Ciarán nodded to the couple. 'Remember when we used to stand in that very spot? It must be the karmic energy there or something.'

Bríd snorted. 'Ah, well Ciarán, it was some kind of energy, but probably not karmic.' She sighed, giving into the loss of solitude. 'Right so, I guess I'll go in and find the karmic energy in the corner with Jimmy and Sean.' She turned to enter the pub.

Ciarán followed her inside. 'Now here I was, thinking that was another place you and I found karmic energy.'

The two of them resumed their seats in the corner. Bríd saw that their numbers had increased by a mighty guitar player and uillean pipes player that lifted the energy and drive to and called her more strongly to play. She picked up her whistle, already feeling the pulse of the music and anxious to express it in the notes. The set pushed her forward and she tried to capture the wave that swept them all along. More tunes rolled past, glasses emptied and laughter and jokes filled the air. Her mood improved, and by the time last orders arrived she felt more at peace.

The night came to a close, and the pub crowd thinned. Jimmy started packing up his concertina and the others followed suit. Ciarán reluctantly reached for his flute case and Bríd handed the whistle over to Jimmy and started to rise.

Ciarán cleared his throat. 'Er, hold on a minute there, Bríd. I'll walk out with you.'

In a generous mood, Bríd smiled an assent and took her seat again. Ciarán finished packing up his flute, all crooked smiles and praise for the evening, and the two waved their farewells and followed other people exiting the pub.

They walked along to the car in idle conversation. Then something twigged in Bríd's mind, like a sudden itch. Ciarán's parent's home was in Ballybeg and she could see no car. 'Where are you staying?'

'Well, that's the thing,' answered Ciarán. 'I hadn't made any definite plans, this being a spur of the moment visit kind of thing. Em, well, you see, I was hoping I could stay at your gran's place, that is, I hope you wouldn't mind and, kind of like, let me have a space on the sofa or the floor. Well, whatever you think.'

His voice trailed off as she stared at him without speaking. Laughter, overwhelming and irresistible, bubbled up inside of her and spilled out.

'Oh Ciarán, if you could hear yourself, so pathetic and

uncertain, at a loss for words. Don't think I don't know what you considered your options might be.' She laughed again when she saw the guilt cross his face. 'All right,' she said after a moment. 'A place on the sofa, and no more.'

Ciarán grinned at her uncertainly. 'I'm happy to beg on my knees. Or would some groveling at your feet suit you better, for the sake of a place to rest me head for the night?'

'I have to say, groveling has its appeal. Come on then, you pathetic puppy,' said Bríd. 'You'd best behave yourself, though, or you'll be resting your head in the road.'

Bríd led him to her car and they made the short journey to the house. Once inside, Ciarán placed his flute case on the floor by a chair. 'Any chance of a cup of tea before we turn in for the night?' he asked.

'You like to push your luck, don't you?' said Bríd.

'I've been known to be very lucky.'

His cheekiness, irritating enough to make her refuse, she ignored only because she fancied a cup of tea herself. 'I'll make some tea, but don't count yourself lucky tonight,' she told him.

Ciarán raised his eyebrows and smiled. His eyes twinkled at her as he shook his head. 'You're a gas man, *cailín*.'

Thinking it was more accurately the reverse, Bríd went into the kitchen and started to fill the kettle with water. Ciarán followed her and leaned against the sink, while she rinsed the teapot and got the other tea things ready. She moved away, over to the cooker and lit the burner. The kitchen, a room of morning sun and quiet chats, was a small addition to the original large kitchen with the fireplace and crane. It allowed only a small table and two chairs across from the cooker and sink. The little fridge took up the corner opposite the doorway that gave space for a piece of carpet on the worn lino. Despite the well-used look, it was clean and tidy, just as Gran always kept it.

'I'm sorry about your gran,' Ciarán said, as if picking up her thoughts. 'She was a fine lady. I know you miss her very much. You can still feel her here in the house.'

Bríd reached up in the cupboard above the sink for two cups and placed them on the table. 'I do miss her,' she said. 'There's so much about her I only now realize was important to me. Her constant advice, strategically placed in pithy proverbs and sayings. And I miss her stories and tales. Especially those about my family. I miss her absolute belief in me and my abilities. I even miss the banter over little things with the shopkeepers in the town.

'"Now Mr Lynch," mimicked Bríd. "From the state of your shoes, I can see why you would mistake this bit of shoe leather for a grilling chop. Let me see your stewing meat then, since even shoe leather can be made tender in soup."

'God, didn't she embarrass me more times than I can count with that tongue,' said Bríd. 'It was a ritual, an exchange they both enjoyed. I can see that now.'

Bríd sighed. Why was it the distance of death brought a perspective, a clarity that gave more patience, more understanding? Perhaps it was the passage of time, uncluttered by new interactions, new memories. The kettle boiled. She poured the water in the teapot and sat down in one of the chairs. Ciarán took the other.

'Ciarán, do you believe people can come back, say, as other people?' she asked. She didn't know why she had mentioned it to Ciarán, except that at this moment she felt the need to hear someone else's perspective.

'You mean reincarnation?' he said.

'No, yes, well, something like that," she said. "More of a soul continuing on, leaving one body and moving on to another after death, not necessarily right away.'

Ciarán searched her face, trying to read it. 'Don't know, really,' he said. 'I mean, I guess I haven't actually thought about it.

When I was young, raised with all that mumbo jumbo about hell, heaven, and purgatory I guess I thought about what that's like, where I might go.'

He frowned and fiddled with his cup, now filled with tea. 'They taught me about it in school with such certainty, and then later I rejected it with just as much certainty. Now, I don't know. I don't really think about it.' He paused a moment, his face cleared and he regained his smile. 'Why, do you think your gran will come back? Maybe as a butcher?'

Bríd laughed, the thought irresistibly funny. 'Now, there's a bit of poetry in that,' she said. 'I don't know what she would choose herself. I'm not sure there is a choice.'

'So you believe it happens,' Ciarán said. His joking grin had vanished and mild surprise stamped his face.

Bríd looked down at her tea. 'Perhaps.' She was sorry now she had mentioned anything, but her thoughts drove her on. 'I think so. It's difficult to explain, but some of the things I have experienced lately have led me to believe its possibility.'

'What now, did the fairies tell you this when you were digging up all those old things?' Ciarán leaned forward, all broad humor and wide grin.

Bríd found herself bristling at his remarks. Was it the manner in which he always slighted her academic work, or was it that Gran always believed in the spirits or fairies of sorts and he was making light of it? Looking at his eyes, which shifted a little under her gaze, she suddenly realized it was his own discomfort that made him joke so. This was not Ciarán's territory. It was a place he didn't even venture, not with anything approaching seriousness.

'Maybe,' she answered and stood up. There was little use in pursuing this any further. It was time for bed. 'Now so, you've had your cup of tea," she said. 'I'm off to bed. You can have the little spare bedroom I used to have. Everything should be there.'

She put her cup in the sink. Ciarán looked at her in a puzzled manner and unfolded his lanky frame from the chair. He followed her up the stairs, the narrow and uneven steps creaking with both their weight. At the top, in the small confines of the landing, he took her hands.

'Look, Bríd,' he said. 'I apologize if I said anything wrong just now. I truly am sorry you lost your gran.' He looked deep into her eyes and placed one hand on her cheek. 'Ah, Bríd, I had it all wrong. I made such a mistake with you, and I've had trouble getting it right since. There, I've admitted it.'

Bríd looked up into his eyes and studied them. Their color, granite-grey and winter seas, contrasted strongly with the deep black she remembered John's to be. The eyes before her now held empty promises. She sighed, and Ciarán, hearing her sigh, took it as acceptance and leaned down to kiss her. He pressed his lips down on hers, the familiar smells of whisky, beer and smoke blended into the sweat of a long night's flute playing, surrounded her and entered her mouth through his. They were smothering her, those smells, these tastes, this touch that she used to revel and linger over when she removed her shirt, or picked up her jacket. She pulled her lips away.

'Ciarán, no. It's over.'

He held her firmly, resisted her efforts to break the embrace. 'Not even for old times' sake?'

'Ciarán!' Bríd shoved him firmly away, quickly entered the room and shut the door. 'Just count yourself lucky you have a bed here for the night,' she said.

She leaned against the door, Ciarán still standing on the other side. A moment passed. There was a light tap. She met it with silence and sighed heavily, her weight still pressed against the solid wood frame. She wasn't surprised at Ciarán. Not really. He always had a strong belief in himself, in his light sure touch with the flute, his clever turn of phrase and a smile that would pick your pocket.

She was surprised at herself. Her anger, hatred and spite had long gone. There was no longing for what might have been. She could even laugh. Bríd knew how rare it was that Ciarán's timing fell adrift. This evening must have derailed him completely. A lesson in a different kind of music. She hoped he'd learn it. Her own lessons seemed to be pushing in on her. Tonight, her own longing was directed at someone entirely different. A longing that once let in, filled her with such strength she wanted to cry.

Bríd switched on the lamp and moved over to Gran's mirror above the small dresser. Her image reflected back, speckled by the worn gilt at the mirror's edge and a faint orange-red stain that bled in from below. An old mirror. How much of it now reflected the parts she was only getting to know? She raised her fingers to her mouth. The taste of beer and whisky still lingered on her lips, but beneath it was the memory of other tastes, other lips. Other hands. Hands that she knew she wanted to feel again with the field-worn calluses and the dirt under the nails.

CHAPTER TWENTY-TWO

Bríd suppressed a yawn as she lit the burner under the kettle. She'd no idea of the time, but her stomach told her it was past time for breakfast. When she looked out the window into the yard on her way down the stairs, she'd seen that Padraig had already been to check on the cattle, his Land Rover just disappearing back down the road. He must have heard she was out late the night before and not wanted to disturb her. She sighed. She should probably get Padraig to sell the herd at the next mart. She hated to give up the last vestiges of the farm, but she had to face facts. She wasn't a farmer and she wasn't likely to marry one.

A knock sounded at the front door, causing Bríd to jump. Who would be knocking? And at the front door, not around the back to the door into the little kitchen? Puzzled, she made her way to the front and opened the door and stared.

'Bríd,' said John, his voice full of relief. He stood before her, a backpack on his back, dressed in rumpled jeans, shirt and hiking boots. His face was drawn and his eyes were tired. 'God, I had no idea it was this far from the bus stop. They said "just up the road and the first farm on the left." No answer on your phone, but, no problem, I thought. I'll just walk.' He looked at her. 'What?' he said, his voice beginning to falter. 'I hope this isn't a bad time. I was going to phone you after I got your message, but I thought it might be best to do this talking in person. I didn't really have much of a chance to let you know. I managed to get a flight right away and when I did try to let you know, I got no reply.' John's voice trailed off.

Bríd continued to stare, unable to believe that he was standing right before her. Her phone. God, she'd left it in the car, since there was no point in having it in the pub when there was no reception there. John cleared his throat.

'Oh, John, what am I thinking? Come inside.' She ushered him through the hall and the old kitchen to the little one at the back. 'Sit down. I'm just making a cup of tea and fixing some breakfast. You must be starving.'

John took a seat at the small table. 'I got something at the airport before I caught the bus. But that was hours ago. I must admit I'm hungry now.'

Bríd busied herself at the stove, trying to still the shaking in her hands. How could he speak so calmly, as though he popped into her house every day? When he stood at the door she hadn't known what to do, whether to hug him, kiss him or what her first impulse had been—to throw her arms around him. Then he seemed so distant, so remote, she could only stand there and do nothing in the end. Tears gathered in her eyes.

'How are you? Are you okay?' His voice was tentative. 'I haven't seen you since you were in the hospital.'

Bríd brushed her eyes. 'N-no. I'm fine now. I was a little shaken and apparently had a nasty bump. But nothing serious. I was lucky.'

'We were both lucky.'

'I thought I heard voices.'

Ciarán entered in bare feet, his shirt hanging out and his

dark hair tousled. He gave a yawn and stuck out his hand. 'Hello. I'm Ciarán. Are you one of the Yanks Bríd worked on the dig with?'

John's eyes darkened. He looked across at Bríd, then back at Ciarán. 'Yes. That's right. I'm John.' He gave Ciarán's hand a brief shake.

Ciarán settled himself in the chair opposite and gestured to Bríd as she placed the frying pan on the cooker. 'You wouldn't throw another egg in there for me, would you?' He turned to John. 'Bríd makes a terrific fried egg sandwich.'

'I'm sure she does,' said John.

Bríd winced. She was sure he was getting an entirely different picture of the situation then he should. 'Ciarán was at the music session at the pub last night and only stopped here because he couldn't get home last night.'

'You don't have to explain anything, Bríd,' John said in a subdued voice.

'Ciarán, why don't you go for a little walk around the yard a minute,' said Bríd. 'I'll call you when your sandwich is ready.'

Ciarán looked at John and then Bríd. With a careless nod, he grabbed a pair of wellies by the door and shoved them on his feet and left. Bríd watched his retreating figure for a few moments before turning to John.

'I shouldn't have come,' said John. 'I'm sorry. I didn't think. I just got on the plane as soon as I could without considering anything else.'

'No, no. It's not what you think.'

'But it's clear you and he...'

'That's past. Long past.'

'I don't think he wants it to be past.'

Bríd sighed. 'I don't care what he may or may not want. As far as I'm concerned, it's over. It's been over for months.'

John sat silently studying her and she tried to put the truth of the words she'd spoken into her face.

'Really?' he said finally.

'Really,' she answered in a firm voice.

'Because I know I've no right to expect anything. We never discussed how we felt. Or I never mentioned how I felt.'

'I thought you were upset with me.'

'What? Why would I be upset with you?'

'Because I insisted on looking for Tlachgta's chamber. If we hadn't driven back so soon, Bob would have handed over the mummy and filled in the chamber before we got there.' She looked down at her feet, trying to control the sudden emotion. 'Then there would probably be more left of your career to salvage.'

John stood up and went over to her, cupping her face in his hands. 'Bríd, I don't blame you. If anything, I blame myself for getting you into such a dangerous situation. I shouldn't have brought you to China. Now I've already managed to tarnish your career.'

She looked into his eyes and saw the concern. 'I'm not sorry I went to China,' she said softly.

'You're not?'

'Not at all.' She leaned up and kissed him, her lips meeting his, firm and tender, then deepening into something more. His arms slipped around her. 'Oh, John,' she said when they finally broke apart. 'When I didn't hear from you, I thought you'd decided you didn't want a relationship.'

He kissed her forehead. 'I'm sorry I didn't get in touch with you sooner. The police kept me busy until after you left and then when I was finished, you'd gone. I had to go back to the university and clear things up there for a day or so. I wanted to get away quickly so I could come and see you. I had to talk to my uncle, too.'

'You talked to Sam?' Bríd was surprised, yet glad that he had finally renewed contact with his uncle.

'I needed to. I had to tell him everything. Somehow I felt that he would help me understand things.'

'Things?'

'What we found in the chambers.' John's eyes darkened. 'Who we found in the chambers.'

'You mean Mog and Tlachtga.' Bríd rested her hand on his arm. 'I have something to show you.'

The kitchen door opened and Ciarán entered. 'Is the sandwich ready?'

John and Bríd pulled apart. 'Sorry now, Ciarán. It won't be long. She began busying herself at the cooker, deferring her revelations for later.

BY THE TIME she'd fed Ciarán and taken him to catch the bus back to his flat in Cork, nearly two hours had passed before she was able to sit down with John. She pushed the internet printouts and the photocopies from the books across the table to John. 'Look what I found. I knew there was something about their names that was familiar to me, so I looked them up at the university library.'

John studied the sheets in silence, the ticking clock the only sound in the kitchen. When he'd finished he looked up at her, amazement on his face. 'It's quite a strong link.' He shook his head. 'But it's hard to believe in some ways.'

Bríd nodded. 'I know. But there's more.' She pulled out the sheet with the symbol on it and reached up around her neck to remove the medallion from around her neck. She placed it on the table next to the sheet. John took the medallion and examined it carefully. He compared it to the symbol on the paper then looked up at her, a question in his eyes.

'It's hers,' said Bríd. 'Tlachtga's. I saw it around her neck in my dream.' She looked into John's eye. 'But she didn't have it in the chamber. That's when I knew really. That Gran's medallion actually belonged to Tlachtga.'

John narrowed his eyes, then looked down and studied the sheet again.

'You think I'm crazy,' said Bríd.

John looked up, surprised. 'No, no. My God, Bríd. I'm the last person who would say that to you. No, I'm just trying to fit it all together.'

She stretched out her wrist to show her tattoo. 'She's part of me,' said Bríd. 'I know it. Tlachtga and Mog are connected to me. And there's Yaloa, too. He's part of the connection.'

'How do you mean?'

Bríd took a deep breath. Would John believe her? 'He's part of you, John. I saw that.' Her voice softened. 'He looks so much like you.'

'Me?'

She nodded. 'You were right. Your clan did come from that area.'

John stared at her, trying to take in her words. Then he leaned his head back and laughed hard. 'Well thanks for that,' he said when his laughter subsided.

'I know you'll probably never be able to prove it, but I wanted you to know. So you could realize that your work wasn't all in vain.'

John smiled. 'No, I don't think that now. Sam helped me realize it. And I don't mind that no one will ever know. Apart from the clan.'

'You told your uncle about Yaloa?'

John nodded. 'I told him everything and he just accepted it. He just said "it was as it should be." That I'd made my journey to the *Sikakowanee,* the Land of the Dead, and come back with the answers I'd been seeking. The real answers.'

'The real answers?'

'That I am who I am. A Tlingit. A Tlingit of the wolf clan, Eagle moiety, whose home is in Alaska.'

Bríd's heart sank at his last words. Was that what he came to tell her in person? She sat back in her seat. 'I'm happy for you,' she said in a small voice.

John leaned over and took her hand. 'That's why I had to come and see you in person. To tell you about what I discovered.'

'What did you find?'

'I wanted to explain that I've decided to get a teaching post in Alaska. To work in the community, among the Tlingit.' His voice was excited as he told her his hopes and plans to promote the culture and the language among his people. His people.

'What do you think?' asked John when he'd finished.

She tried to be enthusiastic. 'I think it sounds wonderful.' She lowered her eyes so he wouldn't see the pain she felt.

'I know it's a far cry from Ireland and your family, but do you think you would consider going there with me? You'd probably have to make trips to the university and here while you complete your PhD, but do you think you could do that?'

Bríd stared at him, her mind racing. 'You're asking me to go with you to Alaska?'

John nodded. 'Bríd, I love you. I've been attracted to you since you first walked into the classroom, and I haven't stopped thinking about you since I left you in the hospital.'

Bríd blinked. Suddenly everything was clear. She knew now why she wanted to sell the herd, why she couldn't let the music go, wherever she might play it. She smiled widely. 'I'll come,' she said.

Read the sneak peek of *Along the Far Shores* at the end of this book, another book of the Celtic Knot Series. (there is no order to read them)

HISTORICAL NOTE

In 1987 Victor Mair, a professor of philology at the University of Pennsylvania, led a tour group through a museum in the Chinese city of Ürümchi in the central Asian province of Xinjiang. During the tour, he went into a newly opened room that showed, under glass, the recently discovered blond-haired mummies of a man, woman and child, with long noses and deep set eyes that were over 3,000 years old. The real shock was that they were Caucasian. Dr Mair was intrigued by the mummies' existence, 2,000 years before the West and East admitted each other's presence. These mummies were among some 100 dug up by Chinese archeologists over the course of 16 years. They came from the Tian Shan Mountains in northwest China and the fringes of the Taklimakan Desert.

Professor Mair attempted to investigate further, but met with some difficulties from the Chinese authorities at the time because of the political climate. Eventually, he led a small expedition to the Tarim Basin and the group found more mummies that were tall and blond, dressed in clothes that were still intact, even woolen plaids that were as brightly hued as the day they were woven.

Professor Mair and others have documented the discoveries from this research trip and some successive ones in books, film documentaries and published articles over the years (for example: *The Tarim Mummies* by Victor Mair and *The Urumchi Mummies* by Nancy Barber). I first discovered his work when reading a National Geographic article on the first expedition and was intrigued by the possibility of what could be a proto-Celtic group finding its way there.

Who were these people? As far back as the second century B.C., Chinese texts refer to alien people called the 'Yuezhi' and the 'Wusun' who lived on China's far western borders. The texts indicate the Chinese regarded them as troublesome 'barbarians.' Until recently, scholars have tended to downplay evidence of any early trade or contact between China and the West, regarding the development of Chinese civilization as an essentially home grown affair sealed off from outside. Yes some archeologists have begun to argue that these so-called 'barbarians' were responsible for introducing things like the wheel and the first metal objects. Professor Mair's own research leads him to believe that these people were Tocharian, an early Indo-European group about whose origins little is known.

I decided to imagine how such a group would come to be there and it led me to create what is mostly my own invention about the mummies and also the small band of proto–Native Alaskans that Yaloa's group represent. The accepted understanding for the Native Americans now is that they migrated from various areas in Asia, in waves; most by boats and others migrating across the Bering Strait at different time periods. I realize that my little group is very late to be leaving the Asian continent and I took a lot of artistic license with it. I hope that it doesn't hinder people's appreciation of the tale.

I would like to thank Professor Mair for his time and patience all those years ago when I first started writing the novel. I would also like to thank my editor, Jessica Knauss, and my writer's group, especially Jean, Jane, Babs, Claire and Karen, for their thoughtful comments and unending support.

AUTHOR'S NOTE

USA Today and Amazon bestselling author Kristin Gleeson is originally from Philadelphia but now lives in Ireland, in the West Cork Gaeltacht, where she writes, plays the harp and sings, in addition to painting the beautiful landscape around her.

She holds a Masters in Library Science and a Ph.D. in history, and for a time was an administrator of a large archives, library and museum in America. She has also worked as a public librarian in America and Ireland. She is a B.R.A.G. medallion Honoree

Kristin Gleeson has also published a commercial biography on a First Nations Canadian woman, *Anahareo, A Wilderness Spirit*, published with Fireship Press and available on other online outlets.

If you have enjoyed this book please post a review on Amazon. It helps so much in getting the book noticed. Also, go to the author website and join the mailing list to receive news of forthcoming releases, special offers and events.

www.kristingleeson.com

ALONG THE
FAR SHORES

KRISTIN GLEESON

An Tig Beag Press

Excerpt

PART I

KINGDOM OF GWYNEDD, WALES, 1169

1

———————

á brón orm. The words of mourning in her Irish tongue hung heavy on Aisling. They'd followed her as she travelled along the fields and through the woodlands on the broken nag with her servant and then across the sea to the kingdom of Gwynedd. They lingered now around the castle hall, mingled with the smoke from the fire and grew stronger, joining the sorrow of the passing of the Gwynedd king.

'Was it the plague that took your mother, our kinswoman?' Prince Hwyel, one of the dead king's sons, addressed her in Latin, for she knew little Welsh.

She could hear the sharp intake of breath from those around her. Some edged away, while others were more overt in their panic, putting hands to their mouths and noses. With a brief flash of anger, she thought of the comments she could make on the ripe odors coming from their elegantly laced gowns and rich tunics.

She caught her brother Cormac's fearful glance from where he stood at the far end of the hall. They were some ways away from Hwyel, who sat at a small table with some of his brothers and other relations to discuss the succession. It was his mother who'd provided the connection years before so that her brother Cormac could be fostered here, far away from their home in Leinster. She'd hoped to escape Hwyel's notice for a little longer, feeling that he would have no interest in a newly arrived sister of his poor and distant kin. But his dark, piggish eyes had missed nothing and she had felt his periodic scrutiny for some time, until after inquiry he'd been told who she was.

Everyone's eyes were on her, waiting for her answer. She resisted the urge to smooth her hair, held in place only by a plain band around her head, or tug on the sleeve of her woolen dress, which, though finely woven, was fashioned in the simple, loose style of her home and no match for the women here.

'My Lord...Cousin,' she said, uncertain what title to give him. 'It's true my mother died of a fever, but it was not the plague.' She responded in Latin, glad for once that her brother had made her learn it, so that she might let everyone know she carried no contagion.

She felt some of the tension ease as false smiles and nervous chatter erupted when Hwyel, seemingly satisfied, resumed his conversation with his neighbor. Aisling felt some relief that attention had shifted away from her, but she could not push aside her astonishment that Hwyel had not even pretended to observe the custom to offer condolences on her bereavement. She looked over at Cormac to see if he found Hwyel's words as lacking in sensibility as she did.

He smiled at her, his face full of determined reassurance, and made his way towards her. He was fair, like she was, though he appeared almost angelic with his honey colored curls and beardless face. She noticed his hands still possessed the slender grace she remembered. Though it had been more than three years since they'd been together, she still found that her heart swelled at the sight of him. Her dearest younger brother. He was all she had left now.

'We'll go to the chapel later and say prayers for our mother,' Cormac said when he reached her side.

She studied her brother a moment, puzzled. 'Yes, of course.' Why would Cormac suggest such a thing? She'd only had a few moments with him since she'd arrived. Just enough time to embrace him and pass on the awful news, before she was told she must go to the hall before Hwyel and his brothers. But surely Cormac remembered that her mother wouldn't have wanted them to pray in a chapel. She'd kept the ancient customs and had paid only lip service to the Christian beliefs to please their father. Perhaps it was the only way he could speak privately to her.

She stood restlessly, waiting for the princes to leave so that she might speak to her brother alone, share with him all that she and her mother had endured these many months. And there was much to be done. She must not lose sight of that. All that time her mother had made her promise to refrain from writing to Cormac had been precious time wasted.

Finally, Hwyel and his brothers rose and made their way out of the hall, dogs crowding their feet. Some of the women followed them, while others lingered, forming small, whispering groups. Cormac moved closer and took her hands.

'Come, I'll take you to the chapel.'

She nodded and followed him through the hall out across the courtyard to a small building. Aberffraw Castle had astonished her when first she viewed it after the rough sea journey. The large stone keep stood atop an outcropping surrounded by a moat and also included a small stone chapel, kitchen and some wooden outbuildings.

She entered the chapel and shivered at the cold. The long, dark winter seemed to have lodged in the stones, and neither the many mass candles wedged in the makeshift rack, nor the feeble fire in the small brazier beside the altar alleviated it. The

short rows of wooden benches looked uninviting. She watched
Cormac approach the altar, kneel and cross himself. She sighed,
despite knowing that it was impossible to think that Cormac
might have set aside his deep Christian beliefs in the years
they'd been apart, but still she had hoped. It had been one
source of difference between them and one that she knew had
secretly disappointed her mother. She took a seat on one of the
benches and waited for Cormac to join her.

Should she try to pray? Pray for her mother, pray for her
father so brutally murdered? Pray for all the land stolen from
them, seized by ruthless noblemen warring with the King of
Leinster? Whom should she pray to, anyway? The Christian God
or the ancient gods of her mother?

'Aisling.'

She jolted and looked at Cormac, realizing that she'd been
caught up once again in the staring absence where no thoughts
came to her, where nothing could touch her—no rage, no
despair, no sorrow. She took Cormac's hand.

'Ah, *mo chroí*, how I've longed to see you again.'

Tears filled his eyes, those lovely sea-blue eyes she remembered. 'And I've missed you so, and now to see you once again
only to be told our mother is dead.'

She nodded and stroked his palm, trying to bring some
comfort.

'I will ask Madog if we may have a mass said for her soul.'

She gave him a curious look. 'You know she would never
have wanted that. She died unshriven.'

Cormac's eyes darkened. 'I'll pray for her then.' He squeezed
her hand and gave her an intent look. 'And you will, too.' She
could detect a note of pleading in his tone, so she refrained from
adding anything more and merely nodded. She told herself she
cared nothing for the prayers that might be said and to whom
they were said.

'Thank you,' he said, his face softening. 'I know that mother has misled you in her own beliefs, but now we can begin to redress that.'

Irritation pricked at her despite her efforts. 'Redress my beliefs? Have you become so much a part of this *Bretnais* court that you have forgotten who your people are?'

Alarm flashed across Cormac's face. 'No-no, you must not think that I am not proud to be Uí Bairriche of Leinster, son of Eoghan. But you should put aside these old ways, forget that our mother wanted you to be a seer.' He eyed her carefully a moment. 'You haven't had the visions come yet, have you?'

'So you still believe it's possible, do you? You haven't entirely given yourself over to the Christian beliefs, then.'

'Yes, I mean, no.' He flushed heavily. 'I have taken the Christian faith deep to my heart and set aside all the old beliefs. But I would warn you that you must keep any talk of visions and seers to yourself.'

She glared at him for a moment, and then relented. Why should she mind about it after all? She'd had no visions; she was not a seer, despite all her mother's hopes and efforts to make it so.

'Let us not quarrel, *a stor*,' said Cormac.

She smiled at him. 'You're right of course. We must make plans instead. There is no time to lose. The rumors are already rife that there will be more fighting in Leinster. Macmurrough thinks to get his kingship back. We can use that opportunity to get back our lands. You're of an age, you can fight—offer your services.'

Discomfort filled his face. 'I know it seems pressing to you that we should return, but it's not that simple. We can't just go. We have nothing, you say. It's all gone. No money, no land, no cattle and no home. Just the few possessions you brought with you. So we're dependent on the favor of this court and now it's in turmoil. The king left eleven sons and many of them feel them-selves fit for the throne. They gather like crows to carrion, some circling from afar, waiting for their chance, while others try to shove and peck each other out of the way. There's a battle coming. Alliances are forming.'

'And which side are you on?'

Cormac gave an uncomfortable smile. 'I'm on no side. I'm on the side of peace, like Madog.'

She stared at her brother, trying to reshape the boy she'd known into this young man that stood before her. He was fifteen, come fully into his height and filled with some of the discernment that life spent among the nobly born required, yet here he was proclaiming himself on the side of peace. Was this the full blooming of the boy poet she remembered? She was more in need of a warrior, though, not a *fili.*

Before she could say more, the door opened and allowed a gust of wind to sweep through. A dark, slim man stepped across the threshold, his footfall quiet and reverent. He moved forward, and, like Cormac before him, knelt before the altar on one knee and crossed himself.. His movements were deliberate and spoke of a great calm, his closely barbered brown hair catching the full light of the mass candles on his bowed head so that it seemed to halo him.

He took a seat on a bench at the front, near the altar and bowed his head. With folded hands, he began to mouth a prayer. His lips moved silently, forming words carefully, his knitted brow betraying their intensity. Here was a man who desperately wanted what he prayed for. Aisling found herself smiling at his earnestness. There was something pure and unsullied about him and she liked it.

Beside her, Cormac folded his hands and took up a posture similar to the man. It was clear he felt he couldn't speak with this man present, so she turned her attention to the front and observed him further.

The prayer took longer than she would have thought and its earnest quality never faltered. When he finally did finish, he rose, turned to them and fixed the most transparently blue eyes on her. It was as if he saw through to her innermost self when he looked at her.

'My lord Madog,' said Cormac. He flushed when Madog shifted his gaze to him. 'I would be pleased to introduce you to my sister, Aisling.'

Madog gave a small bow, which she returned. She had no notion of the customs of this land but she'd been surprised to hear Cormac speak his introduction in Irish.

'You speak our language, my lord?' asked Aisling.

He gave her a warm smile. 'A little. Your brother has taught me.'

Aisling gave him an appraising look, noting his rich but sober-hued garb. This was the Madog whom Cormac had spoken about earlier. The man who would arrange the mass for her mother. The man who spoke of peace.

'Are you a religious of some sort?'

'No, no,' Cormac said quickly. 'He is King Owain's son.'

'One of his many sons.' Madog gave a wry grin. 'I could never aspire to the purity of a holy man.'

'Oh but my lord, you're just as holy as any priest,' Cormac said.

'No, I would never entertain such blasphemous thoughts.'

'Of course not...I only meant that—'

'I know my dear boy, and I appreciate the kind intention by the remark.'

Aisling watched this exchange with wonder. She hadn't remembered this man as one of the identified brothers at the table in the hall, but there was no doubt to his princely bearing. Clearly Cormac had found a mentor he could admire and look up to, but hearing their exchange made her a little uneasy. Was anyone that perfect?

'I'm glad to meet you, my lord, in any case. My brother clearly holds you in great esteem and that alone is sufficient to recommend you.'

'And I'm only too glad to finally make the acquaintance of his treasured sister, though I am sorry it's the loss of your mother that makes it possible.'

His eyes were full of compassion and she blinked back the tears that suddenly came. She could bear the rudeness, the over-sights; it was the kindness that was difficult. While she had nursed her mother in the corner of a squalid hut on the edge of a farm belonging to distant kin, she could manage to face each slight or difficulty with a semblance of equanimity. Now, in the face of true sympathy, she nearly came undone.

Brushing the tears aside, she forced a smile. 'I thank you for your words. It is a sad occasion that causes this reunion with my brother.'

He nodded and glanced at Cormac. 'I will add your mother to my prayers.'

'That's most kind of you,' said Cormac. 'And I will pray for peace, as you do.'

Madog smiled. 'Pray for peace and the success of our venture.'

Cormac's face lit up. 'Our venture? It's been agreed?'

Madog nodded. 'I may begin outfitting the ship as soon as I would like.'

Unease stirred in Aisling. 'What venture is this?'

Cormac gave her a guilty look. 'Prince Madog has read of the voyage of the blessed St Brendan. Some time ago, when we were talking about long journeys to strange and exotic places, I told him the tale of St Brendan's voyage. Well, what I could remember from Father and the bits Bishop Aidan told me on his visits. Madog found them so interesting he wanted to know more, so he wrote to various religious here and abroad and gathered all the details he could. He eventually obtained a copy of *Navigatio Sancti Brendani Abbatis*. We read it through together.'

Once again she was reminded how different Cormac's upbringing was to hers. Regular visits to a priest had given him his education and foundations for life as directed by her father and grandmother, while she had taken an entirely different path guided by her mother.

She gave a pained smile. 'I'm glad you both found it to your liking.'

Cormac showered Madog with an admiring look. 'Prince Madog has been a very good friend and more. He has guided me well these past few years and shaped my skill with words and sword. And now he's asked that I help his dream be made real.' He looked at Aisling, his face shining with purpose and belief. 'He would have me join him on his voyage.'

'Voyage?'

'To retrace St Brendan's journey. He wishes to go to the western lands.'

She was too stunned to say a word at first. 'The western lands? Why?'

Madog put a hand on her arm briefly. 'I know it's hard for you to appreciate how important this is to your brother and to me. We have studied his text these many months and have caught the wonder of his feat. I have prayed long and hard over this and I have felt God's desire that I should seek out these lands. Lands that are unmarred by the strife, the greed and grappling for power that riddle this kingdom and those around us.' His eyes took on a fire that she hadn't seen before. 'There we could establish a new life, one filled with harmony.'

She gave a small nod, uncertain how to respond to something as drastic as he proposed. 'Will there be many of you on this voyage? And will it be far?' As she waited for the answer, the story came back to her, a vague impression of a long sea journey encountering fantastical creatures. She glanced at Cormac and saw the eagerness.

'There are at least twenty men who are willing to accompany me, and now I have a ship and the means to outfit it. As for the length of the journey, I'm not sure. It may take months, maybe more, before we get there.'

Months? That meant many months going and many to return. Something of what he said before came back to her. 'You mean to return, don't you?'

'Of course. Once we've established ourselves. We'll come back for anyone who wishes to settle in this place of peace.'

It could be years before they returned, if they returned. What would happen to her if Cormac accompanied him on this journey? Her mind reeled. This wasn't what she expected. She'd hoped that once Cormac had heard of their true situation back home in Leinster he would do all he could to get some or all of their land holdings back. She hadn't realized his years here had loosened his connection to home so much.

'And you say you have been given approval? By your brothers?'

'Hwyel and my brothers who support him—Morgan, Llewellyn, Rhys. I would guess the others would have no quarrel with it either.' He gave a rueful smile. 'It is one less brother in the way while the kingship is decided.'

She understood more of his desire and the urgency of it. But it didn't detract from her situation, or the hurt she felt that Cormac would wish to part from her once again.

'And in the meantime, while you go off with my brother seeking this land, am I to remain here amid the strife, the greed and grappling for power?' She fought to keep her voice in control. 'That's if your brothers allow it. Take pity on a distant kinswoman who has nowhere else to go, for as I have just told my brother, our lands are lost and must be reclaimed. I cannot do that on my own.'

Madog put his hand on Cormac's shoulder. 'I had no notion that your circumstances have come to such a pass.'

Cormac stiffened. 'Of course, I had not thought for a moment, forgive me, Aisling. I didn't mean to push your welfare aside. I will of course remain behind, with you under my protection, that is, if it's permitted.'

Madog squeezed his shoulder. 'I'm certain Hwyel will allow you to remain with your sister for as long as you like. I'll speak to him.'

Aisling heard the exchange and tried to set aside her dismay that Cormac remembered her position only after she reminded him and Madog expressed his sorrow at it. She weighed the options of Cormac staying behind on sufferance and found that she still preferred that to the separation and the danger he might never return.

'Thank you,' Aisling said. 'I appreciate your help in this.' She noted the barely concealed disappointment in Cormac's face. She sighed, hoping she might find some way to make it up to him. She loved her brother too much not to wish otherwise.